THE
KNIGHTS OF THE
CORNERSTONE

Jim: Hope you enjoy this one! cheers!

THE KNIGHTS OF THE CORNERSTONE

✠

JAMES P. BLAYLOCK

[signature]

ACE BOOKS, NEW YORK

THE BERKLEY PUBLISHING GROUP
Published by the Penguin Group
Penguin Group (USA) Inc.
375 Hudson Street, New York, New York 10014, USA
Penguin Group (Canada), 90 Eglinton Avenue East, Suite 700, Toronto, Ontario M4P 2Y3, Canada
(a division of Pearson Penguin Canada Inc.)
Penguin Books Ltd., 80 Strand, London WC2R 0RL, England
Penguin Group Ireland, 25 St. Stephen's Green, Dublin 2, Ireland (a division of Penguin Books Ltd.)
Penguin Group (Australia), 250 Camberwell Road, Camberwell, Victoria 3124, Australia
(a division of Pearson Australia Group Pty. Ltd.)
Penguin Books India Pvt. Ltd., 11 Community Centre, Panchsheel Park, New Delhi—110 017, India
Penguin Group (NZ), 67 Apollo Drive, Rosedale, North Shore 0632, New Zealand
(a division of Pearson New Zealand Ltd.)
Penguin Books (South Africa) (Pty.) Ltd., 24 Sturdee Avenue, Rosebank, Johannesburg 2196,
South Africa

Penguin Books Ltd., Registered Offices: 80 Strand, London WC2R 0RL, England

This is an original publication of The Berkley Publishing Group.

First edition: December 2008

Library of Congress Cataloging-in-Publication Data

Blaylock, James P., 1950–
    The knights of the cornerstone / James P. Blaylock.—1st ed.
        p. cm.
    ISBN 978-0-441-01653-2
    1. Secret societies—Fiction.   2. Relics—Fiction.   3. California—Fiction.   4. Colorado River Region (Colo.-Mexico)—Fiction.   I. Title.
    PS3552.L3966K55 2008
    813'.54—dc22

                                                                                    2008037152

PRINTED IN THE UNITED STATES OF AMERICA

10 9 8 7 6 5 4 3 2 1

For Viki, John, and Danny

And this time for John Ciarcia and Karen King

Cha Cha and Karen: Here's a book dedicated to the two of you, for years of New York hospitality. The Blaylocks thank you for your love and support. See you soon.

ACKNOWLEDGMENTS

I'd like to thank some people for the help they gave me with this book, starting with my family, all of whom made sensible and useful suggestions when I needed them, and particularly Danny, who gave me the idea of making my main character a hopeful cartoonist and lent me some of his own cartoons to get me going. I'd also like to thank Tim Powers, Lew Shiner, Chris Arena, Paul Buchanan, and Dixie and Bull Durham.

The only way to come to know where you are is to begin to make yourself at home.

—*Lilith*, George MacDonald

Once he heard very faintly in some distant street a barrel-organ begin to play, and it seemed to him that his heroic words were moving to a tiny tune from under or beyond the world.

—*The Man Who Was Thursday*, G. K. Chesterton

KNIGHT ERRANT

Calvin Bryson read the letter a third time, but for some reason it insisted on saying the same thing it had said the other two times. It was from his uncle, Al Lymon, who lived out in the desert along the Colorado River. Calvin was invited to drop in for a stay—as long as he wanted, the longer the better. He had last seen his uncle and aunt at his father's funeral three years ago, and since then Aunt Nettie hadn't been doing well. The letter was cheerful enough, but it had a last-respects tone to it, and its arrival was a little ominous, since he had never gotten a letter from his uncle before, only birthday cards back in his childhood, and then from both of them.

His last trip out to visit his aunt and uncle had been several years back. He had vivid memories of the Lymon house on its shady bend upriver from Needles, where the little town of New Cyprus lay hemmed in by a U-shaped range of barren hills appropriately called the Dead Mountains. Embayed as it was by high cliffs and the green verge of the Colorado, New Cyprus was a half-moon of land isolated from the world, accessible only by boat or by a winding two-lane road through miles of rock-strewn desert wilderness. The house, built of locally cut stone and imported cedar back in the 1920s, had view windows looking out onto the river, and its own little sandy beach on the bay, just wide enough for two or three lawn chairs. He could picture his aunt's antiques and Oriental bric-a-brac, some of it ancient, including a Saracen dagger supposedly from the Third Crusade and said to have belonged to Richard Lionheart.

He looked out through the front window at the street. Two boys played in the sprinklers across the way, just as he had done when he was growing up in this very house. The Eagle Rock neighborhood had taken care of itself over the years, and the old bungalows and Spanish-style houses, most of them built in the early part of the last century, were painted and repaired, and few of them had been renovated into the kind of characterless houses found in nearby neighborhoods. A big, messy carob tree shaded his yard, and he was struck suddenly with the memory of climbing the tree when he was a kid, of the musty smell of the carob pods and the feel of the rough bark on his hands. But he had no desire to climb it now, only a nostalgic regret for times that had passed away—nostalgia called up by the letter in his hand.

But the last thing he wanted to do was to drive out into the desert, especially under these sad circumstances. He picked up his sketchbook and looked at the cartoon he had been drawing when the mail had come in through the slot. It was a picture of two gangly-looking lunatic doctors standing in a doorway, very apparently insane, with tousled hair and with their clothes askew. People on the sidewalk were similarly crazy-looking, with crossed eyes and propeller beanies and their pant legs tucked randomly into their socks. One of the two doctors was pointing across the street at a solitary man who looked like Cary Grant, neatly dressed in a three-piece suit. "That's the one," the doctor was saying. A magazine editor with any sense would buy it. So far none of them had exhibited any sense.

Calvin had gotten thoroughly used to doing nothing during these past months of being alone, unless you counted the cartoons and the book collecting. Elaine, the woman he had been engaged to, had accused him of being aimless, but in fact he wasn't aimless at all. Tonight, for example, he aimed to finish cataloguing his collection of pamphlets from Futura Press and maybe read a book, and then he aimed to go to bed early. Elaine and he had fallen apart at Christmas—maybe the worst Christmas of Calvin's thirty-four years.

He had inherited enough when his father passed away so that as long as he didn't spend his inheritance like a fool, he could live moderately well, and his only real duties nowadays were to himself, or to his collection of rare books and pamphlets, mostly what was known as "Californiana." Over the years he had paid questionable sums for pamphlets printed on garage presses by cranks and crackpots, but there was an element of innocent wonder in the era that produced them that attracted him, and wonder was a commodity that had pretty much gone out of the world.

He didn't like to think of the things that were going out of the world, but not thinking about them wouldn't change the truth. You start coming up with excuses not to visit your old aunt and uncle, and then one morning you wake up in Hell, with your pajamas on fire....

He reread the part in the letter about Aunt Nettie. It was impossible to say for sure what her condition was, but he assumed her cancer was out of remission. Although the letter revealed little about her troubles, it implied a lot about Uncle Lymon's. Calvin had found that living alone wasn't easy sometimes, but there were other things that were more difficult. The Lymons had been married for over fifty years, and Calvin could only imagine what that meant—a lifetime of companionship drawing to a sad close.

He flipped through the Rolodex looking for his uncle's telephone number. Uncle Lymon was a potentate of some sort in a lodge called the Knights of the Cornerstone, which went in for secret handshakes and strange hats. Calvin half feared that the subject of his becoming an initiate in the order would come up again when he visited, as it had last time. If it did, he would demand a suit of armor and a pyramid hat with an eyeball on it. If they could meet his price, he was in. He took out the Rolodex card and reached for the telephone, but before he had time to make the call, the doorbell rang.

He parted the blinds and looked out again. It was a UPS driver at the door. *Books!* Calvin thought, his spirits lifting, but when he opened the door and took the box from the driver it was far too light to be books. The man wasn't wearing a uniform, just a blue work shirt, and the van at the curb was the right color of institutional brown but was unmarked. The driver apparently saw him looking at it. "I'm warehouse," he said. "Your box got left behind by mistake, so they asked me to run it out here in one of the out-of-service trucks. It's an element of customer service."

"I appreciate that," Calvin said, signing his name on a list on a clipboard instead of the usual electronic gadget. He took the box back into the house, watching through the blinds as the van roared away in a cloud of exhaust. Not only was the box too light to be books, it in fact felt utterly empty. The return address was from Orange City, Iowa, from Warren Hosmer, his father's ancient cousin—his *own* cousin, of some odd number and removal. This was puzzling, and if it called for him to drive out to Iowa, he would have to put his foot down.

He fetched a box cutter, and was on the verge of slicing into the multiple layers of tape when he noticed that in fact the box wasn't addressed to him personally, but rather to Al Lymon, c/o Calvin Bryson. That beat all. It would have been identical postage for Cousin Hosmer to ship it straight to his uncle's post office box in Bullhead City, Arizona. New Cyprus was unincorporated territory, and his aunt and uncle collected their mail across the river, taking the round-trip ferry ride a couple of times a week and shopping at the Safeway and the big Coronet dime store near the ferry dock while they were in town.

Then it occurred to him that UPS didn't ship to post office boxes. But why use UPS at all? Why not just mail it? Calvin shook the box, which made a swishy sort of sound, as if there were tissue paper in it, or some other ethereal thing—a million-dollar bill, maybe, or a chorus line of angels dancing on the head of a pin. He was half tempted simply to cut it open and claim not to have looked at the address till it was too late. Except it would be a lie, and there was no use taking up that vice after having mostly avoided it for so many years. Sometimes it seemed to him that if he eliminated human contact entirely, he could rest easy in regard to that particular crime—unless he counted lying to himself, which was admissible because it had its own built-in justice: later on you were sorry for it, or so people said.

A curious thing struck him—the coincidence of the box arriving on the same day as his uncle's letter—and he wondered if he were being invited into a plot perpetrated by the old-timer end of the family, which had always been a mysterious crowd, although there weren't a lot of them left these days. He recalculated the likelihood of waking up in Hell as he went back to the Rolodex and found the number for Warren Hosmer, which he jabbed into the phone. Being lured into other people's mysteries didn't attract him. A couple of well-conceived phone calls would likely solve all problems, or at least shift them to some indeterminate date in the future. The phone rang ten times before anyone picked it up.

"Hosmer," a man's voice said.

"It's Calvin Bryson," Calvin said as heartily as he could.

"Cal! Good! Good! Good! You got the package?"

"I did," Calvin said. "How did you know?"

"Why else would you call?"

"Right. Anyway, I signed for it, and it's sitting on the dining room table. I guess I was wondering whether I shouldn't just take it downtown to the post office and send it on out to Uncle Lymon's P.O. Box."

There was a lengthy silence. "I wanted to avoid that," Hosmer told him.

"Ah!" Calvin said. "I see. Okay. Sure. Why?"

"It's that damned address of Lymon's. You never know how many hands the package will pass through or what kind of curiosity it'll stir up by the time he picks it up."

"All right. I guess I can take it out there myself if—"

"Good. We thought that would be best."

"Like I was saying, I'm not sure how soon...Did you say 'we'?"

"Lymon and me. He said you're taking a little trip out to New Cyprus. He and Nettie are looking forward to it like nobody's business."

"It's in the...planning stages," Calvin said. This was inscrutable. He picked up Uncle Lymon's letter and looked at the three-day-old postmark.

"The sooner the better," Hosmer told him. "I won't sleep much till it's out there safe."

"That suits me," Calvin said. "It's none of my business, really, but what's inside? The box feels empty."

"Well, it's an heirloom, a *family* heirloom. It's a veil, I guess you could call it. A gossamer scarf. Belonged to your aunt Iris. Maybe you haven't heard of her. She's been dead these many years."

"That would explain it," Calvin said. "Like her wedding veil or something?"

"No. The veil she wore when she was calling up spirits. Her séance veil."

Suffering Judas, Calvin thought. He had never heard of any Aunt Iris, let alone that there'd been a spiritualist in the fam-

7

ily, and now he was under orders to haul her magic veil out to the desert in a cardboard box. "When did she pass away?" he asked.

"Nineteen ten. The family got the idea that her ghost was in the veil. It sounds crazy, but things *happened* with it. It kept rising up and sort of floating in the air. They'd open Iris's old steamer trunk and it would drift right out, and no way in hell it wanted to go back in. The thing has a mind of its own, apparently. They'd have to snag it with a butterfly net. I can't tell you much about it, because it was before my time. Thing is, it wouldn't give them any rest till they boxed it up and tied down the lid of that trunk."

Calvin found that he couldn't speak without laughing, which would insult the old man. Unless of course Hosmer was joking, which he had to be, although it didn't sound that way.

"You're skeptical," Hosmer said. "That's good. It'll keep you from trusting the wrong people. This kind of thing with the veil is a matter of *belief*, if you follow me—like having surefire numbers for the lottery. Once it comes into your mind to play the numbers, you've *got* to play them. They might as well be a fact. You understand belief, don't you, son?"

"Sure," Calvin said. "Like not walking under a ladder, even if you don't believe—"

"I'm not superstitious," Hosmer told him flatly. "I don't hold with that kind of thing—ladders, black cats. It's a lot of rubbish. I'm talking about matters of the spirit here."

"Of course," Calvin said. "I was just making a—"

"Well, cut it the hell out. When can you leave?"

"What?" Calvin said. "I don't know."

"Don't put it off another minute. We're all going to be a little bit nervous until Iris is interred in the crypt out there in New Cyprus, God bless her. You feel that way, too, I suppose. You're family."

"Sure I am," Calvin said, throwing caution into the shrubbery. Clearly he was outgunned here. "I'm happy to help. I was just wondering when to take off when the package showed up. The timing couldn't have been better. I can leave this afternoon."

"Then it wouldn't have made too much sense for you to mail it on out to Lymon, would it? If you can leave this afternoon, it'll get it there about ten times as fast in the trunk of your car. What would be the point of mailing it?"

"It made no sense at all. I wasn't thinking. I should be out there before dark if I beat the traffic into San Bernardino."

"*That's* the spirit. Your dad always told me you were a good man, and Lymon says so, too. You take care of Aunt Iris. Don't let her out of your sight, and for God's sake, *don't open the box*. If she gets loose in the car and the window's down..."

"That won't happen. Leave it to me."

"That's what I'm doing. That's why I sent her to you. Like they used to say out here in Iowa, 'If it was easy they'd have got someone else to do it.'"

"There's truth in that," Calvin said.

"Damn right there is. Otherwise I wouldn't have said it. Let me know she arrived safe."

"Will do."

"One last thing," Hosmer said, lowering his voice as if leery of being overheard. "You carry a portable horn?"

"I'm not sure—"

"A *blower?*"

"I don't know," Calvin said. "A *blower*...? Like a leaf blower?"

"A telephone, damn it. A *cellular* phone. A *portable.*"

"Sure. You want the number?"

"That's right. And keep it charged up. But once you're out there in the desert, *think twice about using it.* Assume someone's listening. If it's necessary, *I'll call you.*"

Calvin reeled off his phone number and the strange conversation was done. He couldn't remember the last time he had exchanged pleasantries with Cousin Hosmer—probably at an Iowa picnic back in the late Middle Ages. And now this. He hefted the box. A ghost didn't weigh much. Maybe they actually had *negative* weight, like helium, which is why they float.

"Duty calls," he said out loud. His voice sounded strange in the otherwise silent house. Certainly duty had called in a bizarre way, but who was he to ask needless questions? Like the man in the poem, his was but to do or die. " 'Out of the mouths of babes,' " he said, " 'rode the six hundred.' " And then he laughed, picturing the cartoon, which would be utterly meaningless to anyone who hadn't read the poem, and maybe even if they *had* read it.

He put in the call to his uncle Lymon. "I'm on my way," he said. "I've got Aunt Iris."

"We'll have dinner waiting," his uncle told him. "I cooked it yesterday. And can you do me a favor? There's a little market fifty miles this side of Ludlow out on I-40, the Gas'n'Go. They've got grape Nehi soda in bottles. Pick me up a couple of six-packs, will you? I don't get out that way much, and I can't find it in Bullhead City. I'll pay you back."

"My treat," Calvin said.

"Then make it a case," his uncle said, and both of them laughed.

FRED WOOLSWORTH

The barren peaks of the Dead Mountains loomed ahead, off toward the horizon on the north side of the highway, sharp against the desert sky and bunched together along the Colorado River where California, Arizona, and Nevada merged, and where lay the magical, invisible line that marked the time zone. Calvin looked into the rearview mirror, unpleasantly startled, as he most often was, at the sight of his own face. Elaine had told him once that he looked like a young Jimmy Stewart, and he reminded himself of that from time to time. He was the right build anyway, and he could see the resemblance, but there was some essential quality he lacked—the endearing manner of speaking, maybe, or the twinkle in the eye.

He looked past himself, deeper into the mirror, at the gray

hills of the Bullion Range, diminished and hazy but still visible behind him. As far as he could tell, there wasn't a lick of difference between the two dry ranges—one in front and one behind—except that one was associated with gold and the other with death. Probably the names were the quirk of a geological survey team that had come out from the west and lost its sense of humor along the way, which wouldn't be any more difficult than losing a penny if you were out here in the desert for more than a few days.

He tossed his road map onto the passenger seat and considered the strange fact that a person forfeited an hour merely by crossing into Arizona—a purely imaginary hour, of course, but an hour that could only be regained by turning around and heading back west. Except if one never returned west, then one was an hour closer to the grave, if only in some mystical sense. There was something unsettling in it, although he was unsettled by any number of things these days—a consequence, probably, of some variety of looming midlife crisis, although he was a little young for that sort of thing, which was...unsettling.

A vehicle appeared on the highway ahead of him now, shimmering in the heat haze until it solidified into an old green pickup truck with a bad muffler. It roared past, the sun glaring so brightly on the windshield that it might have been Elijah rattling away in a glowing whirlwind, bound for the Promised Land. Some fifty miles past Ludlow he spotted the grape soda connection, and he turned off the highway into a solitary two-pump gas station, lunch counter, antiques store, and market rolled into one. The sign on the big window read "Gas'n'Go Antiques and Cafe." The place sat adjacent to a dry lake that wasn't dry. Over the last few weeks, late summer storms had strayed in from Arizona and left a few inches of water in the lake bed, which cheerfully reflected the blue sky, tinged with gold from the declining sun.

A gust of wind ruffled the surface of the lake, breaking up the reflection, and Calvin climbed out of the Dodge and into the searing heat, nearly staggered by it after the air-conditioned trip out from Eagle Rock. A hand-painted sign on the gas pump read "Pay First!" in order to ward off bolters, so he went inside, hauling two twenties out of his wallet. He shut the door behind him to keep out the heat, and a little bell jingled, although no one came out. There were the sounds of a swamp cooler working on the roof and a distant radio playing country-western music, but the place was apparently empty of customers.

He smiled approvingly and glanced around, taking in the junk food on the shelves, the groceries, the sign over the lunch counter that advertised chili fries and cheeseburgers. Maybe on his way back out he would stop in for a bite to eat, generate some serious heartburn for the long drive home. He could grab a roll of antacids to keep his aura on the necessary sublunar wavelength. Cases of beverages lay piled on the floor beyond a picnic table with benches, including, conveniently, an unopened case of grape Nehi soda.

The antiques sat against the wall by the deli case—baloney and bologna side by side. There were roadkill license plates, bric-a-brac, oil lamps, a rack of books, and some dusty souvenirs including a small plastic toilet with multiple removable coaster-seats that read "I crapped out in Las Vegas." He was sorely tempted to buy the toilet seat coasters as a gift for his aunt, but instead he stepped across to look at the books, which were mostly Westerns and old cookbooks, but also a few likely looking strays. He felt the familiar surge of interest and greed, the off chance that there would be something valuable, or at least strange enough to be appealing.

The paper was dried out in most of the books and was decomposing and fly specked—the eventual fate of everything in the desert—and at first glance there wasn't much in the racks to interest him. Then he spotted a sort of oversize pamphlet, bound like a book, but with its heavy paper cover stapled on near the spine. It was titled *The Death of John Nazarite, Betrayal in the California Desert* and was published by something called the Fourteen Carats Press in Henderson, Nevada, in 1956. The logo of the press was a flat-bottomed, panning-for-gold pan with the legend "Fourteen Carats" on it. The price was thirty-two dollars, which had to be cheap. The heavy paper cover was chipped along the edges from heat and sunlight, but for a paperbound book with fifty years on it, it wasn't in bad shape, especially considering where it lived. There was a frontispiece in it, a woodblock illustration of a woman standing before the mouth of a cave in a fortress-like cliff, holding a platter bearing a bearded, severed head. The wide-open eyes in the head gazed out longingly over what might have been the Dead Sea, and in the distance stood a range of rocky, desert peaks. The illustration was titled "Bring Me the Head of John Nazarite."

It appeared to be the Salome and John the Baptist story with some geographic curiosities—the Jordan River having become the Mojave, and the Dead Sea exchanged for the Salton Sea. One illustration pictured several men in white tunics with red crosses on the front. One of them held an ornate wooden chest the size of a bread box. The caption read "The Red Cross Knights Receive the Head." Clearly the book was cultistic, a piece of California crypto-history. Calvin was possessed by the certainty that the Fates badly wanted him to divest himself of thirty-two dollars. He looked at the list of Fourteen Carats Press publications in the back of the pamphlet—books on secret societies, desert mummies, saucer cults, the Lost Dutchman's mine—nearly two pages of seductive titles, plenty enough to give his life purpose again.

He would add this happily to his growing pile of paper and ink that virtually no one else on earth had the slightest interest in. One nice thing about being a bachelor, he thought as he turned toward the front counter, was that you could do as you pleased, although it wasn't always clear to him why he was pleased to do as he did, especially when he had no one to please but himself. During the time that he had been with Elaine, he hadn't nearly as often done as he pleased, but he had often been surprised to find that he was pleased anyway.

He put the thought out of his mind and grabbed the toilet seat coasters on the way to the register. He couldn't show up at his aunt's doorstep without a token of his esteem, after all. He recalled that she had a set of salt and pepper shakers that had been owned by a shirttail relative of Elvis Presley, and there was an evident Elvis Presley connection here, too—the King dying on the throne and all—although it was unlikely that he could point it out in to his aunt.

A woman who might have been sixty-five came out of the back to wait on him. She was wide and suntanned and had a naturally scowly look that reminded him pleasantly of Tugboat Annie. She had large arms, as if she wrestled bears and was good at it. "Gas?" she asked him, her voice sounding like gravel on sandpaper.

He considered a humorous reply, and then rejected it. "Pump number two," he said, handing her the two twenties and then rooting a third out of his wallet. "Take the book and coasters out of it first. And that case of grape soda." As an afterthought he grabbed a single bottle out of the cooler. "A cold one, too." He hadn't had a grape soda in years, and he was full of a sudden nostalgia for the taste of purple.

"You've got enough left out of the sixty for about an eighth of a tank," she said.

"I'm only going a few more miles," he told her, waiting while she punched buttons on an old cash register. There was a ringing noise when the cash drawer flew open. "I'm looking for the turnoff over to New Cyprus, down along the river. I haven't been out there for years, and I remember that last time I passed right by the turnoff and drove another ten miles before I knew I'd missed it."

"It ain't marked," she said. "Used to be a red cross painted on the highway right there, but it's been blacktopped over half a dozen times. That's their mark, you know, those New Cyprus folks." She looked at him intently, as if it somehow made a difference whether he knew or didn't know.

He nodded, wondering abruptly whether Uncle Lymon was one of the Knights who had received the head. There wasn't a lot to do in New Cyprus, which was isolated even in a land of isolation, and it was a rare evening that Uncle Lymon wasn't off at the Knight's clubhouse, the Temple—or else the Temple Bar, depending on its function on any given day—wearing a tunic with a red cross embroidered on it and half covered with badges of rank and retired fishing lures.

"You'd think they'd repaint it," she went on, "but New Cyprus is homestead territory, so nobody's in charge of anything. Either that or everybody's in charge of everything, which amounts to the same thing. It's not a bad way to be, either. My old man used to drive out there for lodge meetings, but he's been dead these past three years."

"The Knights of the Cornerstone? My uncle's some kind of officer in it."

She nodded her head as if she had known it all along. "You're Al Lymon's nephew. That's what I thought."

"Calvin Bryson," he said, putting out his hand.

She shook it and nodded. "Shirley Fowler. I see the Lymons now and then when I drive over the hill to visit my granddaughter, but not as often as I'd like. How's Nettie? She doesn't get out much these days."

Calvin shrugged. "Her cancer was in remission, but it's bothering her again, although I don't know how bad. She's had about all the treatments, and there's not a lot that can be done about the pain. She spends some time in the past, too, I guess you'd say."

"Well, the past isn't a half bad place to visit once in a while. Tell her Shirley Fowler sends her regards."

"I'll be go-to-hell!" a voice said behind him, and Calvin turned around to discover a heavyset bearded man, maybe seventy, just then stepping out from behind a rack of Little Debbie snack cakes. Had he been there all along...?

"I'm Fred Woolsworth," the man said. "So you're Cal Bryson? I'm a friend of your uncle's. He told me his nephew was coming out for a spell." He was loaded up with Navajo silver—a big squash blossom on his bolo tie and a watchband that must have weighed half a pound.

"Glad to make your acquaintance," Calvin said. "Woolworth, like the dime store?"

"*Wools*worth, with an *s*. Like 'money's worth', but wool. My daddy used to say, 'When you go out to shear sheep, make sure you get your woolsworth!'" He laughed out loud.

Calvin smiled and nodded, trying to think of a gag line of his own involving sheep, but coming up with nothing but "ewe," which pretty much only worked on paper. If he had his sketchbook he could draw the cartoon. "When did my uncle tell you I was coming? I didn't know it myself till today."

"News travels fast out here in the desert," Woolsworth said. "Believe it or not, I knew your daddy back in Iowa, before he came out West with your mother. Nearly fifty years now. Your daddy moved out on the coast, and I wound up in Bullhead City. Wasn't nothing there in Bullhead but the river back then, and one bridge downriver across to the Needles side. Lots of water under *that* bridge over the years. Now we've got casinos across in Laughlin, and God knows what next. There's talk about moving that big English clock out here—Big Ben, they call it. Set it up in that park next to where they put in the new Wal-Mart. You'd be surprised at the stuff that finds its way into the desert, including people. Anyway, I was sorry to hear your daddy passed away."

"Thanks," Calvin said. Somehow the Big Ben idea just didn't sound feasible to him. Next to a *Wal-Mart*?

"You're out here on account of your aunt's sick, I suppose."

"I'm bringing out a family heirloom, too, but that's not an excuse for coming out here. I just want to spend a little time on the river. See the folks again. It's been a couple of years now."

"Of course," he said, nodding heavily. "Of course. God bless. I didn't mean to suggest you needed an excuse to do the right thing. Just making small talk. You can't be bringing much of an heirloom, though, in that little bitty vehicle of yours."

"Family artifact," Calvin told him.

"*Artifact?*" Woolsworth said. "That's a good word. It's got real weight to it. It elevates a thing above the doodad level, if you know what I mean. Now, that plastic toilet you're buying there, that's a *doo*dad." He laughed out loud again.

Calvin smiled politely at the lame joke. Woolsworth was a real card.

"Tell Al Lymon that Fred Woolsworth says hello. Tell him I'll see him at the Temple one of these evenings real soon. Tell him *sooner rather than later.* Will you do that? Just them words."

"I will," Calvin said. Woolsworth went out through the door, the bell jingling behind him, and he angled across the lot as if he were going to walk back down the highway. Calvin took a step forward to get a better look and saw that there was an old green pickup truck parked at the corner of the lot near the propane tank. Woolsworth climbed into it and a moment later the engine roared to life. The truck pulled out onto the highway heading east toward Needles, its broken muffler making the engine sound like an outboard motor.

"I'll be damned," Calvin muttered, remembering the truck that had passed him earlier, not a quarter of an hour ago, traveling west. It *couldn't* be the same truck. If it was, then Woolsworth must have turned around after passing him and come straight back east. But there was nothing fifteen miles back down the highway except empty desert. Where had the man been going?

Shirley opened the grape soda and handed it to him, and then put the toilet seat coasters into a bag. "He's a real character," she said, referring to Woolsworth. "I didn't see him come in. Did you?"

"No," Calvin said.

"Watch out you don't talk too much to people you don't know out here in the desert."

"Thanks for the tip."

"Anyway, what you do about that New Cyprus road is to watch for it on your left just about exactly two miles past the Henderson cutoff. If you're not looking for it, you won't see it, because it runs down across the wash, and it's usually under a couple of inches of sand. Don't slow down till you get across the wash and back up onto the pavement, or you're liable to find yourself stuck. And give this to your uncle," she said. She reached under the counter and fished out a cardboard box taped shut—a box exactly the same size as the box that contained Aunt Iris's veil. The address was made out to Al Lymon, c/o the Gas'n'Go. It was from Warren Hosmer.

"Thanks," Calvin said, taking it from her. He hefted the

box in his hands—another ghost-infused veil? He started to say something, but gave up. He wasn't going to get any answers out here on the highway. He set the box on the case of grape soda and laid the book and the sack on top, then picked the whole lot up, snagged the open soda bottle with his right hand, and turned toward the door, half expecting to see Fred Woolsworth across the road, lurking behind a yucca.

Outside again, he crammed himself sideways against the car, pulled the door latch with his pinkie finger, and set his armload of boxes on the seat. The oppressive heat was a living presence, like the plague or an axe murderer or Woolsworth's muffler—something that couldn't be ignored. He started filling the tank and then leaned against the fender of the Dodge while the pump worked. He sipped his soda, looking out over the desert.

The same storms that had filled the dry lake had generated a second blooming of wildflowers, and on the rise above the gas station there were patches of blue and yellow blooms. There was no denying that the desert was a beautiful place, especially near sunset like this, when it was cooling down and when the shadows were long and lent an air of mystery to things, but to live out here would be a different matter—impossible in high summer. Still, people *did* live here, for some reason, like Shirley Fowler and Fred Woolsworth, or his uncle and aunt, for that matter. It was the solitude, maybe, that attracted them.

The gas pump shut off, and Calvin hung the nozzle back on the pump. *"Fred Woolsworth,"* he muttered. What a character. The man's talk had had a vaguely ironic tone, like a veiled insult, although probably it was a mere nutticism, as his father would have put it. He felt as if Woolsworth had been sizing him up, though, and had found him wanting. He finished the soda and pitched the bottle into the trash. Purple tasted pretty much the same now as it had twenty years ago, which was comforting in these times of world turmoil and grim change.

As he was climbing into the car it came into his mind that Woolsworth hadn't bought anything at the store, not even the Little Debbie cakes he had apparently been fingering. That struck Calvin as odd—the man joyriding in the desert and then stopping at the Gas'n'Go for no reason at all. He had most likely come in while Calvin was looking through the books and had hung around, lurking out of sight behind the snack food, waiting for an opportunity to start up a useless conversation. There was no reason for any of it, which didn't seem reasonable.

Abruptly he recalled the jingly little bell over the door. If Woolsworth had come in while he was looking at the books, the bell would have rung. But it hadn't rung. What did that mean? The man could easily have grabbed the bell and silenced it if he knew in advance where it hung. Or he could have cut the truck engine fifty yards up the road, coasted into the lot where he wouldn't be easily seen from inside, and sneaked in through the back....

Calvin realized that his imagination had gone into high gear. Perhaps his brain was overheated. He turned the ignition key, immediately seeing that the "trunk open" light was illuminated. He climbed back out, and sure enough the trunk *was* open— not quite latched.

Woolsworth had opened it. He must have. Who the hell else?

Calvin looked inside the trunk. Aunt Iris was gone. His duffel was there but the box wasn't. "That thieving son of a bitch," he said out loud, and it came into his mind to call the cops. He had his cell phone out of his pocket and flipped open before he imagined the conversation and the cop's almost certain reaction: "*What* did he steal...?"

Then he thought of Shirley Fowler handing him the second, nearly identical box, knowing who he was as soon as he asked for that case of grape soda, and Hosmer's telling him to avoid talking on the portable blower out here in the desert. Something was happening, and he had no idea on earth what it was, but probably it didn't want the police. In an hour the sun would have sunk, the desert would be falling into darkness, and it would be cocktail hour at Chez Lymon, where he could look out safely on the puzzling world from the battlements—or in his case the bafflements. Laughing uneasily at his own joke, he shut the trunk, climbed back into the car, and headed east.

THE DEAD MOUNTAINS

Two miles past the Henderson cutoff, Calvin slowed down to twenty miles an hour and looked hard for the New Cyprus road, which he almost certainly would have missed if it weren't for Shirley's instructions. He swung a hard left turn down the embankment, the Dodge banging into a deep rut with a muffler-denting clank and up onto the semipaved track that led into the Dead Mountains and to the river on the other side. He passed a marker farther down, half hidden by greasewood. It was a rock the size and shape of a big headstone with the legend "New Cyprus" and a cross cut into it and then painted red, the paint mostly sandblasted off by the desert wind. It stood like an Easter Island sentinel with no apparent purpose, since it was a couple of hundred yards in—way too far to be made out from the highway.

The narrow road wound upward through craggy hills, and soon he lost sight of the desert floor and was alone in a silent, empty landscape of barrel cactus and yucca and mesquite. After a climb of fifteen hundred feet or so, the road finally began to level out, and he reached a high pass through the rocks that opened onto a broad vista of endless, sun-beaten flatlands, broken here and there by dry ranges.

The river flowed green and swift below, and beyond the river stretched the irrigated fields of the Fort Mohave Indian Reservation. Beyond that, off on the horizon, big thunderheads rose over distant mountains. The city of Needles lay hidden in the southwest, but upriver in the distance, maybe twelve miles, the outskirts of Bullhead City were just visible, and opposite that, on the Nevada shore, the high-rise casinos of Laughlin.

He followed the road downward now, winding through narrow defiles and along the edges of cliffs until he came out onto a sort of plateau several hundred feet above New Cyprus. On either side of the road lay an old rock quarry littered with broken cut stones, many of them immense and set upright like dominoes and reminding him of old Celtic standing stones. A line of narrow-gauge railroad tracks that decades ago must have snaked their way to the desert floor descended into a steep gorge, and an ancient flatcar some twelve feet long stood rusting on the tracks. Greasewood and mesquite grew up around the standing stones and through the tracks and the wheels of the flatcar, giving the place the air of a long-abandoned cemetery.

He rounded a bend, the quarry disappearing behind him,

and there was a clear view of New Cyprus along the river below. He could see stands of cottonwood and thickets of willow on the bank, and the roofs of houses and mobile homes as well as a lone building out on an island connected to shore by a narrow footbridge. That would be the Temple Bar, the lodge headquarters of the Knights of the Cornerstone, where the thieving Fred Woolsworth would allegedly be seeing Uncle Lymon one of these evenings soon. The ferry wharf stood empty at the upriver edge of the island, shaded by a corrugated aluminum roof, blindingly bright in the sunshine.

It occurred to Calvin as the Dodge wound its way downward that he had to be careful of accusing Woolsworth of breaking into the trunk of his car. He had no real evidence of it, and if Woolsworth actually *was* a friend of Uncle Lymon, that sort of accusation would do nothing but poison the well. Calvin had been in the Gas'n'Go for a solid twenty minutes, and any number of people might have breezed into the lot, opened his trunk, and grabbed the box. The very fact that Woolsworth had walked inside to chat argued that it hadn't been him. Most thieves didn't go out of their way to talk with people they'd just robbed. Unless Woolsworth was merely a distraction....Unless he had an accomplice in another vehicle....

A dry stretch of the old riverbed swung into view below, a wide, rocky swath right along the edge of the mountains, and he could see the Y-shape where the new bed had surged away from the old, back when the river had changed course nearly a century ago, shifting a little section of the border between California and Arizona two hundred yards to the east and forming the crescent-shaped piece of beachfront that had become New

Cyprus. The land between the old riverbed and the new had remained unincorporated territory, a couple of hundred acres of essentially ownerless land, open to homesteading. His uncle and aunt hadn't been among the first homesteaders, but they were old-timers by now, and the early homesteaders were long passed away. The sheer cliffs of the Dead Mountains, walling off New Cyprus both upriver and down, killed the potential for further development. Aside from Shangri-la there probably wasn't another city in the world that was so clearly defined and isolated.

He remembered his uncle having told him years ago that the residents of New Cyprus had taken a vote whether they'd live in Mountain Time or Pacific Standard, but couldn't decide, and so had given up wearing watches altogether in accordance with the way things were done in Heaven. During the first visit out here that he could remember, Calvin had innocently asked his uncle what time it was, and his uncle had replied, "Not yet," which had turned out to be a standard New Cyprus response to the query.

The road dipped across the old riverbed, which lay white and sandy in the evening shadows, with scrubby-looking plants growing up between the boulders. On the other side it ended at Main Street near the downriver edge of town. Calvin turned left, upriver, crossing a bridge over a wide wash where storm waters had funneled down out of the hills since time immemorial. It was nearly seven thirty. The sun had dropped below the mountains now, and the town had fallen into evening, gratefully shedding ten degrees of heat. A sign on the roadside read "New Cyprus Town Limits" and beyond that lay a scattering of tree-shaded mobile homes on a surprisingly green, park-like lawn. People were sitting outside on lawn chairs, children and dogs were running around, and there was smoke rising from barbecues. He rolled the car window down, and the smell of the river and the cottonwoods brought with it a sudden childhood memory of playing in this very park, of the cozy interiors of mobile homes, and of sitting on the lawn watching bats flitting through the open spaces between the trees on an evening very much like this one.

Several people looked up curiously as he drove past, and one man waved, as if he knew who Calvin was, which he probably did. Probably they *all* did, for some inscrutable reason. Calvin waved back, then took off his watch and put it into the glove box, switched off the air conditioner, and rolled down the window. His cell phone lay on the seat beside him, and he realized that he wouldn't be wanting it, despite the chance of Hosmer calling him with further orders. Whatever the Bible had to say about a nagging fishwife went double for cell phones. He turned the phone off and put it into the glove box with his watch, and turned right onto a small potholed street that led to the river, past the Cozy Diner cafe, a secondhand store, and the churchyard. Along the river stood several old homes on big lots, one of which was the Lymon estate.

The house sat a few feet above the bank of the Colorado, shaded by a half dozen big cottonwoods. An arbor out front was draped with bougainvillea and honeysuckle and was a tangle of purple and red blossoms. Two swamp coolers perched on the roof, and Calvin could hear them rumbling as soon as he pulled in under the carport and turned off the engine. There was a wooden door set into the base of the wall at the top end of the carport—the entrance to a cellar bomb shelter or some other survivalist quirk. Apparently all the houses in New Cyprus had one, although he wasn't sure about the trailers in the park. Maybe they had some kind of hatch in the floor.

The shelter door stood open now, a light glowing out of it. He sat for a moment in the quiet car, thinking about meeting his aunt and wondering whether she would remember him at all or if she was too far gone. There was a movement in the lighted doorway, and his uncle's head emerged, followed by the rest of him. He carried an empty cardboard box, which he tossed aside, waving cheerfully at Calvin before switching off a light on the outside wall and shutting the shelter door.

Calvin climbed out of the car, taking the box that Shirley Fowler had given him. His uncle stood there smiling, wearing a sport shirt, a pair of Bermuda shorts with suspenders, and beat-up leather slip-on sandals. He said, "Welcome to New Cyprus, Cal. I was just loading supplies into the shelter. Can't tell when the next flood might rise up."

"But do you want to be belowground when the waters rise?" Calvin asked.

"By heaven, you're right," his uncle said. "What we want is an ark. Maybe the two of us can knock one out while you're here." He put out his hand and Calvin shook it. His uncle had the same jolly look about him that Calvin remembered—the same edge-of-laughter smile, the conspiratorial wink. He had always been stout, and the extra pounds gave his round face an almost youthful look. He seemed tired, though, borne down by gravity, as if life had gotten hard for him at a time when he would have been better off taking it easy. *Let that be a lesson to you,* Calvin told himself. Taking it easy wasn't something to be put off.

"Did you bring that grape soda?" his uncle asked.

"Yes, indeed," Calvin said, and he handed over the substitute Aunt Iris box before heading around to the passenger side of the car.

His uncle looked at the box and nodded, not saying anything about the Gas'n'Go address.

"You know a character named Fred Woolsworth?" Calvin asked him.

"Never heard of him," his uncle said. "*Wools*worth?"

"Yeah, like 'money's worth.' He said he was a friend of yours, and that he knew Dad back in Orange City in the old days."

"That doesn't tell me much. I never heard of any Woolsworth."

"Says he lives in Bullhead City. Drives an old green pickup with a bad muffler."

"That sounds like a fellow named Bob Postum. Beard? Heavyset?"

"Yeah. Longish gray hair. Maybe seventy. He's big, but he looks fit enough, like he could take care of himself if he had to."

"That's Postum. He told you his name was *Woolsworth*? That's typical. Lowball sense of humor. It's stretching it a little if he told you he's a friend of mine. We wouldn't let him into the Knights. Wrong pedigree. In fact, he tried to buy the old Brewer place right upriver there through a second party, but it...fell out of escrow, you might say."

Calvin hefted out the case of soda and set it on the trunk. "I might be wrong, but I think he might have stolen the box with the veil in it—the one I got in the mail from Warren Hosmer. I don't say that he *did*, only that he might have. Someone broke into my car when I was in Shirley Fowler's store—she sends her regards, by the way—and when I came out the trunk had been opened and the box was missing. Whoever it was left the trunk unlatched, too, like they *wanted* me to know they'd stolen it."

"Pride goeth," he said. "Are you sure you didn't leave it back home?"

"No chance. Like I say, I don't *know* that Postum stole it, because I didn't see him do it, but *somebody* took it out of the car when I was in the store, and Postum is the primary suspect. I didn't make any other stops on the way out here. Also, there was another weird thing. I'm virtually certain his truck passed me heading west, maybe fifteen miles before I got to the store. Might have been a different truck, because I wasn't really paying attention, and there was a lot of glare, but it was pretty much the same vintage and with the same hole in the muffler. I'd bet a nickel it was him."

"So you think he was *looking* for you? He was cruising up and down the highway, and when he spotted you he turned around and came back to steal the box?"

"I don't know what to think. I guess there're lots of old pickups out here in the desert. Also, how the heck would he know it was *me*?"

"Well, that's a twenty-dollar question. What's important is that he *did*. I half expected something like this, but I wasn't sure it would be Postum. Now we know. Anybody else with him?"

"No."

"Did you tell him your name?"

"He overheard it when I was talking to Shirley."

"Well, he'll be wondering whether you're a player or just a courier, but he won't be able to say for sure. Either way looks likely."

"You think he did it out of spite? Because you turned him down as a lodge member?"

"I don't think that quite covers it. One thing's for sure, though—there's more to Bob Postum than meets the eye. But like I said, I already suspected that. I just wonder how *much* more and how soon we'll find out."

"Well, I'm sorry for losing the veil," Calvin said. "Aunt Iris and all..."

"You can cheer up about that. The veil in the box Hosmer sent you is a fraud. This one you got from Shirley Fowler is the real McCoy. Hosmer and I thought we'd throw out a little bait—see what kind of fish came up out of the river to gobble it up. You follow me?"

Calvin nodded shrewdly at his uncle. In fact, though, he didn't follow any of it and hadn't been following it since the middle of the afternoon. *Bait?* And what would Bob Postum care about Aunt Iris's veil? Perhaps there was some sort of explanation that led back to Iowa at the dawn of the Cretaceous period, some old feud—unrequited love, terrible jealousies, dead toads hung from door knockers. "What were you two fishing *for?*" Calvin asked. "Not that it's any of my business." He picked up the case of soda, the paper sack, and the Fourteen Carats book off the seat, and they set out toward the house.

"*Men,*" his uncle said heavily, "and now here you are, and

Bob Postum, into the bargain." He laughed, as if it were a joke. He opened the front door and Calvin followed him into the dim interior, where the swamp coolers were evidently doing their job. The place had a wine cellar kind of cool to it, at least compared to outdoors—very still and heavy with the smell of water-cooled air, cut stone, lemon-oiled wood, and old books. The furniture was solid and dark, as if it had been built by a medieval craft guild in some distant age, which maybe some of it had been, and there were Turkish carpets on the floor and a long picture window looking out through the cottonwoods to the river. The religious art and relics on the walls and tables lent the place an air of dusty antiquity. Nothing had changed, apparently, from the last time Calvin had been here. Probably nothing had changed for the past fifty years. He liked that. The absence of change had an almost irresistible allure for him, and he could easily picture himself twenty or thirty years from now, safely content within the confines of this very house here in New Cyprus, sheltered from the world by the Dead Mountains and the desert and the desert river.

"Tell me one other thing," his uncle said to him, breaking the spell. "Did Postum see Shirley give you the second box?"

"No," Calvin told him. "He'd already gone out, and she had the box behind the counter, out of sight."

His uncle nodded.

"How's Aunt Nettie?" Calvin asked. He trailed after his uncle into the kitchen, where he set his boxes and packages on the counter.

He took a moment to answer. "She's in some pain, even with the medication, which tires her out. There's not much connecting her to the world that's any good. She likes a can of Bud-weiser now and then, even though it's against doctor's orders, or at least the doctor over in the medical center in Bullhead. Doc Hoyle, the local man, he recommends it. But he's a confirmed toper. Anyway, her mind drifts a little—downriver," he said, not smiling now. "But maybe that's for the best. Why don't you go on out back and see what she's up to? Don't hesitate to make things clear to her. She wants a little encouraging sometimes."

Calvin went on alone in no real rush, through a den deco-rated with odds and ends from an Arab bazaar—draperies and cushions and stamped brass plates and a hookah the size of a potbellied stove. He wondered idly whether the decorations qualified as doodads or artifacts, and then he spotted a basket of woven reeds heaped with hundreds of coins about twice the size of silver dollars, each stamped on one side with the familiar equal-armed cross and on the other with the likeness of a stern-looking man that Calvin couldn't identify. He quelled a sudden urge to pick up a big double handful of the coins and let them run through his fingers.

He saw that his aunt was sitting outside in a webbed alu-minum lawn chair under the big trees along the edge of the river. Her feet were ankle-deep in slack water that eddied slowly over a sandy bottom. A speedboat appeared on the sunlit far side of the river, coming down from the direction of Bullhead City. It was towing a skier, and as Calvin watched, the driver of the boat made a little whirly motion with his hand as a signal to the skier, and the boat U-turned and headed back upriver. Moments later, two figures floating on inner tubes bobbed past, also on the far shore, paddling with their hands to position themselves. They were quickly lost from sight, the river hurrying them along toward Needles. Then a fishing boat putt-putted into view, angling into a little bay half choked by willows. The lone occupant dropped an anchor over the side, picked up an already-rigged fishing pole, and tossed his lure into the water. The ceaselessly moving diorama reminded Calvin pleasantly of a Cascade beer lamp he had seen on the wall of a bar up in central Oregon, and he understood another piece of what it was that kept his aunt and uncle in this far-flung part of the world. His aunt seemed to be gazing out on the river as a person might gaze at the ocean or at a fire in a fireplace. Either that or she was asleep. He steeled himself for the meeting and went outside into the warmth of the evening.

"Hello, Aunt Nettie!"

She apparently wasn't asleep, because she glanced up at him now with an interrupted sort of look, as if he were a door-to-door salesman. Then her expression changed to one of veiled recognition. "So you've come at last," she said.

"Yes, indeed," he told her, trying not to read too much into her demeanor and tone. She was thinner than he remembered, and somehow it made her look taller. Her straight hair, still with streaks of black in it, was cut short, almost bobbed. In the past, though, she'd had a piercing gaze, but now it was dulled, and he wasn't certain that she actually knew who he was at all. Maybe the "at last" business didn't refer to him, but meant that she had been expecting the artifact. "I brought the veil," he said.

She looked downward and put her cupped hand over her eyes, as if to hide her sudden emotion, and then she clutched at his hand and held it, shaking her head. "God bless you," she said. He hadn't prepared himself for this—the change in her, even though Uncle Lymon's letter had warned him. Half of what she had been had disappeared, and he looked out at the river for a moment to try to come to terms with it, which he couldn't do. "You've come to *stay* this time." Her eyes rolled back into her head disconcertingly, as if she were literally searching her mind. "It's coming to pass," she said.

"Sure," he muttered stupidly. "But it was no problem, really. There was a little mix-up out at Shirley Fowler's store, but we got it settled. Shirley sends her regards."

"Shirley?" his aunt asked, recovering herself abruptly and giving him a doubtful look.

"Shirley Fowler, out on the highway—at the Gas'n'Go. She said her husband used to be a Knight. I didn't catch his name."

There was no sign that she understood him. "And you?" she asked.

"I'm doing pretty well," he said. "Better than I deserve. How are you feeling?"

"Are you a *Knight*?"

He smiled widely to deflect the baffling question, wondering again if she knew who he was after all, or whether she was speaking metaphorically somehow. "I...No, not really. I haven't really thought much about it. I've been pretty busy."

"The world is too busy for its own good," she said softly. "I see a Knight in you." And then, looking off into the distance, she said, "Shirley Fowler had a store out on I-40. She's a local girl, from out in Essex. How's Leonard?"

"Leonard?"

"Shirley's husband. Leonard Fowler."

Dead, he thought, but he didn't say it. "He wasn't there, actually. I didn't speak to him."

She nodded. "He hasn't been out here for a good long time. Probably he's passed away, like most of the rest of them."

"I brought you a little something," he told her cheerfully, and he handed her the paper sack, which she took from him while looking deeply into his eyes. "Go ahead and open it. It's not Aunt Iris...." he said, regretting both the comment and the coasters even as he said it. She hauled the plastic toilet out of the bag and took a good look at it, apparently trying to make sense of it. "I mean to say that it's not the *veil,*" he said. "It's a...knickknack. From Las Vegas." There was a time when she would have laughed at it, but now she gave him a puzzled look, lifted off the top toilet seat, and peered at the legend inscribed on it. After a moment she laid the lid back on top of the others, put the whole thing back into the bag, and set it down under the chair. River water immediately began to swirl it away. "I'll just put it inside the house," Calvin said, snatching it up again. "I hear the sounds of supper. Can I bring you anything? Can of Budweiser?"

"They say it's the king of beers," she said, but she was gazing out over the river again. The fisherman in the rowboat was simply a dusky shadow now. Bats flitted through the air, darting and wheeling, and the muddy smell of the shoreline was heavy on the evening breeze. He could see the lights of the Temple glimmering on the water, and the storm clouds that had been out over the horizon a half hour ago loomed now in the darkening sky, creeping closer by the moment.

"Well, if you're all right, I'll just go inside, then," he said.

She didn't answer. Clearly she had gone downriver, as his uncle had put it. Either that or she was so mortified by the toilet seat coasters that she simply wasn't speaking to him any longer. He went in the French doors and through the den, carrying the wet sack. In the kitchen he found his uncle heating a casserole in the microwave.

"Rice, bay shrimp, peas, and crumbled potato chips," Lymon said when Calvin peered in through the glass in the oven door. "It's straight out of Betty Crocker. It's the potato chips that do the trick. When you reheat it, though, you've got to scrape off the old chips; otherwise they get limp. You crumble on a fresh layer, heat the whole mess up, and you've really got something. Better the second time around."

"It looks delicious."

"Your aunt will probably take hers outside tonight. She likes to be out on the river this time of the evening, especially when there's weather."

"I can see why. It's beautiful out there. So how's she coming along?"

"Come see, come saw," his uncle said. "Some days are better than others. The cancer's pretty far advanced. It was in remission for a while, but when it came back..." He shook his head. "She's still all right alone, though. She can take care of herself, at least for short periods of time."

"That's good," Calvin said. "That makes a big difference."

"I point it out because you're free to come and go. I'm heading over to the Temple in an hour for a little meeting. I'd invite you along, but it's an official thing, you know, just the Elders."

"That reminds me of something," Calvin said. "Bob Postum

39

asked me to tell you that he'd see you at the Temple one of these evenings soon. He specifically wanted me to say 'sooner rather than later.' I thought he was being friendly, but now it doesn't sound that way."

His uncle shrugged. "It's a lot of malarkey is what it is—nothing for you to worry about. Did he say 'the Temple' or 'the Temple Bar'?"

"Not the same thing?"

"Well, loosely speaking, but your man Postum isn't loose with his speech. He'll lie to your face, but it'll be carefully phrased, if you see what I mean. The building was meant to be a church, a meetinghouse, and it was referred to as the Temple from the earliest days."

"Is there a Knights Templar connection there?" Calvin asked.

"It's the same jargon. And you've seen the regalia. Sure there's a connection. Anyway, the Temple was built on what looks like a sandbar, although of course it's actually bedrock; otherwise it would have washed away years ago. People still call the island out there the Temple Bar because of the sandbar connection. And when it came to be used for social functions, and they put in the actual bar, then people started calling the *building* the Temple Bar, by which they meant something like a clubhouse. But a clubhouse isn't the club, you know, just like a church building isn't the church."

"So Postum didn't mean that he would stop in for a drink?"

"Not if I had to guess, but a man like that enjoys being obscure. Are you all right with your own company tonight?"

"Sure," Calvin said. "I'll probably hit the hay early anyway."

"Healthy, wealthy, and wise, eh? Good for you. You might think about joining up, though, while you're out here. You've got a better pedigree than Bob Postum."

"I'm pretty much dug in out in Eagle Rock."

"Why not dig yourself out? With the equity you've got in that house of yours, you'd end up with money in the bank moving out here to New Cyprus. We've got a kind of rent control thing going. We like to move someone into a house without listing it—keep everything in the family. Most of the time, money doesn't even change hands. The Knights take care of their own. Did Nettie say anything about it?"

"About what?"

"You becoming a Knight. It's been on her mind a lot these days. When she's…adrift…like she is tonight, she gets an idea about things. You don't want to take what she says lightly, because it might just come to pass."

The buzzer on the microwave went off, and at that same moment the bottom fell out of the water-soaked bag that Calvin was holding, and the tiny toilet dropped out onto the kitchen table, the seats falling off and clattering away, a couple of them dropping to the floor. One of them landed on the Aunt Iris box. His uncle peered at it. " 'I crapped out in Las Vegas,' " he read, and then chuckled. "We used to call it 'lost wages.' If they sold one of these toilets to everyone who crapped out, they'd be rich."

The coaster on the box suddenly shifted sideways, apparently moving under its own power, sliding uncannily along the top of the box as if it were being drawn by a moving magnet hidden inside. It hesitated at the edge, shuddered slightly, and then rose into the air and fell over the side, like one of the Gadarene swine off the edge of the cliff.

His uncle reached across and picked up the box. "It's that breeze off the river," he said. "It sets up air currents." He went out through the kitchen door, taking the veil box with him. The door swung shut behind him, and Calvin picked up the fallen coasters. He dropped one of them onto the tabletop, and it clattered down without the least tendency to float or creep around. Then he went across to the open kitchen window and put his face to the screen. The air outside was dead-still now. It had the ozone smell of a pending storm. If there was an air current of any variety, it was subtle—too subtle to float toilet seats. Moments later the kitchen door swung open again and his uncle reentered, heading straight for the microwave. He spooned casserole onto plates, took one of them outside, and then came back in, opened two grape sodas, and poured them into ice-filled glasses. "Get it while it's hot," he said. "There's nothing worse than cold casserole."

"Maybe it was Aunt Iris, up to her old tricks," Calvin said after they had sat down at the table.

"Maybe what was Aunt Iris?"

"That floating coaster."

"I don't follow you."

"Cousin Hosmer tells me that her veil used to float around the house like a ghost."

"Did he? I guess I never heard about that. That's probably the Hosmer sense of humor coming out. Let's eat. And you give some thought to that offer of a house, too. That wasn't just idle talk."

The offer *of a house,* Calvin thought, puzzling over it. He let it go, however, spotting the book from the Fourteen Carats Press lying on the kitchen counter where he had set it down. He reached across and picked it up, effectively changing the subject.

"Where'd you get hold of that?" Lymon asked him through a mouthful of food.

"From a rack of books out at the Gas'n'Go. It was published back in the fifties by a small press out in Henderson."

"Fourteen Carats. That outfit's in Bullhead City now, down behind the Safeway in the back room of the bookstore. They're a curious crowd, or at least what's left of them. And I mean curious like in a tendency to pay too much attention to the wrong things."

"You know much about them, then?"

"They've been around about as long as I have, although the son's got the press now. The old man passed away ten or fifteen years ago, under what they call mysterious circumstances. This story you've got here involves your man Postum, too, although you won't find his name in it."

"He didn't mention that at the Gas'n'Go. He had to have seen it lying on the counter."

"Let's just say there were crimes committed—the kind where there's no statute of limitations. It's not the sort of thing a man talks about to a stranger. It's too bad that he saw it, though. You called extra attention to yourself with it."

"It's just that I like this kind of local-color thing," Calvin said. "I don't care who was involved in any crimes."

"You and I know that."

"So we're talking about murder here?" Calvin flipped open the book and looked at the frontispiece again.

"It sometimes goes along with the severing of a man's head. There wasn't enough evidence to convict anyone, though, and there were some powerful people involved. And of course back in those days, in the desert, things were a little bit…loose, you might say—frontier justice. You read a book like this and you'd think that the whole thing involved the Knights, but that's not quite the way it was. These clowns weren't the Knights of the Cornerstone, except for one or two renegade types, who got drummed out of New Cyprus before this nonsense came to pass. We don't traffic in severed heads."

"It looks like the story of Salome and John the Baptist, except set locally. What's the *real* story, then?"

"It's too long to tell it all, but there was a casino owner from up in Henderson, named Geoff de Charney, who claimed to be a descendant of the old French family. There's a long line of Geoffrey de Charneys, dating way back. One of them was burned at the stake with Jacques de Molay when the Templars were betrayed. Anyway, he set himself up as Grand Master of a little crowd of would-be Knights in Henderson—young men, mostly. They had more money than sense, which can be a dangerous thing. He studied the old books and came up with the idea that if he reenacted the legends, he could generate some variety of alchemy and conjure up God knows what—a link to the spirit world that would lend them…*vitality* of some sort. Maybe 'authenticity' is a better word. There's an apocryphal old story that the Templars possessed the head of John the Baptist back in the days of the Crusades and used it as some sort of oracle, and that's what de Charney was aiming at. They all took on French names and wore the regalia, but they were no more Templars than the man in the moon, least of all in spirit. More casserole?"

"Sure." Calvin passed his plate across. "Don't skimp on those crushed chips."

"I told you it was good."

"Is Aunt Nettie doing okay out there?" Calvin asked. "I could take her seconds."

"She won't finish the first helping. And she's right where she wants to be. That view hasn't changed in all these years, so she can sit out there and reminisce to her heart's content. She loves a storm, too. We'll just let her be."

Calvin nodded. "So you were saying about these Templars?"

"I was saying that that's what they were *not*. The Templars were put down centuries ago, although I guess you could say they were down but not out, since remnants of what they had are still—what do you want to call it?—*alive* in the world, maybe. De Charney's crowd had *pretensions* along those lines, because of his illustrious lineage. But you can't make book on your ancestors' deeds."

"Why didn't they just start their own organization? Call themselves the Crusaders or the Wildebeests or something?"

His uncle looked at his plate for a moment, pushing his food around with his fork, and then said, "That wasn't what they had in mind, you see—some kind of *service* organization, like the Moose or the Elks. They wanted to step into something that's been around a little longer, something a little higher octane and with a deeper connection to things. Partly it was greed, but that wasn't all of it. Anyway, long story short, they arranged for the murder of a preacher from out in Redlands named John Nazarite, who wasn't doing anyone any harm and a few people a certain amount of good. He used to have big tent revivals out along the Mojave River, and every Easter he'd baptize people at a natural spring out there near Desert Center. The rite, or the murder, or whatever you want to call it, involved de Charney's niece, a girl named Paige Whitney, who was a dancer in one of his casinos. You're right about the John the Baptist connection, too. De Charney was rumored to be having an affair with his brother's wife, who was Paige Whitney's mother. I don't know whether de Charney contrived all this baloney by setting it up, or whether he fell into it by chance, realized the biblical parallels, and it put ideas in his head. Ultimately, though, there was a lot of claptrap and mumbo jumbo—a cult ceremony, like I said—a re-creation, and at least one dead man.

"They never did find the head, and nobody got prosecuted for the crime, because old de Charney had enough money to make it all disappear. The Fourteen Carats sensationalized it in that book you've got there, although it had a little bitty print run, and the whole story looked like malarkey to most people. It was just too far-fetched to interest the authorities, but it turned out to be a mistake that Fourteen Carats printed it, because it put them on the wrong side of some powerful people."

"What about Bob Postum?"

"Not much, except he was one of de Charney's crowd. He was young then, and gambled a little. Made a small name for himself in Henderson and Vegas. He started calling himself Baldwin, after the old Christian king of Jerusalem back in the day, which must have irritated de Charney. That's what I meant by his pedigree: it's a lie in more ways than one, although if a man believes a lie long enough he forgets that it's a lie. He married Paige Whitney a few years later, which put him in the inner circle, but something went bad there, and for a long time the man kept to himself. Then a couple of years back he came out of retirement, you might say, as if he'd been biding his time until de Charney was on his last legs. Even so, until today I wouldn't have pegged Bob Postum as a major player. I would have said he was mostly bluff, which is probably just exactly what he wanted us to think. But that's why we set out that bait, like I said—chum the waters a little, see what comes up out of the depths. Sometimes you get a rock cod, and sometimes you get a sea serpent."

There was the rumble of thunder, and then the sound of rain, quickly growing heavy, and the two men sat in silence, listening. After a couple of minutes Aunt Nettie came inside carrying her half-empty plate, her face and hair wet with rainwater. Although she was moving slowly and probably painfully, there was a look of intense joy on her face, as if she had been waiting out there all this time for the sky to open up. "My land!" she said, setting the plate on the counter. Then she passed out of the kitchen without another word, heading toward her bedroom at the back of the house.

"She likes the weather," Uncle Lymon said, "more than just about anything." He continued to gaze in the direction that she had taken. There was sadness and worry in his face, and again it came into Calvin's mind that the old man loved his wife with a weight that had decades behind it. The realization made him regret what he himself had missed out on. Yesterday he would have bet money that a man couldn't feel honest regret for the loss of something he had never gained in the first place, but that's just what he felt at this moment. He was struck with the certainty that he had been marking time, watching the world through the front window of his house just as his aunt watched it from her chair on the river.

He stood up to help his uncle clear the plates. The kitchen curtains moved now, catching a breath of air with the smell of the river and rain on it.

"There's your ghost," Uncle Lymon said, "blowing in from Arizona."

THE TEMPLE BAR

After supper, Calvin found himself restless and at loose ends in the quiet house. He could hear water dripping from the eaves and the muted sound of the television from down the hall in his aunt's bedroom. He stared out the window for a time, watching the lightning flickering in the east, and then he aimlessly began to look over his uncle's books, which filled dozens of broad cedar shelves book-ended with cylinders of what appeared to be solid silver, stamped on top with the Knight's cross. He hefted one of the cylinders, which must have weighed several pounds. How many were in the room? Forty? He had heard of people putting their money into gold and hiding it under the floorboards, but silver had to be a ponderous way to squirrel away wealth.

He found that he was drawn in by the hundreds of arcane volumes, mostly on historical subjects, some of the books so apparently ancient that he didn't dare touch them. Uncle Lymon had invested heavily in histories of the Crusades, the Grail, the Knights Templar and the Hospitallers, and other holy orders and movements and legends. Many of the most ancient books had titles in Latin or French. *De Antichristo* was easy enough to translate, and the same was the case with the *Histoire de la Papesse Jeanne*, written by a Frenchman named Lenfant. The contents, however, which the titles made sound so promising, were unreadable, French and Latin both being Greek to him, as was Greek.

He found books on the Illuminati, the Rosicrucians, the Assassins, the Mormons, and an array of books on Masonic lore. He took down *Morals and Dogma of the Ancient and Accepted Scottish Rite of Freemasonry*, which looked to be full of mysteries, and sat down to read it. But he was quickly bogged down in a mathematical account of the marvels of the number nine, which apparently could be broken up in a heap of different ways and then multiplied and re-added and cooked at a high heat with parsley and butter and still taste just like the number nine. It was evidently the great mystery number of the universe, but he couldn't fathom what the mystery portended. That was the problem with secret societies, he thought—the secrets too often led down the garden path, finally revealing a view of a birdbath or a head on a plate.

He returned the books to the shelves and then, out of curiosity, he opened the doors of a low cabinet beneath them, expecting to see more books, or manuscripts, maybe—something worth keeping free of dust. What he saw were two cardboard boxes, identical to the two he was familiar with. Both of them had the usual Hosmer address, and both of them were taped shut. He picked one of them up, and then the other. They were either empty or contained—what? Another veil? If there were four of the boxes, he wondered, why not six? Why not eight? Veils crisscrossing the country in the trunks of automobiles, flying out from Iowa in biplanes or floating down rivers in baskets like Moses among the bulrushes. A man like Bob Postum wouldn't be able to tell an artifact from a doodad under the circumstances. It seemed like a fancy way to throw him off the track of poor Aunt Iris's veil.

He became aware that the rain had stopped, and he returned the boxes to the cabinet and stepped to the window. The dark river flowed past in a terrible hurry, bound for the ocean, with its own manifold mysteries. He went into the kitchen, found a grape soda in the refrigerator, and took it outside into the warm night, pulling off his shoes and socks and sitting down in his aunt's chair, letting the river water swirl the unfathomables out of him, right out through the ends of his toes.

It was a moonless night, pleasantly warm, and the stars shone where the clouds had retreated back into the east. He could see the Temple out on its island, illuminated by parking lot lights, and he imagined himself a Knight, sitting on a stool out there in the old building, drinking twenty-five-cent beers and talking with the Brethren. Last time he had visited he had gone over there a couple of times. The Knights all seemed to answer to Whitey and Red and Woody and other adjective names. Immediately he had become Cal instead of Calvin and had fallen into a conversation about the virtues of fishing for striped bass below the dam in low water and about the sad fate of the two-stroke outboard motor, neither one of which subjects he knew anything about, although he wished he knew more. Out here in the desert those kinds of things seemed fundamental, although fundamental to what, he couldn't say, because he was an out-of-towner.

After ten minutes his feet were numb and the bottle was empty. He picked up his shoes and socks and walked gingerly along the bank, then up onto a stone path that led back around to the carport, where he leaned against the hood of the Dodge and put his shoes and socks back on. The rain seemed to have abdicated entirely, so he set out walking, up the driveway and out onto the street that led down to the edge of the trailer park. The dark grounds were mostly empty of people now, the trailers lighted, the windows flickering with the shifting images of television screens. Two rangy-looking dogs appeared from behind a trailer, spotted him, and came across to say hello, but they quickly lost interest and wandered off.

Without having made any conscious decision to do so, he found himself walking in the direction of the river again, down toward the bridge that spanned the fifty feet of moving water between New Cyprus and the Temple Bar. His feet seemed to compel him forward, despite the fact that the Temple itself was off-limits to anyone but the Elders tonight. But the Temple wasn't his destination, really. He had no intention of knocking on any doors or of crashing the party. He would simply walk out to the island and back again, just to air himself out.

When he was out beyond the last of the trailers, he was

faintly surprised at the quality of the darkness—a darkness virtually unknown in the suburbs. Overhead, though, the sky was awash with stars, bright enough for a space traveler to read by, and it was a marvel to him how little of that light actually reached the earth. He set his sights on the pools of illumination in the Temple parking lot and walked up onto the bridge. Away to his right, muddy rainwater washed down the gully from the Dead Mountains and swirled out into the river.

The windows of the Temple had slatted shutters drawn across them, and the interior light shone through in bands. It came to him that he could easily peer unseen through a gap in the shutters and have an eyeful of the secret doings of the Knights—the Elders giving each other the wiggly-fish handshake, maybe. He stopped suddenly and crouched down behind the railing. Someone *was* peering in through the shutters, back toward the rear of the building. There wasn't much light coming through, and because the man was hunched over, it was impossible to make anything out for certain except that he was heavyset and had either blond or gray hair. He held something up to the window, almost undoubtedly a camera.

Bob Postum, Calvin thought. He moved forward warily, crouching along, but almost as soon as he started out, the man turned sharply and looked in his direction. Calvin ducked again, and when he peeked over the railing a moment later, the man was scuttling away toward the river, disappearing into the willows before Calvin could get a good look at him. More boldly now Calvin hurried across the bridge and into the lot, crossing to the edge of the building and looking hard into the darkness along the water, where the willows shifted in the night wind.

The Temple was built of heavy rectangular stones, evidently cut in the quarry in the hills. The back wall of the structure buried itself into the natural rock of the island, which mounded up in a castle-like pile to a height of fifteen feet or so. In the darkness it was difficult to see where the cut stone left off and the rock started, because natural rock and cut stone tumbled away on both sides, overgrown by willow.

He climbed partway up the hill of stone, crouching behind immense blocks and keeping his head low until he could see over the willows down to the river below. He heard an odd noise now, a muted clunk and then a scraping noise somewhere dead ahead—the sound of oars in oarlocks. The river below ran black and swift and reflected a world of dancing stars. Thirty feet out his man was rowing a boat hard toward the far shore, making three times as much leeway as forward movement in the strong current, but drawing away quickly. He rowed backward, facing forward in the boat, so that Calvin could only see his back. It clearly wasn't Postum. This man had shorter hair. He wore a white T-shirt with a dark blotch on the back, what might have been a face or a logo of some sort, and he rowed the boat like an amateur, jerking the oars out of the river when he was halfway through a stroke and flinging water in every direction. In a few moments he was a mere shadow disappearing quickly downriver.

Calvin headed back down toward the Temple, hearing talk and laughter from within. He had to admit that the day had moved from curious to ominous: first the mystery of the Aunt Iris veil, then the theft and the second veil, and then Bob Postum needlessly pretending to be Fred Woolsworth, apparently having quit pretending to be King Baldwin, perhaps because of a murder that was half a century old. Calvin was evidently a pawn, entirely in the dark here—literally and figuratively. And of course there was the levitating toilet seat—another variety of mystery—and his uncle's unconvincing talk about air currents off the river.

That was the problem, though. So far there had been no *convincing* talk about anything. He wouldn't say that anyone owed him an explanation, but surely he couldn't be blamed for *looking* for one.

He stopped just outside the window, where he glanced around, looking back toward the bridge and the trailer park and then out toward the river again. He was entirely alone, and it would be the work of a moment to have one small peek through the window, just so he would know what the lurking boatman had been up to. If nothing was going on except beer and skittles and the mystery of the secret fez, he would go home to bed and sleep it off. Tomorrow he could live the carefree life of the unwitting tourist. On the other hand, if the man at the window had seen something that would put the Knights at risk, then Uncle Lymon would want to know, delicate as the whole matter would be. Half convinced by this rationalization, he peered in through the blinds.

There were six people inside, including his uncle. All of them wore hats, although not the typical fez sort of hat, but something that looked more like a helmet from an old suit of armor, fish-scaled with silver circles the size of dimes. The people were girded with beaded sashes, and wore white tunics with the red cross on the chest. He recognized Whitey someone, who had an unmistakably large nose and bald head, as well as a portly man in suspenders with wildly bushy eyebrows, a retired college professor whom he remembered as Miles Taber. Two of the people in the room, he realized abruptly, were women—something that had been obscured by the costumes and low light and by the fact that he wouldn't have expected any women in the Knights. It was difficult to tell their ages, but one was old enough to be his mother, and the other was slightly younger, with bright red nail polish—something that looked incongruous to him under the circumstances.

The six of them stood around an old wooden table built on a base of slender, gnarled tree limbs topped with rough-hewn planks. Oddly, there were authentic-looking leaves sprouting from the table legs, as if the legs were alive and rooted in the earth. On the table sat the cardboard box that Shirley Fowler had given him. His uncle pushed aside his tunic to reach into his pocket, coming up with a pocketknife with which he carefully slit the tape on the veil box.

He shut the knife and returned it to his pocket before opening the flaps and then removing several layers of folded bubble wrap and drawing out the veil that lay beneath it—a piece of yellowed and tattered muslin-looking cloth. Even from Calvin's perspective it looked to be more like a thousand years old than a hundred. There was a charcoal-like smudge on it that resolved itself unmistakably into a human face as the veil was unfolded, a face that didn't look anything like anyone's Aunt Iris. It was the craggy shadow of a man's visage, seen straight on, as if someone, or the shadow of someone, were looking through the veil from the other side.

Calvin glanced away, consumed by the feeling that the image was an actual physical presence, and that it had looked straight into his eyes. He peered up at the starry sky, and he knew that he had no business being there, that something was going on that he was unprepared to witness, or was disallowed from witnessing. But the feeling was overcome by a stronger curiosity, fueled by the certain knowledge that he had been taken in lock, stock, and barrel by the Aunt Iris myth, which had sounded preposterous even when Hosmer was relating it to him.

He peered back in through the window. The two people standing next to his uncle had edged away, as if out of fear or respect, and everyone in the room seemed to relax visibly when his uncle returned the veil to its box and then put the box away in the open cabinet behind them. Lymon returned to the table carrying a basket holding a loaf of bread, a glass goblet, and a clear, doughnut-shaped glass decanter, flattened on the bottom so that it would stand up. Like the veil, the decanter appeared to be as old as Methuselah. It was half filled with red wine—or what Calvin assumed was wine—and was corked with a red glass stopper in the shape of an equal-armed cross. The company cast their eyes downward, and Uncle Lymon began intoning a prayer. "Amen," Lymon said finally, and the rest of them repeated it, and then after a respectful moment he broke the bread into pieces and handed around the basket, then poured two inches of wine into the glass.

The six of them took the bread and consumed it, drank from the glass, and then Lymon set the glass back onto the table. Then each of them put both hands on the table in front of them and bowed their heads again. Calvin became aware then of a creaking noise, like the lid of an old trunk being raised, or a heavy cellar door swinging ponderously open. He thought he could make out a deep, sonorous music underlying it, and he was struck with a sudden onset of vertigo, as if he were looking down from a height at moving water. The music seemed to occupy the air around him, leaking up from deep within the rocks that formed the Temple Bar. The ground shook then, mildly at first, and then with an abrupt lurch.

Earthquake! Calvin thought, and he clutched even more tightly at the windowsill and set his feet. His heart pounded. Rocks on the mound behind him tumbled loose and clattered downhill. The six inside were riding out the quake by steadying themselves against the table, still with their heads bowed, as if this were part of the ceremony and not an interruption. The circular decanter toppled over, and Calvin nearly shouted a warning. But none of them let go of the table, and the goblet fell to the floor with the muted but unmistakable sound of glass shattering.

The earthquake stopped, the night was silent, and then, as if a tension had been suddenly relaxed, the six began chatting in normal tones, stepping away from the broken glass as if unconcerned with it. Calvin could see a shard of what had been the decanter lying near the leg of the table in a pool of spilled wine. Miles Taber walked across to the open wooden wardrobe cabinet, took out a silver plate, and returned to the table, where he bent over and picked up the piece of glass with his fingertips, laying it on the plate and then picking up other pieces hidden from Calvin's view. He set the cross-shaped stopper among the pieces and straightened up, glancing in the direction of the window and pausing briefly before turning back toward the wardrobe. After a couple of steps he turned his head sharply and looked at the window again.

Calvin ducked away, shoving in among the willows, certain that he had been seen. *What an embarrassment,* he thought wretchedly. What could he possibly say to his uncle that would explain his being there? The crazy idea of swimming for it came into his mind—just sliding into the water and letting the river carry him safely down to Needles where he could take a Greyhound back to Eagle Rock, disconnect his phone, change his name, and retire from the world for good and all.

But nobody came out of the Temple. The night was as dark and silent as it had been. He gave it another minute and then set out hurriedly toward the bridge, keeping to the dark verge of the island, away from the parking lot lights. When he was near the bridge, he turned around and walked backward, which seemed cunning to him. If they came out and saw him now, he would reverse his step and head back again toward the island, and it would appear as if he was just then coming down from the trailer park—coming instead of going. But no one came out, and, feeling foolish and shameful, he turned around and headed home, going straight into the guest bedroom, where he put on a pair of pajamas and climbed into bed, switching off the bedside lamp and calling it a night.

Soon the house and the night outside were perfectly still—a vast silence that was almost like a mass of undifferentiated noises. Lying in the darkness, Calvin listened, unable to fall asleep, and after a time it seemed to him that he could hear a faint pounding in the far distance, from up in the mountains, perhaps, or up in the sky somewhere—Thor with his hammer, maybe, knocking together another thunderstorm. The noise wasn't regular, but would start up and then fade away and then start up again, and there was a ringing quality to it, like a hammer against an anvil. When he finally drifted into sleep, the hammering became more pronounced. Not louder, but as if the ringing blows had multiplied—dwarfs in a mine, perhaps, knocking jewels out of rock walls with pickaxes, the sounds echoing backward through time....

He awakened later to the sound of his uncle coming in. He heard the tread of his uncle's feet moving down the hallway, and then heard the soft click of the doorknob turning. Calvin lay still, feigning sleep, the entire thing reminding him unpleasantly of his childhood. It was past two—strangely late for the old man still to be up and about. Calvin lay awake for a time thinking curious and troubled thoughts before finally descending again into sleep.

TIME AND THE RIVER

In the morning he awoke to the smell of coffee, with none of the confusion of finding himself in a strange place. On the contrary, he knew exactly where he was. All night long he had dreamed of earthquakes and of ring-shaped decanters tumbling to the floor in slow motion and breaking, and of walking through a stone cavern deep beneath the river, with the sound of rock hammers keeping time with his heartbeat. But as soon as he became aware of the morning sun through the window, the dream images fled away and the waking memory of last night's activity replaced them like the same size shoe. It had seemed uncannily mysterious out there in the darkness on the Temple Bar, but now in the light of day it was perfectly clear to him that what he had witnessed had been a small Communion service and a coincidental earthquake. Interesting, but nothing to lose his mind over.

Then it came into his head once again that the six Knights in the bar had seemed to *expect* the earthquake, that they had been ready for it. But there was nothing he could do with that thought other than to file it away in his mind with all the rest of yesterday's unfathomables.

It was early, and through the bedroom window he could see past the cottonwoods to an empty stretch of river that glowed in the morning sunshine. The Dead Mountains were golden with it. Yesterday had been never-ending, what with the long drive out into the desert and all the rest of the tomfoolery. Today he owed it to himself to do nothing, and perhaps tomorrow, too. His aunt had absolutely the right idea, sitting in a lawn chair and watching the river tumble past. Maybe he would go out onto the bridge and play Poohsticks. Maybe he'd take a nap.

He pulled on his pants and shirt, ran his hands through his hair, and went out to greet the day. In the kitchen there was hot coffee in the pot next to a note that read "Help yourself."

"I will," he said out loud, and poured coffee into a mug. Then he found his aunt, already sitting outside in her chair, looking at the water. She had a mug of coffee in a cup holder cut into the plastic arm of the chair.

"Good morning," he said, stepping out into the daylight.

She turned and smiled at him, looking sharper and fresher than she had yesterday evening, which was a relief. He opened a chair that was leaning against the side of the house and sat down next to her. "Need a refill?" he asked.

"I'm all right," she said, and they remained for a time in

silence, sipping coffee and letting the river eddy over their feet. The low morning sun, looking right at them from over the hills in the east, was already heating up, and Calvin was grateful for the shade. "I'm wondering about joining the Knights," he said without thinking about it first. It was only about 10 percent true, but the day had a what-the-heck quality about it that made it perfect for speculation.

His aunt nodded. "I had a suspicion you'd come around," she said. His aunt seemed perfectly sane to him now—sharp, even. If she was bothered by some variety of dementia, it had taken the morning off.

"What do the Knights do, mainly? They're a service organization?"

"Well, the Knights serve a higher power," she said. "They do good works whenever they can, like the Bible recommends. And I mean good *work* too—up and walking good. That's the main part of the equation, you see. When Jesus turned water into wine out at the wedding, it was *good* wine; so the Bible says. The Knights don't bother with halfway measures."

"I seem to recall that most New Cyprus folks are members."

"Pretty nearly all of them are, or have been. Some fall away, lose interest, take a breather, but they're still on the list until they take themselves off, which doesn't happen too often. It was a rule from the first, back after they brought the Cornerstone in from the East and set it up beneath the Bar. In those days it was just a rocky hill in the desert. That was before the earthquake changed the river's course and revealed what lay beneath the island. Hugh Blankfort was Grand Master then. He figured that the land where he planted New Cyprus was neither here nor there once the river swerved out of its bed, but was in between, perfect homestead land. He goes way back, Blankfort does."

"Further back than you and Uncle Lymon?"

"Oh, my yes. *Way* back, his family. Traces his roots back to France in the earliest days. Family had the French spelling, with a *q*, but no one could pronounce it, so they simplified it some when they came out West. Blankfort and the Knights brought the stone out on a flatcar, overland from New Rochelle, right after the turn of the century. That's when the waters parted, and the river turned out of its bed. That's how they knew this was the place. If you ask me, God made the river turn aside, just like in the time of Moses, although you can believe what you want about that. They found a holy place waiting for them right out there beneath the Temple Bar, and they built over the top of it. That's the Fourth Secret. I tell you that because that's why you came out here, at least partly. You'll learn the particulars soon enough when you're a Knight."

"*What* was it they brought out on the flatcar?" he asked.

"The Cornerstone. There was no way to transport a stone that size except by rail, all the way out from New Rochelle. Forty-mule team couldn't do it. They still ran mule teams in those days."

"Sounds as difficult as wheeling West Virginia," he said, repeating one of his father's old jokes, and he was happy to see that his aunt smiled at it.

"There wasn't anything around here back then—just a few shacks over across the river, prospectors, mainly. And the land was worthless unless there was gold or silver under it, which there wasn't much of, leastways not over on the Arizona side.

A lot of Okies came in through Needles during the Depression, and some of them stayed to quarry more stone out of the Dead Mountains, mainly for the funeral industry and to build New Cyprus houses. The stonecutting was a going concern in the thirties. They put it on flatcars running out of Barstow and sent it all over the country. That's why they call them the Dead Mountains. Lots of headstones and urns and crypts cut out of those hills."

"Is that right? I was wondering about that old quarry and rail line. No profit in stonecutting anymore, I guess."

"Once the homes were built, quarry work slacked off, and then during the war most of the men went off to fight and the stonecutting was about over. It's a lost art now, what Hugh Blankfort used to do." She lapsed into silence now and watched the river.

"It's interesting how the Temple is built right into the rocks like it is," he said after a time, and she turned to look at him again.

"That's Blankfort's work. Some of the old-timers called that island the Temple Mount; some of them called it the Temple Bar. All of it's tied right into the Cornerstone."

" 'The stone that the builder refused,' eh?"

" '...Shall become the cornerstone,' " she said, finishing the verse for him and looking straight into his face.

For a moment he was afraid that she thought he was trying to mock her—hauling out a Bible quotation himself before she could get a crack at it. But evidently she didn't. "So the Knights must have a fairly big membership," he said finally. "Probably they don't need an absentee member like me."

"They're not all of them active," she said. "Lots of them are standing by. 'Blessed is he that waits, and cometh to the days.' So says the Old Book."

Calvin nodded. It was a good sentiment—being blessed for waiting.

"Yes, sir. Blessed are those who wait," she said again, maybe to make sure that he was listening. "But you can't wait forever," she said. "Sooner or later you've got to do what it is you were called out to do."

He found he was unsettled by his aunt's easy way of quoting Bible verse. She could find something useful in it without a moment's thought. She had always been naturally religious, ever since he could remember, which had sometimes been an embarrassment to him. Her early efforts to interest him in things of the spirit hadn't exactly taken hold when he was younger, and even now it was a reminder that he had shirked another duty. "What if you weren't *called out* to do anything at all?" he asked. "It's kind of restful that way."

"A person thinks so, but then comes a day when you come face-to-face with it."

"With *what*?" he asked, vaguely surprised that he was actually interested in an answer.

"Well, with whatever it might be. With the *dragon*, I guess you could say." She nodded her head. "We're all sent out to do it battle, you see, only some of us pretend otherwise, and then we start to believe our pretending, and then when it comes for us, we're no match for it."

"Maybe it's best to avoid it. Just don't open the door when it knocks."

66

"Oh, it's already inside," she said. "That I can guarantee. You get to be my age and you can't fool yourself about that. It'll look right out of the mirror at you. And anyway, what're you doing out here in New Cyprus if you weren't called out?"

"Well, sure," he said, trying to deal with this. "I didn't think you were talking about that kind of calling. I mean, on the telephone, or a letter in the mailbox." He shifted in his chair, looking for something more to say, and uncomfortable with the notion that she seemed to be talking to him for a reason now, and not just shooting the breeze. He glanced sideways at her. Her eyes were illuminated by the rising sun. "You look good this morning," he said. "Rested or something."

"I *feel* rested," she said. "Like a desert tortoise waking up to spring weather."

"Tell me about Aunt Iris," he said.

"I don't know the woman. Whose aunt is she?"

He found himself at a complete loss. "I seem to remember stories about an aunt Iris. Apparently she was a spiritualist...?"

"A spiritualist? Not our branch of the family. We don't hold with that."

"Of course not," he said. "I didn't mean to imply..." He let the thought trail away. "Did you feel that quake last night?" he asked. "Round about ten?"

"No," she said. She looked at him curiously, and he had the uncanny notion that she had figured him out somehow—perceived the gears going around inside his soul. "Were you out to the Temple last night?" she asked.

"On the island? Why do you ask?"

"No reason. The ground gets shaky out there is all. Maybe

it's the river pushing on it all the time. We all get shaky with the river pushing on us." She went back to watching the water now, and Calvin kept his mouth shut, having avoided the outright lie.

A pontoon boat appeared on the river, and he watched it sweep past, several people sitting on board. One of them waved, and Calvin waved back. "Another cup of coffee?" he asked her.

"I'm already afloat," she said.

He smiled at the idea. "I'm going to grab a second cup," he said. He went inside and was halfway through the den, heading back into the kitchen, when the telephone rang. He looked back to see if his aunt was going to get up, but she sat there placidly, either not hearing it or not caring, and after the third ring he shouted, "I've got it!" and picked up the wall phone receiver over the counter. "Lymon residence," he said.

There was a silence long enough to become slightly ominous, and then a familiar but flat-sounding voice said, "Identify yourself," which struck him as a strange sort of greeting.

"Warren?" he asked, realizing it was Cousin Hosmer. "It's Cal. Cal Bryson."

"Where's Lymon?"

"Out. I don't know where. He made coffee and..."

"Coffee? What are you talking about?"

"About...coffee. He brewed some up before he left, so I guess he wasn't in any kind of hurry. Maybe he wanted to make the first ferry into town."

"When's he coming back?"

"I don't have any idea. Let me ask Nettie what she knows. Hold on."

He went out through the den again. "Warren Hosmer's on

the phone," Calvin said to her through the screen door. "He wants to know when Uncle Lymon's getting back."

"He'll be back," she said. "He always is."

"Do we have an ETA? Warren seems anxious to talk to him."

"Tell him it'll happen in the fullness of time. Hosmer's always in a tearing hurry. We were out in Grand Junction once, up on the Monument, and there was a thunderstorm coming up. Well, Hosmer was there with the Hyink crowd from Iowa and the Streffs and their tribe. We were setting out a picnic, and I said to Hosmer—"

"Hold on one second. I'll be right back." He returned to the kitchen and picked up the phone. "She doesn't know either. Should I have him call you?"

"Not on this phone. Did you get the item out there safe? No incidents?"

"Yes to the safe part. Or at least I think so. But no to the no-incidents part. There was a little trouble at the store when I stopped to buy grape soda."

"What kind of trouble?"

"Well, there was this character who told me his name was Woolsworth, although apparently he's actually a local named Bob Postum who used to go by the name King Baldwin, so I guess it doesn't really matter what his name is now. He drives a green pickup truck with a bad muffler, and—"

"Get to the point. I don't give a damn about the man's muffler."

"The point is this Postum character apparently stole the box out of the trunk when I was inside buying the soda. Then Shirley—"

"Not over the telephone."

"Pardon me?"

"Name no names, my friend. Telephone's too public, especially those New Cyprus phones. There's something for you to think about before you start yapping. They can tap right into the junction box across the river and get an earful. I've been telling Lymon that for years."

"*They* can? Who are *they*?"

"Ask Lymon. I've got to get a move on. Did Postum see your face?"

"My face? Yeah, we had a long chat. He said he knew my dad back in—"

"Then watch out for him. Everything he says is a lie. If you see him a second time, it's not by chance. First time wasn't either. Do you understand what I'm saying? Not...by...chance."

"Sure. I guess so. Are you telling me he's dangerous?"

"Everybody's dangerous if there's something they want bad enough. I'm telling you that when he finds out that you foxed him with the fake article, he won't be happy. They're going to wonder who you are exactly, and why we called you in."

"Called me in?" *Here it was again.*

"Many are called," Hosmer said heavily, "but few are chosen. And the ones who are, pretty much choose themselves. Remember that. Whatever you might think to the contrary, you set out walking like a duck yesterday, and now you're starting to quack like one. To their minds you're either a by-God duck or else you're a decoy. Right now even *you* don't know which one you are, but before this is through you're going to have to quit mincing around like a parlor monkey and make up your mind one way or the other or else someone will make it up for you. Chances are they won't waste a bullet on a decoy. And you can take the heat as long as you're not stupid. Either that or stay out of the kitchen. Mind your p's and q's. Don't ruffle your feathers. You're family, like I said, and Lymon tells me you're a good man. So was your father. He was one of the best. They got to him finally, but they had to work hard to do it."

"*Got to him...?* Dad died of liver cancer in the hospital. I was there. What do you mean a *bullet...?*"

"I didn't say they shot him."

"No, I mean will they shoot *me*? You said they won't waste a bullet on a decoy."

"Figure of speech. Or at least we hope so. Did you see the autopsy report?"

"On Dad? He was seventy-eight years old. They don't do an autopsy on a seventy-eight-year-old man with liver cancer. It stands to reason what he died of."

"Nothing in this world stands to reason, son. Human beings aren't reasonable creatures. If they were, this whole shebang would be a utopian carnival with a champagne reception. You start believing in the champagne and a man like Postum will sweep you straight under the rug, lay it back down over your corpse, and dance you flat as a pancake. They won't find you to *do* the autopsy on, not out there in the desert they won't."

Calvin almost laughed out loud with relief. This nonsense about his father's death put the rest of Hosmer's talk into perspective—ridiculous perspective.

"Like I was saying," Hosmer went on, "your father was a good man to have at your back, and the apple doesn't fall far from the tree. What I'm telling you is not to underestimate Postum. That could be fatal."

"Thanks for the tip," Calvin said. "A stitch in time saves nine."

"You're right about that. And I mean *fatal*, too, just in case you missed that part. Keep that in mind whenever you start thinking you've got time sewed up tight."

"I'll keep it in mind. Do you want me to give Uncle Lymon a message?"

"Yeah. Tell him I'm going under."

"Under?"

"*Under.* Doggo. Incommunicado. Tell him I don't like the weather. Iowa's too hot. *I'm going under.* You got that? *Under.* He'll catch your drift. He'll know where. Tell him the temperature's rising out in New Cyprus, too. That's the word on this end. And warn that interested party, but make sure you've got a secure line. Tell her they're turning up the heat."

"I will," Calvin said, assuming that he meant Shirley Fowler.

"And about yesterday. You delivered the goods anyway?"

"Yeah," Calvin said. "Everything worked out okay."

"Good. *Then for you chickenshit bastards listening in,*" Hosmer said in an abruptly loud voice, "you can *go* to Hell."

There was the sound of the phone hanging up. Hosmer had gone under. The old man had referred to Hell as if he had meant the place itself, and not just a general-purpose cussing. Calvin heard a double click, and then what sounded like wind blowing through a garden hose, as if the line were still open. Maybe someone—some chickenshit bastard—was tapped into the junction box across the river....

72

He slammed the phone back onto its cradle, wondering suddenly if even his cell phone was secure and whether he should dig it back out of the glove box, but then he remembered Hosmer's earlier warning. And anyway, he had read that cell phone conversations could be picked up by people lurking nearby with a tin can and a string. It was an age of spyware and listening devices and miniature cameras and identity theft, an age when it was impossible to sort out the Postums from the Baldwins and the Woolsworths.

Clearly this was all nuts. Of course it was. But Shirley Fowler had also been "called in," apparently, and the least he owed the poor woman was a phone call to tell her that the kitchen was heating up in Iowa. It might be nonsense, or it might be a stitch in time, but what he needed, apparently, was a pay phone—not a New Cyprus pay phone, but a randomly chosen pay phone across the river, just to be safe. And while he was there, he could pay a small visit to the bookstore where the Fourteen Carats Press was allegedly hiding out.

He wondered how he could contact his uncle, who didn't carry a cell phone at all. Uncle Lymon wasn't exactly a card-toting member of the twenty-first century and probably never would be. He had been in his prime in the 1950s and had held on to that era with both hands, dragging a slide-rule mentality along with him through the computer age. Probably he was better off for it. Almost certainly he was, Calvin thought, rooting through the cabinet drawers beneath the wall phone and coming up with the narrow little Needles and Bullhead City area phone book. He found the number of the Gas'n'Go Antiques and Cafe and wrote it out on a notepad, then tore it off and put it into his shirt pocket. Hosmer had told him to call Shirley Fowler, so he would call Shirley Fowler. This was no time to quit taking orders. It occurred to him that if *they* caught up to him, the phone number would be incriminating evidence—duck evidence. He would have to chew it up and swallow it along with a cyanide capsule. He tried to chuckle at the idea but failed. The only thing that was funny was that it wasn't funny, and even that was only barely funny.

He headed back outside. "I think I'll grab the ferry into town," he said to his aunt. "Need anything? Something from the Safeway?"

"Pick me up a bag of those peppermint stars. They've got them in the produce section, in bins. Couple of pounds."

"Sure," he said. "Say, do you know a character from hereabouts named Bob Postum?"

"I won't touch the stuff," she said. "If a body's going to drink coffee, then drink coffee, not boiled dirt. Grab a two-pound can of Folgers."

"Easy as pie," he told her.

"Apple," she said, "unless there's something you like better. The Safeway makes a good pie."

"I'll get those peppermint stars, too," he said, and walked back into the house, switched off the coffeepot, and went in after his shoes and socks.

AT THE COZY DINER

On his way down to the ferry dock Calvin detoured to Main Street and looked into the Cozy Diner, but Uncle Lymon wasn't among the customers eating breakfast and drinking coffee. A man nodded at Calvin over a stack of what must have been half a dozen tire-size pancakes, and then raised his coffee mug in a sort of salute. Anyplace else in the world Calvin would have assumed he knew the man, but here in New Cyprus it wasn't at all certain. Calvin was apparently a celebrity of sorts, Al Lymon's prodigal nephew. It was comforting in a way, but disconcerting in an equal measure.

They were good-looking pancakes. Buckwheat, unless he was very much mistaken, which he wasn't. He had always been a big pancake man—none bigger. And there appeared to be about a pound of bacon on the man's plate....

He looked at his wrist out of habit and realized that his watch was still in the glove box in the car along with the phone. But what was the rush? This was New Cyprus, where time had no dominion, as the poet said. As far as he was concerned, time *rarely* had any dominion when there were pancakes involved. He spotted a table against the wall and sat down, idly settling in to listen to the conversations going on around him, none of which had anything to do with him. After a moment a server approached the table carrying a coffeepot and a menu. She stopped to refill a cup at the adjacent table, and then turned his way again, and his first thought was that she had an interesting face, both pretty and comical, although that didn't quite do her justice, and she smiled at him in a way that made him aware that he was staring at her. But it was a friendly smile, as if she recognized him.

"Coffee?" she asked.

"Yes. Please." He smiled back at her. She had the light skin and freckled complexion of a redhead, and she had probably gone trick-or-treating as Pippi Longstocking somewhere back along the line. Now her strawberry-colored hair was pulled back in a ponytail like something out of the 1950s. He took the menu from her and laid it on the table without looking at it. "Pancakes," he said, noticing that her name tag read "Donna."

"We've got several kinds," she told him.

"Buckwheat for me."

"You want the Million-Dollar Plate?"

"Million-Dollar Plate? What would that be?"

"Little bitty ones," she said. "About the size of quarters, but a *lot* of them. We're famous for them in these parts."

"I think I'll go for the standard size this time," he said, "with bacon on the side. I'll save the Million-Dollar Plate for tomorrow morning."

"Okay, with bacon. Anything else?"

"Peanut butter, if you've got it." He shrugged at her, as if he knew it was a lot to ask.

"We can do that," she said, apparently having no problem with the idea of peanut butter on pancakes. That seemed to him to be a good sign, but then he wondered why he was looking for signs—signs of what? She might be twenty-eight, he guessed, maybe thirty, maybe his age, but young-looking, and he glanced at her left hand, which was ringless, then looked up hastily. She was smiling at him again, and he gave her a weak, senseless grin.

"You're the Lymons' nephew, aren't you?" she asked. "They were telling me all about you. The whole town's buzzing. From L.A., isn't it? Birdland, or something. Big Rock."

"Eagle Rock," he said. "I'm Calvin Bryson. Pleased to meet you."

"We've already met," she said, "but you don't remember. I used to spend a lot of time here when I was little."

"You have a heck of a memory," Calvin told her.

"Traumatic memories last forever. We were running around in the park, and you pushed me and I fell into a picnic table." She pointed to a scar on her cheek, and suddenly Calvin recalled the incident clearly, although what he remembered was sitting alone afterward, filled with shame. "Oops, I've got food up," she said, and she moved away toward the kitchen.

Calvin studied the menu, half listening to the conversation between a man and woman at the next table, and then startled to hear the man say, "Apparently Warren Hosmer got word to..." But then someone laughed loudly nearby, and he couldn't hear the rest. He looked sharply at the couple, but the man had finished his sentence and was drinking coffee now. The woman waved at Calvin and smiled—a little wiggly-handed wave, very coy. "I'm Wilma Du Pont, dear," she said, leaning toward him, "and this is my husband, Henry." She winked at him.

"They call me Downriver Du Pont," her husband said, "on account of a boating accident I had. Not to be confused with Upriver Charlie Lakeview. He's a Cherokee. How do you like our girl Donna?"

"Fine," he said. "Just fine. Glad to meet you folks." This beat all.

Donna was heading toward him, carrying the coffee. "Calm down, brother," he told himself, having come to the conclusion that she was actually gorgeous. Not all men would think so, but then most men were fools who had no imagination when it came to women. She hurried away again, and he dumped sugar into his coffee and then picked up his spoon to stir it with. The spoon was heavy—apparently silver, which was high-toned for a place called the Cozy Diner. Million-dollar pancakes and million-dollar spoons.

Donna moved among the ten occupied tables effortlessly, setting down plates, refilling coffee. He drank his own coffee and sketched a plate of million-dollar pancakes on his napkin—an enormous plate of them with steam rising into wavy dollar signs and with a little bitty rendition of himself looking at them wide-eyed. Donna came back and set down the plate of pancakes and a jar of Skippy.

"Was my uncle Lymon in this morning?" he asked. "Early?"

"Nope," she said. "Haven't seen him. He might have caught the sunrise ferry. Tomorrow's barge day, so maybe he went into Bullhead City to order supplies for the Temple Bar. Maybe down to Needles, if he needed something in particular."

"Barge day?"

"The barge comes across with supplies from Bullhead City every Thursday and Monday. Big doings on the wharf."

"Maybe that's it, then."

"Your pancakes are getting cold," she said. "Especially if you want that peanut butter to melt. Do you do peanut butter and syrup both?"

"On one-third," he told her. "One-third syrup alone and one-third only peanut butter. Everything in threes."

"Combination plate," she said, and then laid the check on the table. "I'll be back with more coffee."

"I'm already afloat," he said, quoting his aunt, and then immediately regretting it. *Don't talk like a nut,* he reminded himself. That was paramount. Most women weren't amenable to nut talk, especially right away. He had found that out once or twice. Abruptly he remembered why he had chased Donna into the picnic table, and the memory made him blush. She had kissed him, right out of nowhere, and he being what?—maybe five or six years old? He wondered if she remembered that part.

Out of the corner of his eye he saw Downriver Du Pont and his wife Wilma stand up and head for the door, taking their secrets with them. He ate pancakes and sketched a cartoon on another napkin—a centipede in a shoe store. The befuddled clerk was saying, "Maybe when the barge comes in..." It wasn't bad, although outside of New Cyprus it would be obscure. He would leave it for Donna, who, ideally, would get a laugh out of it before she threw it into the trash. He found that he was suddenly in a hurry to be moving. The pancakes were as good as he had hoped, but he shoveled the rest of them down hastily, and he ate half the bacon with about half the attention it deserved. Somehow the out-of-nowhere mention of Hosmer's name had put an edge on the morning. *And so had Donna,* he thought, although in a completely different way.

He put a twenty-dollar bill on top of the napkin with the cartoon and stood up, but he realized that it amounted to a psychotically high tip, and he looked into his wallet again for something smaller so that she wouldn't think he was trying to impress her with his high-roller Birdland sensibilities. But he had nothing but twenties out of the ATM. He left the twenty and made his way to the door and onto the sidewalk without looking back.

In the trailer park people were out gardening and hanging clothes and getting things done before the day really started to broil. There were kids running around and dogs meandering from one trailer to another. The big lawn was trimmed and green and was shaded by lines of trees planted strategically to block the sun as it moved across the sky. The trailers were old Airstreams and single-wide mobile homes with built-on verandas and carports. Flowerbeds were lined in river rock and seashells and glass fishing floats and broken-open geodes and old glass insulators from telephone poles. He saw big cylinders of gray metal here and there, set in the borders. Silver again—the same as Uncle Lymon's bookends and the flatware at the diner.

It came into his mind that for ten cents and a doughnut he would pull up stakes and move out here. Or at least he would consider it. New Cyprus was a long way from designer coffee and freeways and easy access to ten thousand other bits and pieces of popular culture that he had no abiding interest in. He thought about Donna again, and whether he should have asked for her telephone number.

He crossed the bridge to the Temple, which was dark and locked up tight. He saw through the window that there was a dim light coming out from under the closed door of what might have been the office or storeroom. It could as easily be sunlight shining through a window behind, illuminating the room. He knocked on the door and waited, then looked through the window again, and then knocked a second time, but there was apparently nobody stirring inside.

At the rear of the building there was a little trail through the willows—something he had missed seeing in the darkness last night—and he followed it down onto a short stretch of beach, where he could see the groove in the sand where the rowboat had been pulled high and dry so that the river wouldn't tug it free of the shore. It was interesting, but it meant nothing he didn't already know. He spotted the ferry upriver, a couple of minutes out, and he hurried back around the Temple and down the path to the dock, where there was already a woman waiting near the gas pumps, a Mrs. Lazlow, who had a little wire cart on wheels and was on her way across the river to shop at the Safeway. He stood making small talk with her while he surveyed the far shore downstream.

There was another narrow beach opposite, maybe a hundred and fifty yards distant—a good place to pull a rowboat out of the water. There were a couple of clearings upriver, too, and it would be a simple thing for a person to drop a rowboat at the edge of the river upstream, drive downstream a half mile and park the car, and then walk back up to the boat, put it into the water, and row across to New Cyprus in the dark of night for some moderately foolproof spying.

There weren't any downstream passengers on the ferry when it arrived. The pilot was a middle-aged woman dressed in a sort of leisure suit, who immediately told Calvin that he was Al Lymon's nephew, which didn't surprise him at all now. "Betty Jessup," she said. "You can call me Betty." She held out her hand for a shake, and he saw that she was wearing red fingernail polish.

He shook her hand. "Cal Bryson," he said. "Did my uncle take the ferry this morning? Sunrise run, probably."

"Nope. Haven't seen him," Betty Jessup told him. "The Cozy's a good bet."

"He wasn't there."

"I see him now and then shopping in the Coronet, on the highway. It's as close as we've got to a five-and-dime."

"I'll take a look," Calvin said.

"Nettie's not in trouble, is she?" Betty asked.

"No, not at all," Calvin said. "In fact, she's raring to go this morning. New lease on life."

"Well, that's a blessing," Betty said. "I'll stop in to see her when my old man takes over at noon."

He nodded and sat down in the shade of the canopy, watching the Arizona side spin past. The boat ride to the landing above Holiday Shores took about twenty minutes. He got off there along with Mrs. Lazlow and her cart, the two of them trudging up the hill toward the Safeway. Bullhead City was wheezing in the summer heat. He looked back to watch the empty ferry angle away, farther upriver toward the final landing, where another, more active ferry ran gamblers across to the Nevada side, to the landings in front of the Riverside and the Colorado Belle and the Nevada Club.

Calvin found that he was starting to sweat despite the dry weather, and he wished he had a hat for shade or at least had rubbed on some sunblock. He headed straight for the phone booth in front of the Safeway. If this one wasn't a secure line, then they would all have to be insecure, because he couldn't tell one line from another. There weren't any suspicious characters lurking, unless you counted a blue-haired old woman sitting on a bench up the way and two younger women pushing baby strollers into the store. He checked the parking lot for the green pickup truck before punching the Gas'n'Go number into the phone. He listened to the phone ring a dozen times, giving Shirley plenty of time to come in from the gas pumps or to take the hash browns off the fire. A recording picked up. "Gas'n'Go," Shirley's voice said. "Leave me a message."

"Hello," he said after the beep, "this is Cal Bryson, Al Lymon's nephew. I was in the store yesterday on my way out to New Cyprus. I wanted to tell you that I got a call this morning from the man who sent the package, our mutual friend in Iowa, and he said to let you know that they were *turning up the heat*. I don't know what that means, but the man says that he's going south, and that I should let you know just in case. I hope all this makes sense to you, because it doesn't make much to me. Anyway, thanks for your help yesterday. Aunt Nettie says hello. She's doing pretty well."

He hung up. What more could he say? Either it was all a bunch of nonsense, or else it wasn't. And either way he had done his job. It was a little worrying that she didn't answer the phone herself, but there was nothing else for him to do. Right now he was in a mood to look into the bookstore that Lymon had told him about. It was time to investigate the Fourteen Carats Press.

He walked across the parking lot and quickly spotted a line of aging cinder-block shops down along the river's edge. They would be almost invisible from the highway. He saw a couple of carts of sale books out in front of one of the shops and headed toward them, passing an alcove at the edge of the building, a covered parking space. He stopped suddenly, and then glanced around before stepping into the shade of the awning. A pickup truck was parked in the alcove, and resting in the bed was a small aluminum rowboat, shiny-new, with a pair of wooden oars in it. There was river water and sand and dried, muddy shoe prints in the bottom of the boat.

FOURTEEN CARATS

Of course there must be a thousand rowboats in Bullhead City, he reasoned.

But *were* there? How many people went out rowing on this part of the river? A little outboard motor was cheap, and it would run you back upstream in comfort, whereas it would be impossible to pull against the current in a rowboat. But of course you wouldn't want the outboard if you were trying to keep quiet.

He looked past the corner of the building toward the bookstore, making up his mind whether to go in. The man lurking on the island last night might have gotten a look at him—although it had been dark despite the starlight. And if the man wasn't one of Uncle Lymon's crowd, which clearly he wasn't, then there was a good chance that he was one of Postum's, if Postum *had* a crowd, which he apparently did. But Calvin couldn't have been any more than a moving shadow last night. And anybody from New Cyprus might have been crossing the bridge, heading for the Temple. The man wouldn't put two and two together—the math was too obscure.

He paused to browse over the books in the carts, as if he had all the time in the world. He glanced up through the glass door but saw nothing inside except the shadows of ill-lit wooden bookcases. *What the hell,* he thought, and he pushed open the door and went in, waiting a moment for his eyes to adjust to the dim light. The place smelled of old paper and pine shelving. A man sat behind the counter working at a computer. There was a window behind him that looked out onto the river and the ferry dock. Without glancing up, the man asked, "Can I help you?"

"Just browsing," Calvin told him, moving toward the counter while he scanned titles. Certainly this *might* be the same man who he had seen last night on the island. His hair was right, same build.... "Actually I'm looking for small press publications," he said. "Local color stuff."

"In the back, along the wall." He gestured vaguely and then returned to his keyboard. The monitor was turned away. A moment ago, when Calvin had walked in, it hadn't been. The man bent over to pick up a book from a heap next to the desk, and Calvin saw that his T-shirt had the image of a face on the back—the usual bust of Shakespeare sitting on an open book, with the words "All the world's a page" printed beneath it. It was highly likely that the T-shirt had a couple of days' wear on it, with a night or two in between, maybe.

Calvin glanced down onto the desktop as he passed, at a jumble of scattered papers, pamphlets, and photographs, and what he saw made him pause despite himself. Among the photographs, partly covered, was a picture of Bob Postum. There was no doubt at all. He wasn't posed for the picture, but was taking mail out of an old mailbox on a fence rail, with the desert and mountains behind him. There were photos of other familiar people also. Calvin recognized Miles Taber walking across a parking lot along with someone who might have been Cousin Hosmer, and also a photo of the rock pile behind the lodge, mostly hidden by willows, taken from a boat on the river, or from the Arizona shore with a telephoto lens.

The man at the desk straightened up and glanced sharply at him, and Calvin nodded and moved on toward the back of the store, conscious that he had suddenly become conspicuous. For a moment he considered turning around and heading straight back outside. He had the distinct feeling that he had walked into something here, that he was minutes away from giving up his reputation as a decoy. But maybe it would be worse to walk out.

And anyway, he saw now that the books on the wall were far too interesting for him to leave without taking a look at them. There were half a dozen Saucerian and Futura Press productions that had to do with alien activities in the Mojave. He owned two of them, had coveted two others for a couple of years now, and hadn't known about the other two. This was a sort of treasure-trove of New Age literature. A Fourteen Carats book caught his eye, the gold pan symbol stamped into the heavy paper cover above a wood-cut illustration of the Lost Dutchman's mine. It looked to be the same vintage as the Templar volume.

He picked it up and flipped through it with his head bowed, but he sneaked a look through the open door of an adjacent room—a stockroom and workshop apparently, with long countertops, a draftsman's table, an old printing press, a table saw, and some sort of high-tech machine. It looked like a computerized router attached upside down beneath a sheet-metal table. He turned back toward the counter, taking the book with him.

The man at the computer was watching him with no expression on his face. Without taking the book from him or looking at the cover, he said, "Eighty-four dollars and thirteen cents."

Calvin was mute for a moment. He had expected about half that. "I just wanted to ask about it, actually," he said. "I bought one of these Fourteen Carats productions yesterday, out along the highway. They're a local press, aren't they?"

"That's right. Out in Henderson."

Calvin nodded. "I heard that they moved out here to Bullhead City."

"Who wants to know?"

"Pardon me?"

"Who the hell are you?"

"Me? I'm just passing through. I can't drive past a bookstore without stopping in for a look. I was coming out of the Safeway when I saw your sign."

"Is that right?"

The man obviously didn't believe him, and had no reason to hide the fact. "This is a little pricey for me," Calvin said. "I was hoping to *find* the Fourteen Carats Press, actually, and see what they had to offer, maybe if they had any old stock lying around."

"I can't help you there. Like I said, as far as I know they're still out in Henderson. It's right on the way if you're headed toward Vegas. But maybe you're already familiar with Henderson." He looked at Calvin expectantly, as if this *meant* something.

"I'll be heading in the other direction, back out to L.A.," Calvin said. He glanced down at the desktop, where the photo of Postum was still half visible, although the photos had been pushed together into a pile now, so that the rest were hidden. "I'll be damned," Calvin said, "isn't that old King Baldwin?" He pointed at the photo, having no idea where he was going with this rash question.

The man was silent for a moment, with no particular expression, and then he reached down and slid open the top desk drawer, revealing a black revolver with a wooden grip. "King of what?" he asked, leaving the drawer open. "Big-screen TV?"

"He just looks like a guy I ran into once," Calvin said, "a real eccentric. Probably it's not him."

"What can you tell me about him, this guy you ran into?"

"Nothing much. We had a conversation at a gas station. He lives out here in the desert somewhere. Maybe they call him King because he drinks a lot of Budweiser."

"Budweiser?"

"King of beers, like the commercial."

"Could be," the man said. "I was thinking maybe he was an Elvis impersonator, or maybe Elvis himself, incognito. Lots of impersonators out here these days. Pretty much everyone you meet is really someone else. Take you, for example. What you don't know is that I saw you come in on the ferry about ten minutes ago, from downriver. Nobody comes in on the New Cyprus ferry unless they're staying in New Cyprus, and nobody stays in New Cyprus unless they have a reason to stay there that's copacetic with the Knights. Now, word has it that your man the King isn't copacetic with the Knights. You wouldn't see him riding on the New Cyprus ferry. So when you walked in, I wondered what you wanted, because I don't think it's books."

Copacetic with the Knights—that wasn't the sort of thing Calvin would willingly deny unless it was dangerous not to deny it, and suddenly it didn't seem dangerous despite the pistol in the drawer. "Did you feel that earthquake last night, around ten?" he asked, taking a wild chance.

The man stared at him. "Why don't we cut to the chase and you just tell me what you want? I'll answer you a question, and then you can answer me one." He closed the desk drawer. "No offense with the pistol," he said, "but I'm a little worried when I don't know who someone is. You should be that same way, because you're out of your territory here, which maybe you don't know. Or maybe that's a blind. Maybe you're smarter than you look. And for the record, you've found the Fourteen Carats Press. This is it. *I'm* it. I didn't feel any earthquake, so if you did, you must have been at the epicenter, which means you came in here because you saw the boat in the back of my pickup."

"What do you mean, *the epicenter*?"

"You don't know what I mean?"

"No clue."

"But you have to admit that it was you on the bridge last night. The rowboat tipped you off? It wasn't the bookstore sign, which is pretty hard to see when you're coming out of the Safeway, which you didn't come out of, because like I said, you just got off the ferry and then you talked on the pay phone, which you can see if you look through the door right there, past the end of the building." He pointed in that direction, but Calvin didn't bother to look.

"It was the rowboat, just like you say. I figured it was your rowboat and that it was you looking in the window at the Temple last night. I didn't tell anyone, by the way, if that's worrying you."

"Everything worries me. But you didn't say anything because you were up to the same thing. What are you doing out in New Cyprus?"

"What were you doing out on the island?"

"Trying to take a couple of photos, but you came along and screwed things up. Now tell me what you're doing in New Cyprus."

"I'm Al Lymon's nephew. I'm just out here visiting. Photos of what?"

"Never mind that, if you don't already know, although I think you do. You seem pretty curious for someone who's just visiting and who doesn't know anything. A person who doesn't know anything doesn't ask questions because he doesn't know the questions."

Calvin shrugged.

"What put you onto me? I don't think it was your uncle."

"Like I said, I bought one of your books from the Gas'n'Go out on the highway. It involves the Templars back in the fifties— the severed head thing."

"That's my father's work. He actually used to hand-cut the blocks for the illustrations and set the type on that old press in the back. I'm more of a journalist, so I just tell a computer to do the etching. All I do is clamp the block onto the table and then take it off again once the cutting's done. Then I rough it up a little with a chisel and file so that it looks hand-cut. It takes virtually no talent whatsoever. But I don't think there's any mention of King Baldwin in that Templars book you're talking about. How'd you hear his name? Al Lymon?"

Calvin nodded.

"Well, you know what they say about a little bit of learning: it can be a dangerous thing. You don't have any idea what you might have been up against walking in here like that. If I *was* one of them, you'd have been in considerable trouble. Now it's me who's in trouble—that is if they're watching you, which they probably are."

"One of whom?"

"You really don't know?"

"No. Calvin Bryson, by the way." He put his hand out, and the man shook it.

"Lamar Morris. Let me give you a piece of advice. Get on the ferry, head back up to New Cyprus, have a nice chitchat with the folks, and go home. The sooner the better. And don't come back in here, because I sure can't afford it. Don't mention any King Baldwin, either, unless you're talking to your uncle. I say that for your own sake. That 'king of beers' thing won't fly. Not around here, it won't."

"Thanks for the advice," Calvin said. And then he pointed at the computer screen. "Hey," he said. "That's the old quarry." From where he stood now he could clearly see the screen and the photographic image on it. It showed the rusted flatcar and the tracks running downhill through a cleft in the rocky hillside, with several standing stones in the foreground. The image was modified, so that the edges of things were softened, and there was enough added shadow to give it the look of a murky cemetery.

"Me and the computer are turning it into an illustration," Morris said.

"For what? Another pamphlet? What's the subject?"

He shrugged. "I'm narrowing that down. Something's going on, though. Some people would call that earthquake a portent. Allegedly there've been a few over the past three weeks. Did it feel like a portent to you?"

"Felt like an earthquake."

"Now why do you suppose you felt it and I didn't?"

"You were on the river, I guess."

"Could be, unless I was already across the river, in which case you'd think I'd have felt it."

"I don't know what I think," Calvin said.

"Could be the quake has a localized effect. There're a lot of mysteries over there in New Cyprus. If you happen to run into any, and you snap any good pictures, I can work out a trade for some Fourteen Carats stock that I've got in the archives. Take a look at this."

Morris opened another drawer in the desk and took out an old pamphlet that was more crudely done than the Templars book. It had a buff-colored cover with black hatchet lettering that read *War in Heaven*. He took it carefully out of its plastic wrapper and opened it to the center, which was covered by a two-page etching of what was unmistakably New Cyprus with the Dead Mountains behind.

"This here's the very first Fourteen Carats publication—nineteen forty-eight," Morris said. "At least it's the first one ever distributed. You can ask your uncle about the one that wasn't distributed. Anyway, this is the only known copy. I used to think there must be more copies of it somewhere, although there was no way to find out. My father only printed fifty in the first place. I looked through every bookstore between San Bernardino and Yuma and came up empty-handed. Then I found this one by accident, at a desert museum out in Hesperia. It probably cost me a thousand dollars in gas money searching for it. But now with the Internet you can run down copies of nearly anything you want in an instant, and so I can tell you that there's not another copy of *War in Heaven* listed on any relevant site—or at least not this *War in Heaven*. There've been a few of them over the years."

"Heaven must get a little tiresome without a war now and then," Calvin said. "Nothing but harp playing and celestial choirs."

Morris obviously wasn't amused. "What I mean," he said, "is that there might be a copy or two in some old trunk somewhere, but this is pretty nearly the Grail if you're a Fourteen Carats collector. I had an offer of eighteen hundred dollars for it, but I turned it down." He slipped it back into its plastic cover and laid it back into the drawer.

"What's the gist of the piece? Trouble in New Cyprus?"

"That's another one you could ask your uncle, although he might not have been out here then. There was trouble of some kind—a power play involving a casino owner out in Henderson who wanted to be Grand Master."

"That would be de Charney? Of severed-head fame?"

"That's right. Only in this case it's de Charney the elder. He tried to buy New Cyprus outright. I mean the *whole* of New Cyprus. He challenged the deed that the Knights had been granted, which was essentially a land grant of some kind, written up fifty years earlier. The place allegedly wasn't worth anything at all outside of the value of the houses themselves. Nothing around here was worth anything till twenty years ago or so. There were rumors, though, that there were mines under New Cyprus. A lot of nonsense, maybe, depending on who you talk to, but de Charney had to be after something."

"Was there actually some kind of *battle*, or is the title just artistic?"

"According to the book, which was written by my father, there *was* a battle of some kind, but it was kept on the downlow. The last thing the Knights wanted was the authorities poking around. *Neither* side wanted that, and still don't. The Knights are an independent crowd. That's what got them in hot water with the Pope back when they burned de Molay and the rest of them at the stake."

Calvin nodded. "Now you're talking about the Knights Templar, the historical Knights Templar."

"That's just what I'm talking about."

"All right. So let me guess. This challenge of de Charney's failed, and so old de Charney and his crowd were out, and a few years later de Charney's son made some kind of magical play for power involving the reenactment of the death of John the Baptist, which in this case was John Nazarite, the preacher from— where was it? Redlands or somewhere?"

"That's the long and the short of it. Old de Charney disappeared—maybe dead in the fighting, but there were rumors that his son murdered him, although it might have been your man Baldwin. Another story says he was struck by lightning, which is so perfect it might be true. Whatever happened back then, these people weren't screwing around. I tell you that for your own good, because they're *still* not screwing around. Something's happening out there now, though. It's all coming to pass."

"And that's why you were out on the island? You wanted to see what was coming to pass?"

"You could say that, although I already *know* what's happening, or at least part of it. I know what it was they brought in, and I can tell you there's a book in it—maybe a larger print run. The Templars are big news right now. Ten years ago nobody but historians and conspiracy nuts ever even heard of them, and now housewives know all there is to know, or at least think they do."

Calvin found that his mind hadn't moved on with the conversation, but had remained hovering around the phrase *what it was they brought in....* "What kind of photos are you looking for?" he asked.

"I'm looking for anything out of the ordinary. Old things, maybe—antiquities out of the Holy Land, let's say. Whatever. People say they hear things at night from up in the hills, like someone's still working the stone. Nobody ever sees anyone. I've been up there half a dozen times, and *I've* heard things, but then there's nothing there—just the standing stones, maybe a coyote looking around. Hell of a creepy place when you're out there alone. Makes you understand what the word *haunted* means."

"I bet it does," Calvin said, but he was thinking about falling asleep last night, hearing what had sounded like dwarfs chiseling away deep in a mine. This morning it had seemed a lot like an aural hallucination. Now it sounded like he didn't know what. "I doubt I'll stick around long enough to take any photos," he told Morris.

"Well, that's the smartest thing you've said since you came in here." Morris got up and walked around from behind the counter, moving across to where he could look out through the tinted-glass door into the parking lot. "If you come up with something, though, give me a call. I've got some overstock I can part with. But we'll find someplace else to meet." He handed Calvin a business card. "That's my cell number. I'll ask you not to share it with anyone."

"Sure," Calvin said, and he edged past him, pushing open the door and squinting in the sunlight, just then remembering the Saucerian and Futura Press pamphlets that were still on rack inside. There was no going back in now, though. Maybe later he'd make another trip across the river, although the mail would work just as well.

"One more thing," Morris said, and Calvin stopped and turned around, holding open the door. "Just for fun, ask one of the checkers in the Safeway if they felt that quake."

LIKE A MILL WHEEL

They hadn't felt the quake. They didn't get quakes out here in Bullhead City very often. Maybe, the checker told him, Calvin should call it a night a little earlier over at the Colorado Belle. Those free drinks and all that noise from the slots could make anyone tipsy.

"I didn't want to leave before I hit the big one," Calvin said cheerfully.

"Did you hit it?" she asked.

"No," he said. Then the checker told him that her sister-in-law had hit thirty thousand on the Big Spin, and it was just like that—her last spin of the night, and right when she was telling herself that she should have gone home an hour ago. How was that for irony?

"That's irony," Calvin said, "but going home an hour ago is almost always good advice anyway." He went out with a bulky double sack containing the coffee, pie, and peppermint stars, and thinking that despite the Big Spin he should write the admonition down on a three-by-five card and carry it in his back pocket: "Go home an hour ago." *Better yet,* he thought, *don't leave home at all.*

He headed along the shaded front of the store toward the hill that led down to the ferry, wondering whether he should call Shirley Fowler again. It had been an hour, after all, and it wouldn't take but a moment. No need to leave a second message if she wasn't there....

He glanced over at the pay phone, and nearly turned in that direction, when he saw that there was someone already talking on it—Bob Postum, who was looking straight at him, smiling through his beard. The man waved, said some last thing, and hung up the phone. Calvin waved back and picked up the pace. He could easily make it to the ferry dock ahead of him, and if the ferry was there, there was no way Postum would get on board, just like Morris had said. Then he saw that there was a small man loitering at the top of the hill, smoking a cigarette, getting fried by the sun and apparently doing nothing at all. Except that no one stood around in the Arizona sun without a reason.

Calvin stopped, opened his grocery sack and looked down into it, then slapped himself in the forehead. "I'll be damned," he said out loud, and reversed direction, heading hurriedly back into the store. The automatic door closed behind him. "Restroom?" he asked the checker with the lucky sister-in-law.

"In the back," she said. "Center of the store. In meats."

"In meats!" he said stupidly, forcing himself not to look back and making his way down the bread aisle. The butcher counter loomed ahead of him, and he saw a wide passage alongside it, leading into the back. He had no intention of going into the restroom and being shot to death in a toilet stall, but somewhere back here there had to be a way out.

A sign read "Restrooms" and pointed into an interior hallway cluttered with unopened boxes and without any apparent exit. He walked straight past it, spotting a pair of double-wide doors ahead, sheathed in steel and with small windows in each, glowing with sunshine. A butcher came around the corner out of what was apparently a cooler, and started to say something to him, pointing back toward the corridor to the restroom, but Calvin redoubled his pace, ignoring the man, and pushed straight through the doors, finding himself outside again on a four-foot-high concrete loading ramp.

He could see the ferry dock easily now. It was empty, and there was no sign of the ferry either up or down the river. Of course there wasn't. The ferry was hourly, and it probably wasn't the top of the hour, although he couldn't know for sure because he had put away his watch and cell phone in order to be copacetic with the Knights. He told himself that Postum wouldn't try anything in broad daylight, although what he meant by "try anything," he couldn't say. Morris had spooked him with the pistol and the obscure warnings. But then Morris had also said that he was probably being watched, and clearly he was.

Calvin jumped down from the end of the loading dock and walked downriver fast, taking a quick look behind him at the asphalt expanse of the lot. There were pallets of flattened card-board and trash bins and scattered pieces of steel ribbon and packing materials. He thought of hiding in a trash bin, except that it would merely provide a convenient place to ditch his body. On his right lay the river itself, with the casinos on the far side. Ten quick steps and he could be in the water, swept away toward New Cyprus. Hard luck for the groceries.

He stopped at the edge of the Safeway, the lot still empty behind him, and looked up along the wall toward the front parking lot. No one. He went on farther, past the front of Morris's pickup and boat and behind the row of cinder-block shops that housed the bookstore, walking along the edge of the river itself. He thought briefly of simply going in and asking Morris to hide him, but he ditched the idea. He couldn't betray the man's trust like that, especially when it probably wasn't necessary anyway. Within moments Calvin was angling across a weedy lot, away from the river toward the highway. He looked back, but saw no sign of Postum or the small man.

There was no reason in the world, of course, that the small man and Postum knew each other. Nor was there any reason, he told himself, to think that Postum wasn't simply buying gro-ceries. Then he remembered Hosmer's *not-by-chance* warning, and right now Hosmer was looking more and more sane, and the decoy was looking like a by-God duck again. Playing stupid would have been far more useful than hiding behind buildings, but it was too late now.

He found himself in the parking lot of the Coronet store, with a lot of dime-store ads painted onto the front windows. He hurried inside. He could browse around until the top of the hour and then head straight for the ferry at a run. There was a teenage girl leaning on the counter, and she looked up from a book of Sudoku puzzles and smiled pleasantly at him. "Do you have the time?" he asked, and she pointed toward the wall behind him, where there was a big round schoolroom clock. Twelve minutes till ten.

"Can I help you find something?" she asked.

"Just browsing," he said, and he wandered toward the back of the store, spotting the hallway to what must be a stockroom. There was no visible rear exit this time, but there *had* to be one. They wouldn't haul stock through the front of the store. He came to rest in a small aquarium section, with five- and ten-gallon tanks containing common tropical fish and goldfish. It smelled weedy and wet, like the river in the evening, and there was the comfortable sound of bubbling on the air. He watched several fat fantail goldfish swim awkwardly in their tank, and after a time he glanced up again at the clock, surprised to see that only three minutes had crept by.

"Front or back?" he asked himself. Front was a sure thing. The back exit, if it existed, might easily have an alarm. Also, Postum would know that sooner or later Calvin would try for the ferry. All Postum had to do was wait him out, and if that was the case, then bolting out the back door made no particular sense. "Front door," he said to himself, and, as if it had been a command, the front door opened, and Postum himself walked in addressing a hearty hello to the girl behind the counter, calling her by name.

"Cal Bryson!" he shouted, waving at Calvin. "You old son of a gun!"

Back door, Calvin told himself. He set out down the aisle through the yardage section, his eye on the door to the stockroom. When he was five feet from it he smelled cigarette smoke, although he couldn't see anyone. Postum was ten steps behind him, moving along quickly. Calvin turned up a perpendicular aisle through shelves full of wading pools and swim fins and swimmer's goggles, and then, glancing at Postum, he turned again toward the front of the store. Postum smiled and jerked his thumb toward the door, and Calvin saw that there was a third man standing just outside. Of course there was. Calvin was out of options. He nearly shouted at the girl to call the police, but then remembered Morris's statement about neither side wanting to involve the authorities. And anyway, there was no crime going on, only Bob Postum, old-timer, having a chat with Cal Bryson, old son of a gun.

"*You're* a slippery fish," Postum said to him when he caught up.

Calvin blinked at him. "Just out doing a little shopping."

"Just like yesterday down at the Gas'n'Go! You must have burned through all them little bitty toilet lids already. Pays to buy the economy size package down at the Wal-Mart. I've got a proposition for you, though, and then I'll let you get back to your shopping. I've been doing some checking up, and I find that you're an innocent man."

"Innocent of what?"

"I mean to say that I'm *fully* convinced you're just out here paying a visit, like you told me yesterday. Now, I don't know what you were doing in the bookstore talking to Lamar Morris, but right now I'll give you the benefit of my good nature and say that maybe you're just a man who likes books."

"That's exactly right. I'm a collector. Californiana. The Fourteen Carats Press is at the top of my list."

"I'll bet it is. It's at the top of my list, too. Morris's daddy used to be at the top of the list, but he disappeared off it. The good news is that unlike his son Lamar, you're not on the list at all yet. There's no reason for you to be on it. But what I wanted to tell you is that there's a rumor going around that someone stole your artifact out of the back of your car yesterday while you and I were inside the store chewing the fat. I feel a little bit responsible, holding you up like that while someone purloined your property."

"I appreciate your concern."

"There's a further rumor that there's more than one of these artifacts, but that only one of them is the genuine article. That one of yours might have been a fraud. I don't suppose *you* know which one is genuine and which ones are fakes. Maybe you don't even know what it is, this artifact."

"Sure I do," Calvin told him. "It's a spirit veil belonging to my aunt Iris. She used to wear it when she'd hold séances. The family is under the impression that her spirit went into it when she died."

Postum stared at him for a moment, apparently trying to figure out whether he was serious. "A *spirit* veil," he said at last. "That's what they told you?"

"As far as I know, that's what it is."

"They had you drive out here on a tomfool errand, thinking you had this séance item in your car—drive straight into who knows what kind of trouble? And you don't have any kind of *problem* with that? Cal, I'm afraid you're what they call a chump."

"Why should there be any trouble over Aunt Iris's spirit veil?"

"Well, there *shouldn't* be. No trouble at all, if that's what it is. I'll tell you what, though. You've got a ferry to catch, and I've got business to finish, so I'm going to make you an offer you can't refuse, as they say." He glanced back toward the girl who was studiously working away at her puzzles, and then spoke in a lowered voice after winking at Calvin conspiratorially. "You come up with the *right* veil, and there's profit in it for you. I don't mean peanuts, either. I mean money that it'll take you a while to count. Your aunt Iris doesn't care where she lays her head—on this side of the river or on that side. And pretty soon it'll be the same thing anyway. I'd treat her with *great* respect. Tell you what. We'll work out a drop-off spot on your way out of town—call it two days from now—down at the Gas'n'Go like yesterday. We play it the same way. You leave the item in the trunk, go inside, and eat a cheeseburger. No need to look in the trunk when you come out. It'll be there—what I'm talking about. Just get into that buggy of yours and head west. You know what I'm saying?"

"So far, so good," Calvin said.

"Then let's make that a date. Noon, Friday." Postum's voice had taken on a softer, more even tone, like a crisis counselor talking someone down from the ledge. "That'll give you time for a visit with the folks," he said. "Meantime, that's just what you do, *visit with the folks*. Stay close to home. No need for you to be over here on the Arizona side or up poking around in the hills. No need to be talking to Lamar Morris, either. That kind of thing raises suspicions, and then first thing you know, your name's on someone's list, right up near the top. Think of it this way, Cal—play this right and three nights from now you can be sleeping in your own bed, with your head on a pillowcase full of paper money, getting a *hell* of a good night's sleep."

He paused as if to let this sink in, and then said, "If you want it the other way, you can be sleeping with the fishes, in that deep water below the dam. You follow my drift here? The water comes over the spillway and sets up a current like a mill wheel. A body just goes around and around till the bones are picked clean by the striped bass."

Calvin nodded.

"In other words, we'll be waiting for you at the Gas'n'Go, come what may."

"I get the point," Calvin said.

Postum nodded. "That's good," he said. "I'm glad we had this little chitchat." He looked at the clock on the wall and so did Calvin. "You might have missed your ride," Postum told him, "except usually they're late because of that grudge the Knights have against timepieces. You hurry, you might make it yet."

Calvin turned and walked toward the front of the store, past the clerk and out through the door. The man who had stood outside was gone now, and the coast was clear. When he got down to the dock, the ferry was just pulling in. Calvin had rarely been as grateful. Betty Jessup waved him aboard, and he sat down under the awning, facing the Nevada side for the ride back to New Cyprus.

The wind and spray off the river were cooling, and he let his mind wander, trying to take it all in. Sixteen hours ago he had driven out into the desert to a place where nothing ever changed, and immediately everything had changed. He had been offered money or—what? A *bullet*? A new job as fish food and then eternity as a rotating skeleton?

A chump, he thought, although he didn't want to believe it. He *had* been set up, obviously, but Uncle Lymon had been honestly surprised to hear that Postum had approached him at the Gas'n'Go. Hosmer hadn't outright told him to go into Bullhead City this morning, and Morris hadn't invited him in for a chat. All of that was his own curiosity at work. If he was a chump, then he was mostly his own chump.

New Cyprus, thank God, was looming up fast on the starboard side now. He was nearly home. Aunt Nettie wasn't in her lawn chair on the beach, and the place looked deserted. Probably she was inside, out of the heat. What was the likelihood, he wondered, his mind taking another turn, that Bob Postum would give him a second thought once he was out of town? The trick was simply to avoid the man and get out of the desert. There was no way that the long arm of Postum would reach all the way to Eagle Rock. Leaving discreetly, and soon, would solve all problems. He felt a certain relief as he picked up his bag and stepped off the ferry onto the dock.

THE VEIL

He found Aunt Nettie feeling spry—a night-and-day difference from how she was apparently feeling last night or even this morning. She was mopping the kitchen floor when he got home, and she chased him out from underfoot. Uncle Lymon, she said, was under the weather, and he had gone down to the Temple for some peace and quiet. Her own pain, mostly in her stomach, had virtually gone away, she told him—for the first time in what seemed like ages. And she was taking advantage of the blessing by doing a little bit of work.

Calvin strolled down to the Temple Bar, which hadn't changed a bit from when he had been inside it before, although seeing it now took him by pleasant surprise. The bar itself was built of black-washed knotty pine, with a swirly black and gold, bamboo-framed Formica counter that almost certainly dated back to the fifties. There were half a dozen bar stools built of bamboo and faded black and gold Naugahyde and another half dozen tables and sets of chairs that matched the stools. All of it had been kept in good repair, and the place was faded but clean. There was a kitchen in back and a menu on the wall above the pass-through window—eggs and hash, burgers and fried fish, and spaghetti Bolognese. Two men sat at the bar drinking coffee—old Whitey and Miles Taber—but Uncle Lymon was nowhere to be seen.

"Well, if it isn't Cal Bryson," Taber said, getting up off the stool and coming across to shake hands. "Miles Taber—maybe you remember me. It's been a while."

"Good to see you again," Calvin said. "Sure, I remember." Somehow Taber had an air of authority about him, despite his comical appearance—the high-waisted trousers with multiple pockets, the suspenders, the faded aloha shirt. "Whitey, isn't it?" he asked the second man.

"Whitey Sternbottom," he said. "Welcome to New Cyprus. If you're looking for your uncle, he's in the back lying down. He's feeling a little bit old-fashioned."

"I guess I won't bother him, then."

"When were you out here last, Cal? Six, eight years ago?" Taber asked. He paused for a long moment, and then said, "I don't mean out here on the *island*, I mean to New Cyprus."

"Maybe five years," Calvin told him, wondering what he *really* meant—not by the question, but by the clarification. Had Taber recognized him through the window last night?

"Glass of beer?" Whitey asked, gesturing at the taps.

"A cup of that coffee, maybe."

"It's mud by now," Taber warned, "but it was ground this morning."

"Give the guy a break, Miles," Whitey said. "He just got here. You start working out on him right away with your jokes, and he's going to turn right around and head back to L.A. before we've had a crack at him."

"Your problem is that you don't know funny when you hear it," Taber said to him. "You've got the sense of humor of a catfish. Anything else?" he asked Calvin, pouring coffee into a mug. "Couple of fried eggs? Kitchen's closed on weekdays unless something's going on, but we can rustle up something easy. Sandwich, maybe? BLT? Bag of chips?"

"I'll wait," Calvin said, settling down on a bar stool and having a look around. The ornately carved, leafy table that had sat near the window last night was nowhere to be seen. He noticed that the cabinet where his uncle had stowed the broken glass decanter and the rest of the strange Communion things was apparently not locked. Next to it were some wall shelves with books and stacks of jigsaw puzzle boxes and board games. "When did my uncle show up?" he asked. "I was looking all over for him this morning."

"Early, I guess," Taber said. "Long before we got here. Lymon's up with the sun, usually. What's going on? Nettie's all right?"

"She's fine, actually. Uncle Lymon got a call from Iowa. I don't know how urgent it was."

"Iowa?" Whitey said. "Warren Hosmer?"

"That's right. Do you know him?"

"You won't find anyone out here in New Cyprus who doesn't, except a few of the new folks. He was Grand Master in his day, but he gave it up years ago. Moved back to Orange City, Iowa, to be near the kids, but he's always kept his hand in. When was that, Miles?"

"I make it early eighties, so they'd be grandkids he's living near now. I was new here then, that's how I remember. He was going into *recruitment*, he said. And he sent a few good people our way, too. He's a persuasive man when he gets started. You don't want to argue with Warren Hosmer."

"Not me," Calvin said truthfully.

"Should we wake Lymon up?" Whitey asked. "What did Hosmer want?"

"Not much except to say that he was 'going under.' Those were his very words. He said they were turning up the heat back there in Iowa. I got the impression he thought there was some kind of general threat, but I don't know what."

"Well," Taber said, "I don't see waking Lymon up over that, but you're free to if you want. There's always a general threat, and if Hosmer has already made himself scarce then there's nothing we can do to help. To tell you the truth, we're a little worried about Lymon. He didn't look so good this morning, although he told us not to call Doc Hoyle, and we said we wouldn't. He was walking like he'd been hit in the gut. Whitey and I have got to get going into Bullhead to take care of barge business, but if you can hang around for a while...?"

"Sure, I can stay," Calvin said. "I've got nothing going on, and Aunt Nettie wanted me out of the house. She's cleaning the place up."

"*Is* she? She must be feeling her oats," Whitey said. "That's good. That should pick Lymon's spirits right up. It's been months since she's been out of that chair of hers. She's either there or in bed."

"You might want to check in on Lymon later on," Taber said. "Make sure he's all right. He says it's nothing, but then that's just what he *would* say. Doc's number's on the desk in the office. Give him a call if you think you should. There's no harm in getting him over here while he's still sober."

"Sure," Calvin said. "Anything need doing?"

"You could sort the pieces in those jigsaw puzzle boxes," Taber said, and then laughed.

"Or not," Whitey said.

The two men went out, and Calvin got up to have a snoop around. He went behind the bar and had a look at the bottles and the barware, and then wandered over to the shelves and looked over the books, but they were mostly Readers Digest Condensed from thirty or forty years ago, titles like *The Seagulls Woke Me* and *Up the Down Staircase* and *Sail a Crooked Ship*—books that struck him as being curiously innocent now, and attractive for that reason. Condensed or not, he could easily imagine working through some of them to while away the idle New Cyprus hours.

He stepped across to the closed-up cabinet, thinking that it looked like a seriously old piece of furniture, very plain—no carvings except the Templar cross, evidently hand-cut into each of the upper panels in the frame-and-panel doors. The wood smelled of age and lemon oil. He had no business snooping around inside the cabinet, or anyplace else for that matter, but he pulled on the iron handle anyway, glancing back first at the room where his uncle was resting. The cabinet door stuck just a bit before it scraped open. Inside lay piles of folded tunics and sashes, with table linen on a shelf below. There were more books, but not casual reading—more of the sort that his uncle had in his library at home. There was no broken glass on a silver platter.

There was a shuffling behind him, coming from the office, and he hurriedly shut the cabinet door. Uncle Lymon appeared in the doorway of what must have been the office, looking rumpled and done in, the usual cheerfulness gone out of his face. He seemed weary and pained and ten years older than he had yesterday.

"Why don't we call the doctor?" Calvin asked him. "Miles tells me the number's right in there on the desk."

"Miles will tell a man anything," Lymon said. "I know what ails me. It'll pass, or else it won't. Anyway, I took some aspirin just now."

"Aunt Nettie's feeling pretty well. She's cleaning up a storm."

"That's good to hear." It appeared as if he meant it, because he nodded and looked shrewdly at Calvin, then made an effort to pull himself together, standing upright and letting go of the doorjamb. "Grab us a couple of 7UPs out of the fridge, will you? It's time we had a little chin wag."

"Sure," Calvin said, walking around behind the counter by the food window and opening the refrigerator. His uncle sat down at one of the tables and Calvin carried the cans over and took the seat opposite, popping open the sodas.

"Here's to your coming out to New Cyprus," Lymon said, raising his can.

"Cheers," Calvin said. He set the can down and waited for his uncle to get started. It was plain that he had something on his mind.

"Let's cut to the chase," his uncle said. "By now you realize there's a certain amount of…activity…going on with the Knights."

"I guess so," Calvin said. "I mean, with the box and Bob Postum and all. I hope I haven't caused any problems."

"Not at all. Not at all." He sat thinking for a moment. "You might have walked into one, but you didn't cause it. You know that your father was a Knight?"

"Was he? I *didn't* know that. Did he go to meetings and all that?"

"No, except when he came out here for a visit," his uncle said. "We kept in touch, though, and he did work for us now and then. Some of the members fly under the radar like that. It gives them a certain leeway."

Calvin nodded. Now that he knew, it made as much sense as anything. His father had a few mysteries hovering around his life, strange comings and goings, mainly, and abrupt disappearances, but Calvin had always assumed the reasons for them were mundane, and his mother had promoted the idea. "I almost forgot," he said. "Hosmer called in this morning after you left. He said to tell you that he's *gone under* and that things were heating up. He said to let Shirley Fowler know. I went into town and left a message on her phone, but I didn't talk to her directly."

"Good. That was the right thing to do, although you've got to watch yourself, going into town alone like that."

"So I discovered. Tell me something about Cousin Hosmer, unless you don't want to, of course. Is he...?"

"He's the sanest man I know."

"Well, that's interesting, because he suggested that Dad had been murdered. He didn't say how, only that 'they got to him somehow.'"

His uncle considered it. "There's a good chance they did. Hosmer wouldn't have said it if he didn't think it was true."

Calvin was stunned. "Are *they* still around?" he asked. "Hosmer seemed to think that I had to watch out or they'd get me, too."

"Like I was telling you last night, there's no reason for them to bother you. You're a courier. You're free to head back home and go about your business and keep your nose out of it. Thing is, you don't *want* to know too much. Too much information and you reach a sort of critical mass, and then you're drawn inside whether you like it or not."

"I'm maybe already there. I ran across Bob Postum in town. He offered me money for bringing him the veil."

"'*Or else,*' I suppose he said. That's typical. A man that can be bought thinks that *all* men can be bought. And if they can't be bought, then they can be threatened."

"That was the gist of it. Maybe you're right about me not wanting to know too much, but since I had a hand in bringing the veil out here, and since Dad was a part of it, there's one thing I *would* like to know."

"Shoot."

"It's not Aunt Iris's veil, is it?"

"No. We figured you'd be better off thinking it was. Turned out to be a good idea, too, when Postum cornered you out there at the Gas'n'Go like that. We didn't want you knowing anything at all."

"I'm okay with that. I'm glad to have brought it out, whatever it is."

"And we thank you for it. Your father thought it was worth the trouble himself, and I can tell you it's been plenty of trouble over the years."

"Can you tell me what it is?"

His uncle went pale all of a sudden, grasping his stomach and doubling over. His eyes drifted shut, and he breathed through his open mouth.

"Let's call that doctor," Calvin said, standing up and turning toward the office, but Uncle Lymon waved his hand and shook his head. He was already recovering, or pretending to.

"It's not necessary," he said. "Just a little heartburn. I'll drop around and see Doc Hoyle myself. We don't need to make the man put his shoes on. Sit down until I have my say."

Calvin did as he was told, and his uncle continued. "The point is," he said, "you heard what I said about knowing too much. I don't suppose telling you about the veil qualifies as too much, but it puts you closer to the center. You might be wise to make like the three monkeys, no matter who you're talking to. This is one of those cases where what you don't know won't hurt you."

"I heard that same kind of thing from Lamar Morris today, after he threatened to pull a gun on me."

"I'm not surprised. He'd be a little leery of strangers."

"He suggested I go home."

"He's a sage."

"But I honestly went in there to look at Fourteen Carats stuff. Then I saw a photo of Bob Postum on the desk, and he had another photo of the old quarry on his computer screen, and I got hasty and said something that tipped him off. He opened his desk drawer to give me a look at the gun."

"An ounce of prevention, to his way of thinking."

"We got along all right once he figured out which side I was on."

"There's the problem. You're already thinking about being on one side or the other. Lamar Morris has you figured out. Bob Postum has you figured out. The only one who doesn't have you figured out is Calvin Bryson." He sat silently for a moment and then mopped his forehead with his sleeve and started up again. "I don't mean to be talking like some kind of Dutch uncle, even though that's what I am. But while I've got you here I'm going to admit that Nettie and I thought it was a shame about you and Elaine. We only met her the once, but we liked that girl. Things fall apart, though, if you let them, and sometimes even if you try like crazy to stop them."

Calvin nodded, surprised at the sudden change in the direction of the conversation. His uncle was looking at him seriously, as if he had something important to say and not much time to say it.

"Seems to me some people live alone because it's easier to be *apart* than to be a *part* of something," he said. "You take my meaning?"

"Sure," Calvin said.

"I thought you did. You like doing for yourself. That's a very independent state of mind, and that's okay as far as it goes. It just doesn't go very far. You've got your books and whatnot, your folks' house out there in Eagle Rock. You can while away the days till kingdom come, and you'll never have to get up in the middle of the night to get the person you love a glass of water. And there won't be anyone to fetch a glass of water for *you*, either." He sat in silence for a moment, and then said, "I apologize for horning in, but I owe it to your dad to ask you what you think you're doing, burying your talents under a bushel like this. So Elaine wasn't the one. All that means is that the one is still out there."

"Sure," Calvin said. "I guess so."

"Don't get on your high horse here," his uncle said. "I told you I was going to Dutch uncle you, and now I'm doing it. What I mean to say is that living apart can be like slow poison. Drunks and dope addicts and zealots live apart, even when they're married. Everything else is secondary to the drink and the dope or whatever else they can't live without. And the longer they live apart, the more they want to stay that way. When you live outside the fold, you can let your own shortcomings roll right along, like a snowball. It's restful for a time, but then one day that snowball will bury you, and you won't see it coming, because you've lost sight of who you used to be."

Calvin nodded, but kept silent.

"Sermon's over," his uncle said. "Sorry it sounded like one. Some kind of fit came on me. You're free to tell me to mind my own business."

"I appreciate your concern," Calvin said, the ready-made phrase sounding as hollow as a Ping-Pong ball. It was hard to argue with anything his uncle had said. Calvin's books were ideal companions. The conversation was always perfect and most often perfectly predictable, and paper had no expectations. He wasn't still in love with Elaine by any means, but the memory of the past months still worked on his mind like a hot griddle. He was afraid to touch it, and maybe he was afraid of the idea of another hot griddle in his future. He wondered suddenly whether it was Bob Postum that he feared or whether it was Donna. What exactly was he anxious to avoid? A bullet, or another romance...? Calvin sat back in his chair and took a sip of his 7UP. Sun shone through the windows, illuminating the floor, and he watched the dust motes moving in the light.

"Now it's your turn," Lymon told him. "What do you want to know?"

"Well," Calvin said, "you said Morris was a 'sage' for telling me to go home. Postum gave me the same advice, except with an incentive. After that little talk just now, I'm not sure what *you* think about it."

"Safest thing would be to go home. But if I really thought that way, I wouldn't have agreed with Hosmer to call you out here in the first place. If a person always chooses the safest route, and never goes out of his way, sometimes he doesn't end up anywhere worthwhile."

"You agreed with *Hosmer* to have me bring out the veil?"

"Yes, I did. But if that was all of it, I wouldn't have been bending your ear these past ten minutes. You want more of my thinking?"

"That's why I asked."

"Then I'll just say it. What I mean to do is talk you into staying on. You're custom built for the Knights. You might not think so, but you're no judge of character, especially your own. You sell yourself short. Nettie and I have pretty much done our part. We're short-timers now. We've got no kin but you, and our house, like always, goes to the Knights when we pass away. If you were a Knight, it would go to you as next of kin. Think about that. It's in the Cornerstone Resolutions. This isn't the kind of thing I could make clear over the telephone or in the letter. By coming out here you've got a small look at what it means. Why don't you poke around New Cyprus a little more. Get a better idea of things. But bear in mind the cost. You'll be all-in if you decide to join. You live in New Cyprus and you're a citizen of New Cyprus. You're not an independent contractor."

"I'll bear it in mind," Calvin said. "What exactly happened to Dad? Do you know?"

"*Exactly?* No. He had the cancer, just like Nettie's got it, but my guess is poison. They claimed responsibility for his death, but there's always the chance they were lying."

"Why didn't they just leave it up to the cancer? He was nearly gone anyway."

"They're big on statements. They wouldn't have made such a dangerous one, though, except for the veil, which had just recently come into play. But they didn't get any closer to it. It was out of your dad's hands by then anyway."

Calvin considered this—his father's leading a double life. But what could his father have told him about it that was sensible? "Son, I'm a secret member of a secret society that traffics in

120

secret magical stuff...." "We keep sidetracking away from the veil," Calvin said. "What is it?"

"Fair enough. It's what you'd call a religious relic."

"Like a piece of the true cross or something? Saints' bones?"

"Like that. People throw pieces of the true cross on the table when they mean to belittle the whole idea of relics—with good reason, too. Most of it is fraud. Enough pieces of the true cross have been sold over the years to build a hotel. But that doesn't mean that there wasn't a cross, and that there aren't pieces of it out there somewhere. I know for a fact there are. There've been princely sums paid for relics a whole lot more mundane, and I mean *princely*. The money Postum offered you is chump change, whatever it was."

Calvin laughed. "You've got that right. He made the offer after he called me a chump. But whose veil? Mother Teresa? Joan of Arc?"

"A woman named Veronica. She's a tentative saint. Legend has it that when Christ collapsed from pain and fatigue while carrying the cross to Golgotha, she stepped out of the shadows and blotted His face with her veil, and in so doing she assumed His pain and weariness. The image of His face remained on the veil, which became a holy relic."

"Sounds like the Shroud of Turin."

"It's been confused with it, along with a couple of other things, although there's no reason to confuse any of them, since the transference of visages of one sort or another is common throughout history."

"Even on tortillas," Calvin said.

"I don't know about that, but I don't see that it necessarily makes a lot of difference—a tortilla or a piece of cloth. The thing is, the Knights Templar took the veil out of Constantinople after sacking the city in the thirteenth century and brought it to Rosslyn Chapel in Scotland, which was a Templar church. Later, no one knows when, it was stolen. Long story short, it surfaced a few years back and stirred up some people's interest, particularly your man de Charney."

"And so that's the Veil of Veronica? In a cardboard box?" He realized that he wasn't as surprised as he sounded. He had seen the thing unveiled last night, so to speak, and although he wouldn't call himself a believer, really, he could understand the nature of the belief. The easy wisecrack about the tortilla had been stupidly thoughtless.

"It's the very same veil," Lymon said. "I'd tell you that it's *said* to be the same, but that's not accurate. It is what it is."

Calvin nodded. The thing was clear now. Uncle Lymon was convinced of it and apparently his father had been certain enough to die over it. Where that left Calvin Bryson, he couldn't say. "Postum's crowd wants it because of its *value*, then?"

"Not its monetary value. Money is only a means to an end. It's not the end itself. The value of the thing is a little bit more esoteric. It requires that you believe in magic."

"Magic? They want it for some kind of ritual, like with the man's head? What was his name? John Nazarite?"

"Like that, but that's not what I mean. Turning water into wine—that's magic. Talking snakes in the garden. Drawing water out of a stone. There's good in that kind of magic and there's bad in it, depending on who you are. That's Postum's downfall—who he *is*. If he heard of a talking snake, he'd want to own it and put it to some kind of use—have it tell fortunes or something. But you can't *own* a miracle. It doesn't belong to anyone or anything on earth. The Knights have an ancient, vested interest in the veil. We'll give it a rest and give it a home. Maybe we can *take* it home. Our interest in it isn't open for assessment, by the way. Comes a point where you either believe or you don't. I wouldn't blame you for not believing any of it. That kind of doubt won't keep you out of Heaven when the time comes, at least as far as I know."

They drank the rest of their 7UP while sitting in silence. Finally Uncle Lymon nodded a couple of times and said, "That's about it."

THE QUARRY

The smart thing would have been to wait until later in the evening before venturing out into the desert, but Calvin wanted some time to think, and that meant getting away. And anyway, the folks were resting, and it was a convenient time to slip out without explaining where he was going. He had a small ice chest packed with bottles of water, a ham sandwich, a box of Cheez-Its, and a slice of the Safeway pie—exactly what he needed for a desert adventure. There was something about the old quarry that had stirred his curiosity, something that had come out of the discussion he'd had with his aunt earlier that morning. The entire idea of Hugh Blankfort working the quarry had sounded more than half mystical, and so did the odd night noises that Calvin had heard, or thought he had heard, when he was falling asleep. He reminded himself that there was no reason to go overboard here. If you hung around with eccentric people long enough, you ran the danger of becoming one yourself.

He turned off the road to take another look down at the river before the hills swallowed him, and, just like yesterday, he was swept away by the view and by the strange existence of a swift-running, cold-water river in the desert. New Cyprus, lying along the river's edge, was stranger and more alluring than it had been when he had first sighted it, and his uncle's offer of a house of his own was like a door opening on another realm and another life.

Or at least a potential door. In a single day Calvin had decided to turn down a pillowcase full of cash *and* a house on the river. In the future he would look back on this day from a safe distance and marvel. But this just wasn't his fight, and he missed the comforts of home. Whoever had coined the word "homebody" had people like him in mind. He swung the car back onto the road and headed up into the Dead Mountains.

It seemed to be slightly cooler as he rose into the higher elevations, but maybe it was the deep shadows of late afternoon that made the difference. He rolled down the windows and shut off the air-conditioning. The heat seemed to have actual weight to it, and for the moment it wasn't unpleasant. Just when he'd had enough of it, the landscape opened up, and he was in the quarry, where he pulled off the road and parked in the shade of a steep little hill. He sat for a moment listening to the unearthly silence, watching a thin white vapor trail appear as if by magic in the sky, marking a momentary highway on a map of the heavens, a highway that was fading like invisible ink even as it was being drawn. The quarry had the air of an ancient ruin, the work of people long passed away, and Calvin was overcome with a lonesome emptiness. It came to him suddenly that he had just retrieved his lost hour, and that he could keep it if he simply kept driving west, but instead he shrugged off the inclination, got out of the car, and opened the back door to grab a bottle of water from the ice chest. He set out around the edge of the hill, heading toward the railroad tracks.

Only fifty feet or so of tracks remained. It was apparent where they had lain years ago, just the vestige of a path now, descending into the valley toward Interstate 40, obscured by sparse undergrowth but with a ghostly imprint on the desert floor here and there. Why anyone would have gone to the trouble to dismantle the rail line was a mystery. Perhaps once the quarry was played out the Knights wanted to further disconnect themselves from the world. He walked down to where a litter of enormous rectangular stones lay broken in the mesquite, like a cemetery after an earthquake, and then climbed uphill toward a cleft in the rock, where he had a broad and ethereal view toward the west, with the highway laid out like a ribbon, transecting the desert flatlands. Behind him, far below, his car sat in the sun, the windows rolled down, and it came to him now that he had left the keys in the ignition.

"So what?" he muttered. If there was ever a place in the world where it didn't matter...He headed downward now, out of sight of the car, walking between steep rock walls and thinking again about his conversation with Lamar Morris and his aunt's reference to a "passage" and the "Fourth Secret." There were shadowy holes in the scattered heaps of rocks, but none of the holes were large enough to qualify as a potential tunnel. He opened his water bottle and drank half of it before he stopped himself. He was mummifying in the dry heat. He should have shoved an extra bottle into his back pocket.

He saw something then—a place where someone had apparently shifted a number of rocks aside to reveal a dark little hole in the ground. There were empty beer cans tossed around, and the litter looked very recent, the cans shiny and clean. Someone had been at work here. He took out his camera and shot pictures from half a dozen angles. He pitched a rock into the hole, listening as it clattered away downward and then was silent. He had no idea if it had fallen five feet or fifty feet. If this was the Fourth Secret, it was of interest mainly to rabbits and rattlesnakes.

He took another swig of water, which nearly finished off the bottle, and realized that he was either going to have to head back down to the car for another one or die of thirst, but before he had taken three steps back along the trail he heard the sound of an engine—a car coming up the grade. He hurried back to the hilltop, where he looked down again at his own car parked below. There was a white compact pickup truck just rounding the bend now, ascending from the highway. It entered the quarry, slowing down, then turned off the road twenty feet in front of his car and sat there with the motor idling.

He crouched down, well hidden by boulders. There were two men in the cab of the truck, sitting still and looking at his car. They shut the pickup engine down, climbed out, and glanced around into the surrounding hills. One of them was rail thin and tall; the other was stocky. He couldn't swear to it, but the thin man appeared to be the same one who had been waiting out-side the Coronet store earlier. He wore the same hat, John Deere green. Postum had warned Calvin about "poking around" up in the hills, and now he had driven straight on up here.

The two stood in front of the truck talking, and then the thin one turned and walked in Calvin's direction, scanning the hills intently. The other man walked toward Calvin's car. It occurred to him now that leaving his keys in the ignition had been moronic, slightly more moronic than leaving his cell phone on top of the bureau in his bedroom back at the Lymons' house. He half stood up and aimed his camera at the pickup truck, pushed the little zoom button, and clicked off several pictures of the truck and the boxes and tools that littered the bed. He heard a shout, and realized that he had been spotted. The thin man took off running up the hill toward him, his John Deere hat fly-ing off his head. Calvin headed back down toward the rocky defile where he had been just a few moments ago. He had seen a trail leading downward from there in the general direction of the river, although how far it went and where it ended up he couldn't say. Without water he wasn't going far in any event.

The trail angled downward more steeply, and he found him-self slipping and sliding on loose rock, the scree clattering, mak-ing a perfect racket. The area had seemed to be full of hiding places, but now that he needed one, no place was available. He looked for a weapon, but aside from getting into a rock fight—pinned down, probably, from above—nothing suggested itself. And if the man was armed...

He angled downward across a broad, flat rock, feeling the heat through his shoe soles and burning his hands when he clambered down off a ledge. He found himself in a little box canyon with nowhere to go but down into open country, where he could do nothing but keep running. He waited, listening hard, hefting a grapefruit-size rock in his hand. Footsteps passed by above him, and he waited until there was silence again, then counted to thirty before scrambling out from behind the outcropping, following the hillside back around toward the quarry, climbing back up the rocky slope.

He reached the top of his little hill, finding himself fifty yards or so above the litter of beer cans and rock. Another hundred yards below that sat his car, with the front door open. The heavyset man was sitting in the driver's seat now, and as Calvin watched, he climbed out of it, dangled the ignition keys on his finger, and then pitched them into the nearby brush. Calvin tried to fix the brush in his memory—maybe ten feet from the car, a stand of mesquite....

There was nothing to do but wait, and it wasn't long before the thin man walked out of the rocks below and turned to look back, shading his eyes with his hand. He picked up his fallen hat and put it on his head. The heavyset man opened the rear door of Calvin's car and took out the ice chest, opening it up and handing his friend one of the waters. Then he fished out the foil-wrapped slice of pie and unwrapped it. Together they ate the pie and Cheez-Its, and then dumped the trash onto the ground. Then they both returned to the pickup, grabbed a pick and shovel out of the truck bed, and started off in Calvin's general direction, no doubt heading toward the work site.

There was no point in sticking around. Calvin made his way downward as silently as he could, leery of being caught in the open, and soon he heard the two coming up toward him. He edged behind a rock and waited for them to pass.

"I don't know," one of them said, "but a couple of extra sticks and what you end up with is rubble. We want to open it up, not bury it. That well out in Oatman that Henry blew just about took out the farm."

"There's no farm here, so who gives a damn?" the other one said. Calvin could hear the scuffing of their feet now. "The thing about blasting is you use enough dynamite to blow the hole clear. If you don't use enough you get the rubble. Where do you suppose that asshole went?"

"Henry? I heard he was working out in Henderson again."

"Not Henry, dipshit—that *other* asshole. The one you couldn't catch."

"Oh, him. I don't give a damn. He's just a complication. It's too late in the afternoon for a complication. We just have to dig that hole out enough to get a good look, and then it's Miller time."

"It won't be Miller time if he's up to something out here and Bob finds out we let him walk away."

"Then *you* look around for him. I damn near died of heat stroke trying to chase him down. Who cares if he's up here?"

After a moment Calvin heard the sound of pick and shovel work. He picked his way downward among the rocks, keeping out of sight. At the bottom of the hill he kept walking, straight across to the stand of mesquite, but saw absolutely no sign of the keys anywhere. He crammed himself in among the low branches, looking down into the gravel and dead weeds, pushing branches aside, but there were apparently no keys.

He hunched out of the bushes and headed toward the pickup truck. He had no compunctions about stealing their car. The Knights would know what to do with it—how to return it, if that's what they were inclined to do. As far as he was concerned, they could push it into the river as a fish habitat. But of course there were no keys in the ignition. He opened the door and felt under the mat, and then bent across the console and checked the other mat before opening the console itself, which was a litter of snuff cans and rolled-up smut magazines.

He backed out and straightened up, looking into the hills, where the thin man was coming down the trail again. The man saw him, stopped abruptly, whistled twice, and then headed down toward him at a sprint. Calvin bent back into their pickup truck, released the brake, yanked the gearshift into neutral, gave the car a good shove backward down the hill, and headed straight down the road toward New Cyprus at a dead run. It would be close, but if he could get far enough ahead of them, there was no way they'd catch him without a car. The heavy one would have a seizure before he had run a hundred yards.

Calvin looked back, elated to see their truck picking up speed, rolling deeper into the desert, the thin man hanging on to the front bumper now, trying to slow it down. With any luck it would roll itself right off a cliff or into soft sand. Calvin hadn't run ten feet farther, though, when he heard a crash, and he glanced back again to see that the truck had smashed to a stop against something. The heavyset man had reappeared. In a few moments they would simply run him down in the truck.

He picked up the pace, around the bend in the road and out of sight. The ruse with the truck would gain him about a hundred yards if he was lucky. Clearly he had to get off the road and hide again, because otherwise the sun and heat were going to kill him. They'd find his bones by the roadside.

A car came around the bend fifty yards ahead, bearing down on him, just like that, appearing out of nowhere—a car from New Cyprus. He waved his arms and ran straight down the lane toward it. The car slowed and stopped, and he ran to the passenger side and threw open the door, climbing in uninvited. Donna sat in the driver's seat, staring at him. "Turn around," he said, interrupting whatever she had been going to say. "They're after us."

Without a word, she swung a U-turn, the tires spinning on the loose gravel of the shoulder before getting traction. He looked back—no use trying to hide—and there was the truck behind them, picking up speed.

"Did you say something they didn't like?" Donna asked him. She was smiling, but only faintly, and she glanced into the rearview mirror and sped up, taking the turns in the road with an abandon that shocked him. He gripped the grab bar overhead and held on, his right foot working an invisible brake.

"I was out looking around in the quarry, and they showed up. They've been working out there—something involving dynamite. They probably recognized my car."

She looked into the rearview mirror again. "They're persistent."

The pickup had run up to within twenty feet of their bumper now. "I wish it wasn't you," he said. "I'm sorry."

"Really? Thanks. Who would you rather it was?"

"I don't mean that. I mean I think we're in trouble. Both of us now, instead of just me."

"You don't have to tell me that. Another couple of miles,

though, and they'll turn back. They won't follow us down into town."

There was a crash and the car slammed forward. Calvin straight-armed the dashboard and jerked around to see the cab of the pickup directly behind them, the pickup's engine revving as the truck swerved and shot into the adjacent lane, half on the shoulder, and tried to pass, but Donna stepped on the accelerator and surged ahead again, the pickup swerving back over, nearly clipping their bumper. Calvin half expected a pistol to appear in the big man's hand or for a tire to blow out or for the car to spin off the road. The tires squealed, and they shot past the roadside viewpoint, nearer to the edge than was comfortable, and Donna accelerated again, throwing Calvin halfway across the seat. He hauled himself back, fastened his seat belt, and turned around in time to see the pickup skidding sideways behind them.

It took him a second to see that the pickup was out of control, slowly starting to spin, falling farther behind, the faces of the two men appearing and disappearing and then reappearing. Donna rounded the next curve without slowing down and pulled out onto a straightaway, picking up speed again. The seconds passed and the pickup didn't reappear.

"A pickup truck is no good for high-speed curves," Donna said, watching the rearview mirror. "They're a little better if you've got half a ton of sandbags in back."

Calvin nodded his head in response and forced himself to calm down. "Thanks," he said. "They'd have had me for sure if you hadn't come along. Where were you headed? Not that it's any of my business."

"Essex," she said. "It's on the way out to Amboy. My grandmother's house."

"Then I owe your grandmother an apology."

"She'll understand," Donna said, looking at him and smiling. "I guarantee she'll understand. You look like you could use a drink."

"That's a fine idea," he said. "I'm buying, unless you've got to turn around and head back to Essex. I'm worried about your going back out that way by yourself, though."

"I'll give Gran a call. But I could pretty much pay for the drinks with that tip you left me this morning."

"I hope that didn't look crazy. I didn't mean anything by it. I could have waited around and got change, I guess."

"I'm not complaining. I love an overtipper."

He glanced at her, and she smiled at him. "Is that sunburn," she said, "or do you embarrass easily?"

The Fates had apparently dealt him an ironic hand. He had nearly been murdered—or something—by Laurel and Hardy, only to be delivered out of potential death to...whom? To a highly competent, cheerful waitress who drove like a madwoman, and who, he was reminded again, was beautiful, and who had kissed him in his youth—his first kiss. The Pippi Longstocking comparison had been apt, but it was only half the story. "Why doesn't your grandmother live in New Cyprus?" he asked. "It's got to be an improvement over Essex."

"Business," she said. "She owns the Gas'n'Go out on I-40. She's been thinking of selling out ever since my grandfather passed away."

"That would be Shirley Fowler?"

She looked at him skeptically. "You've met her?"

"We go way back. I stopped in for gas on my way out here and ended up spending sixty bucks. It turned into a small adventure."

"She can't bring herself to sell out. She and my grandpa ran the place for thirty years."

"So it's Donna what? Fowler?"

"Brewer. Fowler is my mother's side of the family."

"Have you always lived out here?"

"Off and on," she said. "Currently on. I moved down to San Diego, went to school at U.C., then lived in Leucadia for three years, two blocks from the beach."

"What degree? Waitressing?"

"Business," she said. "I'm a market analyst. Waitressing is a sideline. Two mornings a week. Breakfast and lunch. Kind of a hobby."

"Otherwise you work online?"

"Yeah. I do a little traveling when I need to. I like it, living out here. I thought I'd get island fever after a while, but that hasn't happened yet. There's more to this place than meets the eye."

He nodded, not needing to ask what. They rolled out onto the flatlands now, and Donna turned up Main Street into New Cyprus. He realized then that he was immensely relieved to be home, and then he was slightly surprised that in his mind he had worded it just that way.

"I've got a trailer in the park," she said, turning down through the trees and pointing to a big Airstream sitting in the shade of a cottonwood. There were flowerbeds surrounding it and a little lanai off to the side built out of redwood lath and with a corrugated tin roof. "It used to belong to Henrietta Blankfort, but I bought it when she passed away."

"Related to Hugh Blankfort, I guess."

"His great-granddaughter."

"Hey," he said, "I took photos of the stuff in the back of those guys' truck—dynamite, I think, and tools."

"*Dynamite?* How do you know?"

"I got a good look at a steel case that was back there, and I overheard a conversation they were having about blasting." She turned down toward the Lymons' house, pulling into the driveway and shutting the car down. "You coming in?" he asked hopefully.

"You said you were buying the drinks. You think I'm going to let you sneak away?"

He smiled at her and climbed out of the car, happier than he could have imagined being just twenty minutes ago, except that his car was still up on top of the hill.... They pushed inside and found the place apparently empty. "Aunt Nettie's probably out in back," he said, looking out through his aunt's den. She sat as ever, contemplating the river, and he went out to check in with her, waving Donna along. He hoped that this morning's good health was still with her. "Hello, Aunt," he said. "Let me introduce Donna Brewer."

"Hi, Nettie," Donna said, rolling her eyes at him. "You look great. Feeling better?"

"Yes, indeed," she said.

He felt like a fool—as if they could have lived a stone's throw from each other in New Cyprus all these years and not been acquainted. He realized that his aunt was smiling at him with raised eyebrows, and he was suddenly embarrassed. "Is Uncle Lymon around?" he asked.

"He's lying down. You can roust him, though."

He walked off toward the bedroom, feeling suddenly awkward when he was outside the door. He hesitated, and then knocked. "Hello," he said. The door opened and his uncle came out, walking with an effort. He looked beat—pale and done-in. "Did you run into Doc Hoyle?" Calvin asked.

"Not yet," his uncle told him. "He was across the river. I'm feeling a little better, though. I took a good nap. What's up with you?"

Calvin told him the story on the way into the kitchen. "So we don't know whether they wrecked their truck or not," he said. "They might be out there bleeding to death. And my car is still up there."

"We'll have a look," Lymon said, picking up the phone. "Miles," he said into the receiver, "round up some of the boys, would you? There was some trouble up to the quarry. Calvin ran into a couple of guys with blasting gear." He listened for a moment and hung up the phone. "You say you threw your keys into the *bushes*?"

"*I* didn't throw them into the bushes. One of the others did. I looked for them, but I had about a minute before they came back down out of the hills and saw me, and I had to take off fast."

"We'll bring a metal detector. He looked out through the den to where Donna and Nettie sat by the river. "That Donna's a good girl," he said. "You two get to talk much?"

"A little."

"Well, leave your car to us. We'll get the keys, and Miles can drive it back down here. If these two characters in the pickup are hurt, I guess we'll be a while, because we'll have to transport them to the hospital in Needles. I'll bet they're long gone, though, if either of them was in good enough shape to use a cell phone."

"I can go along," Calvin said. "I can drive my own car back down."

"No need," his uncle said. "You need to back off a little bit, not that you did anything wrong. But it's not really your fight. It's your car, but not your fight. You just happened to get in the way of it. It's lucky you went up to the quarry, if they're up to something with the blasting gear. Leave this one to me, though. You all right with that?"

"Yeah," Calvin said. "I understand."

"Good. You've got more important things to do anyway. Why don't you take Donna out for a bite to eat? And not the Cozy Diner, either. Take her over to the steakhouse and buy her a steak. Here." He pulled out his wallet, took out four twenties, and handed them to Calvin. "My treat," he said. "Tell her I said thanks for saving your worthless hide like that."

"Of course I'll tell her," Calvin said, following his uncle back up the driveway. Miles Taber pulled in then, in a GMC Jimmy, with two other men in the backseat, as if they'd all been waiting at the firehouse for his uncle's call.

Uncle Lymon got into the passenger side carrying the metal detector, and they turned out onto the road again and roared off, and just like that Calvin found himself standing in the driveway alone with eighty bucks in his hand. He had never had a chance at his lunch, and the idea of dinner at the steakhouse was brilliant. He stood there for a time, though, asking himself how he was going to play this—what he would say to Donna. Would it be a lie if he failed to mention that he was leaving New Cyprus? The crime of omission had a lot of ugly guises when you looked hard at it, which you most often didn't want to do. That had been one of the problems with Elaine—what *hadn't* been said. Over time what wasn't said had pretty much written the history of their relationship. *Go into this thing with a little honesty,* he told himself flatly, *or don't go into it at all.* For the space of about five seconds he felt pretty good, but then he asked himself, what *thing*, exactly, was he going into?

UPSIDE DOWN

"So how about you?" Donna asked him. She ate like a trooper, putting away pieces of filet mignon and steak fries like they were going out of style—which they probably were, everywhere but in New Cyprus.

"Literature degree," he said. "U.C.L.A. In graduate school I specialized in the work of New Age writers and small press publishers in the L.A. area. So it was more like pop history than literature."

"New Age? Like Shirley MacLaine? Auras and pyramid hats and things like that?"

"Things like that, although what you're talking about is the eighties' version, which isn't as interesting, at least to me. I'm pretty much mired in the past. Back in the early fifties it was a different world. The canals on Mars hadn't been drained yet. There were lost worlds at the center of the earth. Explorers built spaceships in the backyard, with onboard greenhouses for oxygen."

"*Those* were the days," she said. "Now we've got, what?—tanks of air? Factory-built spaceships?"

"Don't get me started about what we *don't* have," he said. "The New Agers were a very earnest crowd. They had conventions, printed pamphlets, made purification treks out to Mt. Shasta. They did a lot of communing with space aliens out here in the Mojave—called them 'the brothers upstairs.'"

"I like that. I wonder if there were sisters upstairs."

"Back then there were whole families upstairs—alien ships with white picket fences around them and a mailbox on a post. The sisters wore aprons and stayed on board with the kids, but they were the secret movers and shakers, like Donna Reed and June Cleaver. Then the world turned upside down, and most of that vanished along with what passed for wholesome TV. All that canal land on Mars turned out to be a real estate fraud."

"I sense a Nickelodeon fan here. In fact, is that a tiki around your neck?"

"Yeah," Calvin said. "I used to collect them. This one's carved out of an old beef bone and dyed with coffee." He took the tiki out from under his shirt and showed it to her—a tiny, stretched-out head with a long nose and goggle eyes. "There's serious mojo in these, but only if you're a believer."

"I still have my troll dolls," she said.

"Then you know what I'm talking about. Give me that old-time religion."

"What do you do with a degree in tikis? Teach classes in nostalgia?"

"I taught a class or two for a couple of years, but there's not a lot of demand for my kind of expertise, you might say, so I mostly taught composition and literature survey courses to students who would rather be dead. Then when Dad passed away, I didn't have to teach anymore. Now let me ask you one," he said, putting down his fork. "What's a nice girl like you doing in a town like this? I can picture *myself* here, because I'm attracted to the place's...aura. It's like things *haven't* turned upside down here yet. Maybe they never will."

"They won't if the Knights have anything to do with it. They've pretty much stopped the clock, or at least slowed it down. Anyway, how come *I* can't be attracted to the place's aura? You've already got that territory staked out?"

He shrugged. "I'm considered an eccentric back where I come from."

"Then you'd fit right in here."

"So I'm told. One thing I was wondering, though, is where does everybody *work*? The ferry must be busy come Monday morning. I can't imagine anyone commuting through the Dead Mountains."

"Mostly they work right here in town. There's a few that take the ferry up to Bullhead City and Laughlin. And some of the Knights are Knights pretty much full time."

"They draw a salary? That's the job I want if I grow up to be a Knight."

"The Knights have what is called the Blankfort Endowment Fund, which pays good dividends, but lots of people would rather work, and they bank their dividend. When you're living in the desert, doing nothing gets old pretty quickly."

"So they say. I'm kind of an expert at it, actually. But tell me something else. I'm a little bit worried about the mysteries of the place, if you know what I mean. There seems to be a lot *going on*. Sometime I'm going to buy one of the Knights a beer and pry some secrets out of him."

"*Him?* You're talking to a Knight now."

He stared at her stupidly for a moment. "Really...you're a *Knight?*"

"What did you expect? A Dame?"

Witty responses flickered in his mind, but he needed a pen to sketch them out. "Another beer?" he said.

"No, thanks. I might get silly."

"How am I going to pry anything out of you if you don't get silly?"

"*Pry something out of me?* Is that some kind of romantic euphemism?"

"My favorite romantic euphemism is 'pitching woo,'" he said evasively. "That was my mother's term. You can't use 'making love' in that sense anymore." He realized he was blushing.

"Are you any good at it?" She smiled at him, putting him on the spot.

"At *what?*" he asked. It sounded a little bit like a brazen overture to him, which was another of his mother's terms.

"At pitching woo," she said. "You seem a little rusty at it, like the Tin Man. I sense a tragedy involving a Munchkin maiden." She smiled at him, but she seemed to be serious. "Are you waiting for someone to pick up an oilcan?"

He searched his mind for something to say, but came up absolutely empty. He couldn't remember ever having run into a woman much more forthright. The waiter appeared, setting plates of apple pie and ice cream on the table, which they hadn't ordered.

"On the house," he said, and moved away.

"Heck of a nice place, New Cyprus," Calvin said. "Everyone's got your best interests in mind."

"Remember that," Donna said. "Now I've lost track of what I was saying."

"You accused me of being rusted," he said, throwing caution to the wind. "There're things that can do that to you, I guess. This one's name was Elaine."

"Elaine—very romantic name. You still think about her?"

"Not too often these days."

"There's nothing wrong with thinking about her. What's the value in having a disposable past?"

He shrugged, and they sat in silence for a moment. Then she asked, "What were you doing up there alone, anyway? At the quarry."

"Nothing, really. Just taking a look around."

"It probably wasn't smart. What possessed you?"

"Just curious, really."

"Curious about what? You said you wanted to talk to a Knight, and now you're talking to one, and she's been plied with drink. All of a sudden you've got nothing to ask?"

"All right," he said. "Here's one for you. The last couple of nights when I was falling asleep I thought I heard a pounding noise, like someone hammering on stone. Lamar Morris at the bookshop over in Bullhead City had told me about that—that it came from up in the quarry. Maybe the conversation put the idea in my head, and then I just dreamed it or something, although it didn't seem like a dream."

"It wasn't," she said.

"So what is it? Ghosts?"

"Why not? You don't believe in ghosts? You're okay with space aliens but you draw the line at ghosts?"

"Do *you* think it's ghosts?" Calvin asked.

"Maybe."

"Go ahead. Tell me. I'm not in the mood to ridicule anyone."

"I'll tell you about something that happened to me about a month ago. I couldn't sleep. I don't know what time it was—late, though. Past midnight. I was lying there in bed trying to figure out whether to get up and work for a while, or shut my eyes again, when I heard a kind of clanking outside, and voices talking, really low. New Cyprus is maybe the safest place on earth, but it creeped me out a little bit, which made me kind of mad."

"It made you *mad*?"

"At myself. I just *hate* fear. I just want to poke it in the eye, you know what I mean?"

"Sure," he said. "Me, too. Fear lives in fear of Calvin Bryson. You can ask anyone. So who was it outside the trailer?"

"I don't know, really. I looked out the window, and there were half a dozen men walking across the park in the shadows, carrying tools. They were nobody I recognized, which wasn't right, since I've seen pretty much everybody in New Cyprus about a thousand times. And they were dressed in antique clothes, too, like they were going to a costume party as miners or something."

"Maybe they were," Calvin said.

"Except they were transparent. They walked straight through a picnic table and a barbecue without slowing down. Then they walked into a patch of moonlight and disappeared entirely, and then I saw them again farther on, in the shadows again."

"And that's it?"

"That's it. I asked my grandmother about it, and she wasn't surprised at all. Her idea is that there are things about New Cyprus that...interfere with *time*. That's how she put it."

"So you think you were looking at something that happened in the past—that you were seeing some kind of temporal discontinuity?"

"That's very fancy. Now you're talking like you *earned* that degree."

"But that *is* what you're talking about?" Calvin said.

"I guess it is. Turns out my grandmother was right. Everyone in New Cyprus has stories to tell. If you want to call these things ghosts, then there're more dead people walking around New Cyprus than live people. We're thinking of giving them a day-old breakfast discount at the Cozy Diner. Yesterday's food for yesterday's people."

She smiled at him, but he knew she was serious. All of this was serious. But what did that mean to *him*? How serious was *he*?

The waiter passed by just then, carrying a load of plates. "Coffee?" he asked.

"Not me," Donna said. "I'm done."

"Me, too," Calvin told him. "I guess we'll want the check." The waiter nodded and moved off.

"We should get back," she said. "In order to show your uncle the photo." She had printed out the results of Calvin's spy work on the equipment in her mobile home—half a dozen enlarged photos of the truck and the littered work site.

When the check arrived, Calvin pulled out his uncle's eighty dollars and handed it to the waiter. It covered the tip and all. He didn't have to add a dime. Donna, however, fished her wallet out of her bag and tried to hand him forty dollars.

"The Lymons' treat," he said. "My uncle gave me the eighty bucks."

"All right," she said, putting the money away. "Let's go thank him."

They went out into the warm night and walked back toward the trailer park, both of them looking up into the starry sky. With a little more tilt, the Little Dipper would spill out an ocean of starlight, or whatever it was full of.

"I read that the cavemen used to think the stars were little lanterns burning in the sky," Donna said.

"The cavemen had lanterns?"

"Made out of pumpkins."

"I like that," Calvin said. "A sky full of jack-o'-lanterns. Do you think they were right?"

"Even a caveman can't be wrong all the time," she told him.

The park was settling down for the night, but there were still people out and about, and even in the lamp-lit evening Calvin noticed the winks and smiles. Did Donna notice the winks and smiles? He glanced at her, but she looked away to say hello to an old woman who was sprinkling her flowerbed. The woman said hello back, and Calvin could see that she was checking him out, maybe wondering if he was good enough for their girl Donna. Was he? Did it matter? Was all of this just water under the bridge? They walked along in silence, and he could see the lights of Chez Lymon coming up on the port bow. Suddenly he wanted the moment to last, to be able to walk around forever under the stars on this warm desert evening. "Oilcan," he said in a squeaky voice. Donna laughed.

He had never been as happy as he was now, and he was on the verge of saying so when Donna pointed and said, "What happened to your *car*?" It sat in the drive, looking strangely mottled. At first he thought that the cottonwoods were painting it with weird moon shadows, but then he realized that he was looking at dents. Someone had hammered the crap out of it—with boulders, apparently. When they got closer he saw that the rear windows were pulverized, and the backseat was covered with glass.

"Wow," Donna said, gaping at it.

"Wow, indeed," Calvin said. There wasn't a door panel left that wasn't dented in three or four places. The trunk had been cratered, and the hood, too. The rear bumper was smashed inward, which would have taken some work. They had run into it! Of course. The front windows were intact, and so were the tires, which wasn't surprising. The car had to be roadworthy day after tomorrow so that Calvin could keep his appointment at the Gas'n'Go in order to sell the veil to Postum for a bag full of kapok. "What's my insurance man going to make of this?"

"Tell him you were driving through the desert and the car was caught in a meteor shower."

He stared at her for the moment it took for his sense of humor to switch back in. "Looks like one of the meteors is still inside," he said, pointing through the shattered rear window at a head-size rock on the seat.

"We found it like that," his uncle said, having come out onto the porch. "Your men were nowhere around. No sign of them, although there was broken glass and pieces of metal on the shoulder a few miles up the road, like they ran into something when they went out of control. We found your keys with the metal detector and drove her back down. It's a mess, but it runs like a top."

"Thanks," Calvin said. "That's good news." He kept any irony out of his voice. There was no use complaining. What had happened to his car had happened to his car, and it could be that they had taken the time to pound it to pieces because he had taken the time to roll *their* car down the hill. Too bad it hadn't gone off a cliff....

"You two have a good meal?" Lymon asked. "Nice chat?"

"Yes, we did," Donna told him. "We talked about astronomy. Thanks for dinner, by the way. Calvin told me that it was your treat."

"My pleasure," he said.

"Here you go," she said, handing Calvin the photos. "I'm going to call it a night. I've got some work to catch up on."

"I'll just step inside," Lymon told them, taking the photos out of Calvin's hand and heading in. "You two want a moment alone."

That's awkward, Calvin thought, watching the door whisper shut. "That was easily the most enjoyable dinner I've had in years," he said woodenly. "The food was good, but it's the company I'm talking about."

"Me, too," she said. "Tomorrow morning, then?"

"Tomorrow morning?"

"You said you were coming in for the Million-Dollar Plate."

"That's right, I did. It's a date."

"I'll see you then," she said, casting him a big smile.

"You need a walk home?"

"This is New Cyprus. Nobody needs an escort in New Cyprus." She leaned forward and kissed him, and he nearly lost his balance. "Maybe we can look for that oilcan sometime. See you in the morning." And then she was gone, fading into the darkness down the driveway. He stood watching for a moment, took another long look at the stars, and went inside.

He found Miles Taber standing in the living room with Uncle Lymon, Taber squinting at a photo through Lymon's big magnifying glass. Lymon was sitting on the couch, looking as if gravity were asleep on his shoulders. "Blasting, core drilling, wells, and excavation," he read. "Beamon Construction Services, Needles."

"Ned stinking Beamon," Lymon said. "He's a hoser of the first water. If there was any justice in the world he'd have blown himself up by now. Hoisted himself on his own petard."

"Well, there isn't any justice in the world," Taber told him. "That's why they call it 'the world.' It's what men sell their souls for. There'll be justice enough for all of us in the hereafter, and don't we hope there're no surprises in store for us there."

"Amen to that," Lymon said, sounding oddly serious. "It's obvious that they're getting set to blast."

Taber set down the magnifying glass and looked hard at Lymon. "You don't look too good," he said. "Worse than this morning. You aren't keeping any secrets, are you? You sneaking over to the medical center when you make those runs into Bullhead City?"

"No," Lymon said. "I haven't seen anyone except Doc Hoyle in the past ten years. He says I'm as fit as a draft horse. I've got a touch of the bug, that's all." He started to get up, then sat back down, then made a bigger effort, moving into the kitchen in a sort of headlong way. Taber looked at Calvin and shook his head doubtfully. After a moment Lymon came back in with three grape sodas and handed them out. "Cal knows all about the veil," he said to Taber. "It's no secret to anyone by now. Lamar Morris knew about it, too."

"Good for Cal. I don't know whether it'll be good for Lamar."

"What are they going to blow up?" Calvin asked.

"Probably that heap of rock where they've been messing around," Taber told him.

"Just for the heck of it? They're into explosions?" After a period of silence, Calvin asked, "None of my business?"

"Well," Taber said, "not strictly speaking. Sorry to put it that way, especially after they worked your car over, but…"

"I'm okay with that," Calvin said. "No need to explain. I think I know anyway. Morris tried to talk me into taking some pictures of anything that might be construed to be a passage or a tunnel—some secret way that they used to get the stones down into New Cyprus without hauling them down the road."

"Why don't we just invite Lamar Morris into the club?" Taber asked. "Satisfy his damned curiosity."

"He'd turn us down," Lymon told him. "He's like his old man. He'd rather stay on the outside so that he can write about it." Then to Calvin he said, "Postum and his crowd are maneuvering to open up New Cyprus—jockeying for position. You and I talked a little about their activities back in the early fifties. They pretty much fell apart for a time after that, but they've *regrouped*, you might say. We're not sure what they intend—how serious they are."

"I don't know what that means," Calvin told him. "Open up New Cyprus?"

"We think they're fixing to sack the town," Taber said. "And just in case it's true, we're fixing not to let it happen. Greed has a lot to do with it, like it always does."

"I thought they wanted the veil?" Calvin said. "If they intend to sneak in through the passage and steal the veil, why don't you just hide it somewhere? Bury it in the hills?"

"Like I said, they want the *world*," Lymon told him, "and they're willing to sell their souls to buy it—although I'm beginning to think I mean 'he' instead of 'they.' The veil is the high-ticket item, like you say, but hiding it won't put a stop to this. I'm not sure we *can* stop it. We have to play our part in it."

"Speaking of Lamar Morris," Taber said to Lymon, "you forgot about that box he sent over."

"By golly, I did," Lymon said. "Morris sent you a box, Cal. It's heavy, like books. Tubby Wingate brought it up. Apparently someone left it with Ms. Jessup, but she was busy running the ferry, and so Tubby snagged it a couple of hours ago and dropped it off. I put it in your room."

"Thanks," Calvin said. "I'll take a look and let you two powwow."

"I powwowed my last powwow," Taber said. "I'm through."

"I've got a couple of things hanging fire, too," Lymon said. "Let's call it a night."

"It's a night," Taber said. He shook hands with Calvin and went out, and Calvin headed off, caught up in this new mystery. *Books?* That made no sense at all, although it was a pleasant idea. The box lay on his bed, taped shut. He yanked the tape loose, and found the books—a good-size pile of them, including a dozen Fourteen Carats productions, titles that hadn't been for sale in the shop. Morris clearly had an inventory of back issues. Calvin sorted through them, marveling at his luck. *War in Heaven* was in there, along with another Knights piece called *Death in the Dead Mountains*, which looked particularly interesting. There was another piece called *The Illuminated Island*, maybe the most interesting of the lot, with a woodcut illustration on the cover that was clearly the elder Morris's work. It was a picture of the island where the Temple now sat, except there was no building yet, just rock and willows and the river beyond an open rectangular pit from which emanated an unearthly glow. Aside from the Fourteen Carats stuff there was an old, falling-apart copy of *Journey to the Center of the Earth* that was worth just about nothing unless someone wanted to frame the illustrations, a copy of Walter de la Mare's *Memoirs of a Midget*, and what was apparently a film script that was printed on three-hole-punched paper with a single brass brad holding it together. It was titled *The Last Battle*, by someone named Robert P. Wolverhampton, LL.D. Calvin flipped through it, looking for something to make sense of it. It appeared to be a Crusades-era adventure story involving the siege of a walled city, and, he saw, it had several alternative endings, as if the author couldn't make up his mind. Apparently someone had been using the script as a coaster, because the top pages were discolored with ground-in dust and coffee stains, and the whole thing smelled of stale beer and cigarette smoke.

What had inspired Morris to send him all this? Was the man going to ask him for some kind of immense favor and wanted to sweeten him up first? That had to be it. But Calvin wouldn't be of much help. He had nothing to show for his troubles today but some photos of a pickup truck, to which Morris was welcome. Maybe the blasting paraphernalia in the truck bed was worth something as a piece of information, but it couldn't be worth this stack of books, at least not the Fourteen Carats imprints. It was all Calvin had to offer, though, and from now on Calvin was a short-timer, and he was sticking close to home—no more photographic adventures.

On the other hand, he wasn't interested in giving any of the books back. He wondered how he could finesse this—*if* he could finesse it without telling lies or making promises. He found Morris's card in his wallet and stared at it for a moment, debating. The books were a *gift* from Lamar Morris, after all—no question of that. There would be nothing served by simply handing them back with a smarmy "no thank-you." That sort of thing could be holier-than-thou and self-righteous, he told himself, and at best it committed the sin of looking a gift horse in the mouth, which every mother warned her children against. Probably it was one of the seven deadly sins.

And it was Morris who had recommended that Calvin leave town in the first place. So...what? The man tried to persuade him to leave and then had sent him a bribe to stick around for some undercover work? Possibly Morris was a schizophrenic.

Calvin sat thumbing through the books for a few minutes, reading a paragraph here and there. Abruptly he made up his mind, stood up, and went out into the kitchen to use the phone. There was no sign of his aunt and uncle, who had probably gone to bed. He considered what he would say to Morris. A simple thank-you would suffice. There was a good chance that Morris wouldn't pick up anyway, since he was so evidently spooked, and Calvin could leave the thank-you on his voice mail. Morris could call back at his leisure and make demands if he wanted to, which Calvin could apologetically decline depending on the circumstances.

If he had to he would have Betty Jessup run the books back into Bullhead City. Morris could pick them up on the dock. He punched in Morris's number and listened through a half dozen rings. Then a recorded voice came on, and he felt an instant relief. He could simply leave the message....

But it clearly wasn't Morris's voice. It sounded a little like Bob Postum, but weirdly disguised, as if he were talking through a pile of buttered toast. There wasn't a hint of humor in it: "Lamar Morris isn't here anymore," the voice said. "He's dead." Then there was silence.

Calvin hung up the phone fast. His heart was going like a jackhammer. *A prank,* he thought. It had to be a prank. Morris must have a hell of a dark sense of humor. He hadn't seemed to have *any* sense of humor earlier in the day, but clearly his sending *Memoirs of a Midget* couldn't be serious....

Wasn't here *anymore*? That just didn't sound like a prank. Calvin thought again about Morris being offered eighteen hundred dollars for *War in Heaven* only to turn it down, and he found himself heading fast through the living room. This was something that his uncle needed to hear. Their bedroom door was slightly ajar. "Hello!" he said, rapping on it harder than he meant to. It swung open another inch, and he saw into the interior, where his aunt lay on the bed, apparently asleep on her back. His uncle sat in a chair next to her, bent over, his forehead in his hand. He was moaning softly, as if in barely sufferable pain. Over his aunt's chest and stomach was draped the Veil of Veronica, the image on it staring up at the heavens, as if the ceiling were invisible. The veil seemed to glow with its own aura, although surely it was merely the bedside lamp reflecting off the old muslin. His uncle's right hand hovered over the veil, glowing in the light that flickered around it. There was a weighty presence in the room, as if the air were as heavy as mercury.

Calvin was silenced by what he saw. He stood for a moment, waiting to see if his uncle had heard him, but Lymon was obviously utterly distracted, perhaps with pain, perhaps with some sort of spiritual ecstasy. Calvin turned around and walked quietly back down the hallway. Whatever he had witnessed—whatever was going on—was simply none of his business, and would never be his business. He badly wished he hadn't seen it.

But his understanding of the veil had shifted now, as if the world of New Cyprus had been jolted by another earthquake and he had been dumped into the river and swept into deep water. His house back in Eagle Rock, and the comforting life he lived there, looked almost exotically plain and homely to him.

BARGE DAY

Calvin expected the barge to be the size of a freight car, maybe pulled up the river by a team of oxen, but in fact it was a moderate-size pontoon boat with a flat, open deck and with a shallow draft so that it could use most of the river to turn around in. People who didn't drive—which was half the population of New Cyprus—could have furniture or computer equipment or a television set shipped down from Bullhead City or up from Needles, and then they could run it home on a hand truck. There were a couple of dozen people milling around now, trying to stay out of the way till the pilot shouted their names.

The ferry had come and gone during the time that Calvin waited with Miles Taber, watching boxes being off-loaded, and once again Mrs. Jessup hadn't seen Uncle Lymon, who was perhaps lying down in the office like he apparently had been yesterday. Calvin had his cell phone with him today. After yesterday's shenanigans he didn't intend to be without it. It was nearly ten o'clock when he left the Cozy Diner, where he had consumed the infamous Million-Dollar Plate—more pancakes than he had ever eaten in his life or would ever eat again—conspicuously more than any other diner was eating, stacked up in a pyramid on an enormous plate. He suspected that Donna had told the chef to come as close to a million as he possibly could, and the chef had come very close. After the heroic way Donna had gone after her food last night at the steakhouse, though, Calvin wanted to come off as a trencherman and not some kind of lightweight who couldn't finish a tub of dollar-size pancakes and a side of bacon. Next week sometime he would be able to eat again.

"Thanks for giving me a hand this morning," Taber said to him. He held on to a flatbed cart with heavy casters, which looked like it could hold about half a ton. "I hauled one load back already. There's only one box left for us, but it's heavy. God knows what it is—something Lymon ordered."

"I kind of thought I'd find him here."

"Apparently he expects me to unload the goods myself. Whitey didn't show either, but I expected that. He went on up to Laughlin to have breakfast with his daughter. She's a blackjack dealer at the Riverside."

"I'm worried about my uncle."

"He's too damned stubborn and tough for his own good," Taber said. "He should get himself a real checkup, over across the river."

Or something, Calvin thought, replaying in his mind the strange scene he had witnessed last night. There was no way he could mention it to Taber, although he would have liked to have his take on it. His own take on it involved things that he didn't have the capacity to believe.

"He didn't put on the coffee this morning like he usually does, so I figured he was still in bed when I went out about eight," Calvin said. "Nettie was up, though. She's having another good day. She had me get her sewing machine out of the cabinet and set it up on the kitchen table. She was actually talking about going into town to buy yardage."

"Good for her," Taber said. "If you'd have seen her last week, you'd call it a miracle. Probably it *is* a miracle."

The man from the steakhouse finished loading up a little Pullman electric cart, small enough to navigate the footbridge, and whirred away, and so Taber and Calvin walked up the gangplank, Taber pushing the cart ahead of them. Calvin was struck with the intensity of the heat rising from the deck. He was already sweating like a pig. "Bear a hand with this crate," Taber told him. "Lymon must have ordered a couple of sacks of concrete and some fence block. No wonder he left it for me."

With the pilot's help, they muscled the box onto the cart and set off, maneuvering down the gangplank and along the dock with Taber hauling and Calvin steadying it. It was a tight squeeze through the door of the bar, and Calvin had to heave on the cart to bump the rear wheels up over the threshold. There were half a dozen other boxes sitting in the middle of the floor, waiting to be opened. One of them had already been emptied out, and there was a pyramid of toilet paper rolls and other paper products sitting alongside.

"Suds?" Taber asked, drawing himself a glass of beer.

"Sure," Calvin said. "Should I open this thing up?"

"Be my guest. Might as well empty it out right there on the cart. It's a little like Christmas, isn't it?"

Calvin picked up the box cutter and slit through the several layers of tape, folding back the cardboard and exposing a heap of foam popcorn. Taber came around from behind the bar, setting the glasses on a table and hauling the emptied-out carton alongside.

"Shovel it into this," he said. "We recycle the packaging material down at the Bullhead Mailbox."

Calvin dipped out a double handful and then another, but when he shoved his hands into the box for a third, his fingers bumped into something that made him jerk his hands back out—what felt like human hair, attached to a human head. "Jesus," he said faintly, nodding at the box. "I don't know what it is, but…"

Taber took over, bailing out foam. He stopped for a moment when they saw what it was, and then he kept bailing until the man's head and shoulders were exposed. It was Lamar Morris, stuffed into the crate, hunched over in a sitting position. Shakespeare looked up at them from the back of his T-shirt. Probably they had gotten to him yesterday, Calvin thought, after he had babbled to Postum about being a Fourteen Carats collector.

"Poor son of a bitch," Taber said.

"What do we do?" Calvin asked. "Call the cops?"

"Yeah, we'll phone out to Essex. There's a substation out there. Shirley Fowler's son. He'll take care of it."

Calvin stared at him. The implications of "Shirley Fowler's son" were enormous. It meant that this would be covered up, and he'd be complicit in it. Did he care?

"That would be your girl Donna's uncle."

"Okay." His *girl*? There it was again.

Calvin stared at the dead man. Right now the smartest thing he could do was get out—climb down off this merry-go-round before it picked up any more momentum. "You know those books that Morris sent over yesterday?" he asked. Taber nodded. "Well, I called back to thank him, and there was a strange message on his phone."

"Let's hear it," Taber said. "Ring the number right now."

Calvin fished out Morris's card again and made the call on the bar phone. He handed Taber the receiver, and Taber listened for the moment that it took, and then hung up again. "Sure," Taber said. "I could have figured it out for myself. Bob Postum murdered Morris and then sent the books along as a message to you—kind of a double-barreled incentive."

"It's a pretty clear message," Calvin said, knowing absolutely that it could have been him in the box and not Morris. Killing Morris had been utterly senseless.... "Tell me something. Can Shirley's son take care of this without *me*?" he asked, watching Taber shovel out more foam. "I kind of wanted to be on the road tomorrow morning."

Taber nodded. "Sure. George is a good man. And this doesn't involve you anyway. Your testimony is irrelevant. Whatever you have to say, it won't do Lamar Morris any good. Right now those books don't mean anything as far as I can see. Go ahead and put the damn things in your suitcase." He grasped the corpse's hair and pulled the head back. "Garroted," he said. "I've got half a mind to take the body back into the hills."

"Won't George Fowler want to see it?"

"I kind of doubt it," Taber said. "The less evidence the better in a case like this. And anyway, maybe we won't bother to call George now that we've got this figured out. And one other thing," Taber said. "Lamar Morris lived alone—no next of kin, either. There's no one to mourn for the man except us, which is a shame, but you don't have to worry about anybody's justice here."

"That's good to know," Calvin replied. "Look, I'm thinking I won't wait for tomorrow morning to leave." As soon as the words were out of his mouth he felt small, but then he looked at Morris's body in the crate. He looked away again.

"You're right," Taber said. "It's going to get worse before it gets better, and it's moving pretty fast, too. I can tell you that Lymon and Hosmer didn't figure you'd be a target when they set you up to bring the box out here. Tell you what: why don't we have Betty Jessup run you up to Laughlin tonight after dark? We'll get a party of Knights to go along, as if they were just going up to the casinos to play the slots. We'll outfit you with a wig and a dress. All you need is to look like someone else from a distance. I'll phone Whitey and have him rent a vehicle while he's up there today. You can pick it up in the parking lot of the Riverside and head straight home, call it ten o'clock. Get the hell out of here while the getting's good. You can cross over the Laughlin Bridge and drive back down along the Arizona side."

Calvin's head was reeling. "Are you serious?" he asked. "About the wig and all?"

"Damn straight," Taber said. "Why not? It's right out of Shakespeare. It's literary. We'll make sure you get out of town safe. Maybe you should head down through Needles, though, and stay off I-40 as much as you can. Don't even *think* about Henderson and Vegas."

"Sure," Calvin said. "I've already got a route picked out. What about my car?"

"We'll have a couple of the Knights drive it back out to L.A. in a day or two, after this blows over. Postum and his bunch won't mess with them. They won't care about the car by then. What's important is that you get out of here now that Postum's got your number."

Calvin felt deflated. Still, it would be an ironic twist if Calvin ended up like Morris, message and messenger both....

"Don't have too many scruples here," Taber said to him, dumping foam back into the box. He found a tape dispenser behind the bar and taped the box shut, sealing Morris into his paper sarcophagus. "This isn't your fight. You've done your job. Right now I envy you. You can walk away. It might look a little bit craven to someone who doesn't know the facts, but I can assure you it's not. I used to have a tenured position at U.N.L.V., teaching medieval lit, and I gave it up for a Knighthood. Took an early retirement. What I've got to show for it right now is a dead man in a box. So quit worrying. Lymon will turn up. He always does."

He told himself that Taber was right. He didn't owe anybody anything here, except maybe Donna. The thought came to him to ask her to come along with him, and for a moment it looked like a perfect plan, and his spirits lifted. She could lock up the trailer and spend some time in civilization, a sort of dual citizenship....

But the idea was idiotic. She wouldn't have any interest in going back with him to Birdland. She had just put the rat race behind her, and of course he had nothing to offer her—nothing at all. Back in L.A. he had nothing to offer *himself*, for God's sake, except a place to hide.

"I guess I don't have to tell you that nothing good will come of talking about this murder," Taber said, looking at him seriously.

"Will anything good come of *not* talking about it?"

"By 'good' you mean will Bob Postum be paid out for the crime?"

"That's part of it."

"He might be. We don't go in for revenge, though, like some folks would—even if Morris had been a Knight. Postum and his people would be ecstatic if they could move us to violence, and we don't want them to be ecstatic, although we won't let our people come to harm, either. And for sure we won't let a man like Bob Postum define the rules of engagement. When the time comes, we'll define the rules ourselves."

"It seems to me like the time has just about come," Calvin said.

"Yes, it has. That's why it's important you're on the road tonight after the sun goes down. Take my advice and don't look back."

Calvin nodded. But under the circumstances Taber's admonition sounded like more than a mere piece of advice, as if Calvin's ignoring it would turn him into a pillar of salt as he fled into the hills, or as if Taber were about to offer him a handful of pomegranate seeds.

"Why don't you take the afternoon off?" Taber said. "I've got a nice little boat, a Boston Whaler. Take Donna out for a spin on the river. Put some lunch and a bottle of wine in an ice chest. It'll be a last hurrah." He smiled at Calvin, but the smile was thin. He looked like a man in a hurry now.

"I never really drove a boat before," Calvin said. "I'm not sure..."

"You'll like the Whaler. It's a humdinger—unsinkable foam hull, almost no draft. You're right down on top of the water. Donna's a crackerjack in a boat. She knows every sandbar and turn in the river. She can teach you a thing or two. Meanwhile, I'll look into what you've been telling me. You're done with all of it. You might as well relax."

Calvin nodded at him, half stupefied.

"Help me roll this into the back," Taber told him.

"All right," Calvin said.

"Do you mind if I take a look at those books that Postum took out of Morris's shop? Then I'll call Whitey and set up that rent-a-sled, and then I'll head on up myself."

"Sure," Calvin said. He steadied the cart again as Taber wheeled it toward the rear of the building.

"Since you're leaving town, I'd like to show you a little something that's usually reserved for Knights—something we call the 'relics antechamber.' You've got the right to have a look, after what you've been through. Who knows if you'll ever be back out here. I'll have to ask you to look away for a moment, though."

Calvin did as he was told. There was the sound of ratcheting iron, surprisingly loud in the small building, and then the grinding and creaking of iron gears and stone sliding over stone. He felt a cool whoosh of air, and smelled stone dust and a cold cellar odor—what he would imagine King Tut's tomb to smell like. *Of course,* he thought, *a secret door.* He should have foreseen a secret door. Lamar Morris would have turned this into a first-rate illustration.

"Through here," Taber said.

Calvin helped maneuver the cart through the head-high opening that had appeared where several big stones had slid aside. Inside was an antechamber maybe twelve feet square. It was dim, and it took his eyes a moment to make out the details of the stone corridor leading away downward on the other side of the room, which was lit by wall lamps connected by heavy black cord strung from porcelain insulators, as if the place had been wired in about 1915. The floor was wet, probably from the river seeping in, and in one place the water pooled up deeply and ran through a long crack between the stones of the floor. Against the wall, a heavy, dark chest stood on carved legs alongside the Communion table that Calvin had seen through the window two nights ago. There was no sign of any leaves growing out of the legs now. What that meant, he didn't know.

On top of it sat the decanter and the goblet on the silver plate—except the decanter wasn't broken. It was whole, and once again there was wine in it. *An exact replica of the decanter that broke the other night?* It didn't make good sense that they would have a case of the things in storage. It was evidently hand-blown, the glass cloudy and heavy and with streaks of what must be minerals. But the shards that Taber had swept onto the plate had certainly *looked* like pieces of this decanter, and the red pool had looked a lot like wine....

There was something in the heavy, silent air that was distinctly strange, and Calvin realized that the hairs on his arms were standing up straight. It wasn't just static electricity; it was something he could almost *hear*, like antique music playing at some low-level frequency—as if the stones themselves were the instruments. It was deeply resonant, and he thought of the planets turning in the void, setting up a harmony of vibrations. For a moment he picked out an actual melody, but as soon as it came into his mind he lost it again. Abruptly he was dizzy, and he leaned against the wall for support. Taber watched him closely.

"That's the Cornerstone you're sensitive to," Taber said in a low voice. "The Cornerstone level lies below us, but it's off-limits unless you're an Elder. Some people can hear it, and some people *see* things—lights and shadows, ghosts. First time I was in here, twenty-five years ago now, I was still wearing a wristwatch, and the thing went wild, hands moving all over the place. Then it died. I had a watchmaker look at it, but it had permanently lost its mind."

Calvin nodded. The idea would have been crazy a couple of minutes ago, but now it seemed plausible. The effect of the Cornerstone—if that's what it actually was—diminished just a little bit, as if he were adjusting to the pressure.

"Now that table there," Taber said, "that's built with wood from the Holy Thorn, out of the very same tree that was planted at Glastonbury by Joseph of Arimathea, or at least that's the story that's been following it around for the last eighteen centuries. It's a living miracle—capable of growth, putting out limbs and leaves pretty much instantly. You ever see anything like that?"

"The other night, actually. Through the window."

Taber nodded at him. "I thought that was you," he said. I couldn't be sure, but thank you for coming clean. So tell me, what do you think of miracles?"

"I've never thought much about them at all," he said evasively.

"Until you came to New Cyprus, and looked into the right window? From now on you'll have plenty of reason not to think about them. Or the opposite, if you see what I mean."

"I'm not sure I do."

"I mean that once you've witnessed one or two, you can't occupy that middle ground anymore. You've either got to accept them or deny them. It's simpler to deny them, just like being asleep is simpler than being awake. Take that music you're hearing... You *are* hearing it?"

"Yes," Calvin said.

"It would be easy for us to put a couple of speakers down below and generate it ourselves. Even the table putting out leaves and branches—you can see that kind of stage effect in any decent theater. This whole thing might be a fraud set up in order to lure you in. You sell your house out there in Eagle Rock and move out east to New Cyprus and throw in with us. You could have the hat and the handshake after you put money into the offering plate."

"It's not all that uncommon."

"No, sir, it's not. A person wants a healthy dose of doubt. Keep your hand on your wallet. The thing is, you've stumbled into a den of believers here, Cal. It's hard not to see that when you talk to a woman like Nettie Lymon. But let's move on. We can talk while we walk. That is, if you want to take a walk...?"

"Sure," Calvin said. "Now that we're here."

They wheeled the cart around a corner where the passage turned inland toward the Dead Mountains, straight as a desert highway. "We'll park him here," Taber said. In the distance, no telling how far, the floor seemed to rise, but the tunnel was a perfect illustration in perspective, narrowing to a vanishing point. "You look like a man with unanswered questions," Taber said to him.

"Not more than about a dozen."

"Go ahead and ask. I'm in an expansive mood."

"All right. I thought that maybe you spotted me through the window night before last. I came out to the island and found Morris sneaking around, trying to get photos through the blinds. He took off when he saw me, and I had a look myself. I had too much curiosity after bringing out the veil and all."

"I'd have done the same when I was your age," Taber said. "And I don't mean to be condescending. Go ahead and ask what you're thinking."

"Okay. That round decanter on the table back there—I saw it break when it fell off the table during the earthquake. You picked up the pieces. Now it's whole again. Or else you've got more than one."

"Just like we've got loudspeakers under the floor. There's never been but the one decanter. Its origins are pretty cloudy, but the Knights Templar took it out of Constantinople with the Veil of Veronica and other holy relics. It's what Hugh Blankfort called 'the Second Secret.'"

"You're telling me it mends itself?"

"I'm not really *telling* you anything. It does what it does. We don't ask *how* it does it, or why. We're not scientists. If it repairs itself, then that's what it does. It's not that far-fetched, Cal. Every creature born of man and woman can put themselves back together again if they really want to. If you don't want to think of it as a living miracle, then think of it as a living metaphor. Let's walk on a ways. I want to give you a couple of more things to think over."

They left the cart behind and headed deeper into the passage. Other tunnels angled away into the darkness now and then. After walking for maybe a hundred yards Calvin could feel that they were moving uphill. "Here's where the river flowed in the old days," Taber said. "You can see the mineral discoloration in the rock. That was back before the quake." He pointed at the ceiling of the tunnel, which was streaked with glittering veins of white.

"Nettie told me something about it," Calvin said.

"No reason you shouldn't know. What happened was that Blankfort and his Knights brought the Cornerstone right out across the desert after Blankfort had some kind of vision, or so the story goes. They camped along the Colorado, and when the sun rose in the morning there was an earthquake that turned the river out of its course and broke open the Temple Bar so that they could see down into the earth, into a sort of grotto. Blankfort took it as a sign that they'd reached the Promised Land, and they laid the Cornerstone down in what they called the Deep

Cellar. And right when they had the last shim set, and the stone was square and plumb, there was another quake, and the river flowed out around the Bar on either side, turning it into an island. They built the Temple and cut this passage over the years that followed, and of course they built New Cyprus in the new land along the mountainside."

"*What* cornerstone?" Calvin asked. "Why haul a big stone all the way out here from New Rochelle and bury it where it serves no function?"

"The word 'function' is a little tough to define. The thing is, that's what they did. That's what happened. The Knights Templar brought the Cornerstone into Europe at some point between the First and Second Crusades—the Cornerstone of the Temple of Solomon. It was common knowledge that the Templars were excavating the Temple Mount, and heaven knows what else they found, but they hauled the Cornerstone back into France by ship and hid it. It was Blankfort's family that brought it on across the Atlantic into New Rochelle, and Blankfort himself who brought it out West along with some of the other relics. What happened when they laid the stone down in the Deep Cellar wasn't something he anticipated."

"And that's the First Secret?"

"No. The First Secret's a secret. All I told you isn't any kind of secret, except the origin of the Cornerstone, which doesn't really have to be kept secret because it's too far-fetched to be true. And anyway, the Vatican claims it's got the Cornerstone, which makes *way* more sense than its being out here in the desert. The unbelievable secret is the best kind—it pretty much keeps itself."

"The Vatican doesn't have it?" Calvin asked.

Taber shrugged. "They've got something. We've got something else."

Calvin was distracted now by movement farther up the passage—a shadow, strangely shaped, like a man hunched over a wheelbarrow or cart. For the space of an instant it seemed to flesh out, and Calvin saw a man leaning over a cart full of something—rock, maybe—and then he vanished utterly when he moved into the lamplight. Then he saw it again: the identical movement, shadow to flesh to nothing. No mistake. He watched for it to return. "What *is* that?" he asked Taber.

Taber turned to look, and they both stood silently for the space of twenty seconds before the vision renewed itself, like a loop of film endlessly repeating. "Move forward," Taber told him. They started along the passage again, watching carefully, but the vision didn't return. They came upon iron tracks laid into the stone floor, but there was no need to ask about them; their purpose was obvious.

"Now it's gone," Calvin said. "Why? Matter of perspective?"

"That's just what it is. And I'm not sure either of us understands all the definitions of the word 'gone.' I can tell you this sort of thing isn't rare, though—not in New Cyprus. Of course it would be easy to fake...."

"Sure it would. Just like the rest. Do you think they're ghosts?"

"I don't speculate on it too much, but, no, I don't think they're ghosts. I saw one in the relic antechamber once, and I'm convinced it was Al Lymon. But Al was down at the Costco buying paper goods. A man can't be in two places at one time.

Unless he can. There's always that alternative. Anyway, speculation's futile. I do know that you can't strike up a conversation with any of them. They're a silent crowd, although you can hear footsteps sometimes. Let's stop here."

A chamber opened off to the right-hand side, and Taber stepped into it and felt around on the wall. Lamps came on, revealing a large room hewn into the bottom reaches of the Dead Mountains. Calvin stepped into it, hearing the vastness of the place in the silence and seeing right away, with a shock of horror, that it was a catacombs. It was lined with niches hollowed into the walls and edged with cut stone. Shrouded skeletons lay in many of the niches, scores of them.

"Everything stays cool and dry down here," Taber said. "Nothing to disturb anyone."

"Do all the Knights end up down here?" Calvin asked in a hushed voice. Somehow he couldn't imagine Donna choosing to pass away into eternity entombed in a catacomb.

"Oh, no," Taber told him. "It's like anywhere else. Some of them are in the churchyard topside, and lots of them are shipped home—wherever home was before New Cyprus; close to the kids, maybe. Some have their ashes scattered over the river, like your dad. We crated Whitey Sternbottom's kid brother up two months ago and sent him back to Des Moines. And Hosmer, of course, is strictly an Iowa man. I myself mean to stay. I've got a niche over there on the west wall. Better view." Calvin managed a grin.

"So this is still in use? I'm surprised it's legal."

"Still in use. And what passes for legal in unincorporated territory like New Cyprus can seem a little bit arcane to outsiders. Anyway, that's the ten-cent tour," Taber said. "There's a two-bit tour, but right now it's beyond your means. Take a look up there in the back corner though, at that glint of light. Do you see it?"

"Yeah. Looks like a lens. Camera?"

"Slick, eh? We're old dogs, but we've got some new tricks. You never know when you need a third eye. We'd better get back up the passage—get you squared away for tonight."

They left the catacombs and started back downhill, walking in silence. They hadn't taken ten steps, however, when it abruptly dawned on Calvin what was wrong with his uncle. "I know why Uncle Lymon's sick," he said. Taber stopped and waited, a look of anticipation on his face. "He's doing it to himself."

"Doing *what* to himself?"

"He told me a little bit about the Veil of Veronica—what it is and where it came from. He said that when Veronica blotted Christ's face, and the image appeared, she assumed His pain, or something like that. *That's* what was going on last night after you left. That's what I saw." He told Taber about the partly open bedroom door, the strange aura that he had wanted to think was a table lamp, and his uncle's evident pain and his hand resting on the veil.

"I think you're probably wrong," Taber told him. "I don't mean I think you're *lying,* I mean I think you mistook something. Probably it *was* just a table lamp. Al wouldn't...*employ* the veil that way. Even if he was convinced it was necessary, which God knows it would be in Nettie's case. He'd have told us what he intended to do. He's got scruples about that kind of thing. The veil doesn't belong to him or to anyone else on earth, and he knows that as well as I do." They walked on now, a little more quickly than before.

"If it were me," Calvin said, "I'd toss the scruples into the trash if my wife was suffering." Immediately he knew that this was a moderately egotistical thing to say. He hadn't ever been called upon to act heroically, even in small ways, and it was easy to make grandiose claims when you weren't going to be put to the test.

Then he wondered whether he might soon *be* put to the test. He recalled what Aunt Nettie had said to him—when was it? Yesterday? *"What are you doing out here in New Cyprus if you weren't called out?"*

They passed Morris's cart, Calvin trailing his hand over the cardboard surface of the box that contained the body. The next moment they were back in the antechamber where the Communion table stood. Taber opened the door of the cabinet next to it, looked inside, and then shut it again.

"It's not there, is it?" Calvin asked.

Taber shook his head. "No, it's not."

"How powerful is it? Can he kill himself with it?"

"I don't know. The cancer was close to killing Nettie. If he takes the disease away from her along with the pain…literally, I mean." He shook his head. "This changes things. If Lymon takes himself out, we've got to look at things a little bit differently." He shook his head, as if grappling with possible futures. "It just doesn't seem gentlemanly to confront him on it. It would shame him, I can tell you that. And if he's already done it anyway…Damn it, you don't just *use* a miracle."

"Why not?" Calvin asked. "When Moses got the water out of the stone, everyone had a drink, didn't they? When God parted the Red Sea, they all went right on across. They didn't stand around and marvel at it. You don't waste a miracle, either."

"Yes, they *did* make use of it, but that was thousands of years ago. If you were caretaker of that stone today, you wouldn't set up to sell bottled water. You would if you were Bob Postum, but not if you're Al Lymon."

Calvin shrugged. "I guess not," he said. "But your argument is a little abstract. Aunt Nettie's not abstract. She's real, and so is the cancer."

"Well," Taber said, obviously composing himself. "It's something we'll have to deal with, and by 'we' I mean the Knights."

Calvin stood still for a moment, listening to the strange sounds in the air around him, thinking about his aunt and uncle. "I think I'll pass on that offer of a rental car," he said finally. "I think I'll stay."

OVER THE RIVER

They flew along atop the river in Taber's Boston Whaler. Calvin had anticipated something out of *Moby-Dick* when Taber had first referred to it—something with a front end that flared upward and wooden seats with oarlocks beside them, maybe a harpoon and a tub of rope. But the Whaler was nearly flat, so low to the water that Calvin could drag his hand in the river while Donna piloted them upstream, cruising along near shore in the shade of the Dead Mountains to a little beach she knew about.

It was a quiet afternoon, the river nearly empty of boats. The ferry had passed them heading back down to New Cyprus, and so had a couple of skiers on the back of a boat, jetting along with music blaring, but there was no one besides themselves along this stretch. In an ice chest he had a bottle of champagne and two glasses as well as assorted goodies to eat. Donna wore a bathing suit top and a pair of shorts, and her hair was tied back into a ponytail. Calvin had to make an effort not to stare at her. By any sane definition it was shaping up to be a perfect afternoon.

The boat swung in a wide arc now, around a sheer wall of rock that edged the upriver end of the Dead Mountains, which cut off a little still-water cove from most of the rest of the river. Donna killed the engine and ran the boat straight up onto a shady piece of beach, stepping out over the prow and tying up to a clump of willow. "This is it," she said. "We used to come up here when I was a kid. What do you think?"

"It's beautiful," he said, handing the lawn chairs over the side. He grabbed the ice chest and climbed out, looking up at the tumble of rock towering away overhead, the upper reaches lit by a halo of sunlight in a deep blue sky. He set up the chairs in three inches of water, Aunt Nettie–style, kicked off his flip-flops, and sat down, watching Donna fish the champagne bottle out of the ice chest along with two glasses. She tore off the foil, unwound the wire, and edged the cork out of the bottle without any ostentatious popping and fizzing, and a moment later he found himself holding a glass of champagne that was colder than the river water swirling over his feet.

"Cheers," Donna said to him. Her smile was more than a little bit coy, as if she had his number, which of course she did.

"Over the river," he said, clinking her glass and taking a sip.

"What does that mean?" she asked. " 'Over the river'? I heard Miles Taber say it once."

"I don't know," he said. "I think I got it out of a Steinbeck novel. It seemed apropos under the circumstances—you know, with the river and all....Except I think that it probably means another river."

They sat in silence for a moment, and then she said, "You know, I knew Lamar Morris. Back when I was in high school. He asked me out, actually."

"*Really?*" Calvin said. "Now that's weird. It's a small world."

"Out here it is," she said, looking steadily at him. "But what's weird about it? Now and then I get asked out. Sometimes I've got to get a little bit pushy, I guess. I've got to borrow a boat from a matchmaker like Miles Taber in order to hook the timid ones and talk them into a date."

"I didn't mean weird *that* way. I meant..." He found that he was completely speechless, and that Donna's smile had turned into a grin. "I meant that there's too much synchronicity to things sometimes. I run into one of Lamar's father's books at the Gas'n'Go, and then the next day I meet Lamar, and then the next day he's dead, probably because I met him, and now I find out you dated him, and of course your grandmother owns the Gas'n'Go where I bought the book, and...Well, now here *we* are."

He gestured at the rocks, the river water and willows. Something seemed to be pending. It was definitely pending. He was being given an opportunity here. "You ever go out at Halloween as Pippi Longstocking?" he asked her. "With the sideways braids and all?"

"Do you even have to ask?" she said. "My grandfather even built me a playhouse behind the Gas'n'Go called Villa Villekulla, and I had an imaginary monkey named Mr. Nilsson, and an old wooden rowboat with a little cabin built in the middle called Hoptoad."

"The cabin had a name?"

"*Hoptoad* was the name of Efraim Longstocking's ship—Pippi's father. Do you want some more champagne?"

Calvin nodded. "I thought the name of the house was Vena Vena Cava." He held out his glass and let Donna fill it.

"You mean like the vein in the heart? That's *really* weird. That's even weirder than me being asked out by Lamar Morris."

"That's what it sounded like in the films."

"So you didn't read the book? You only watched the movie?"

"I *might* read the books now that I know they've got a ship in them called *Hoptoad*. I remember she was always going on about her father coming home to take her away to some tropical island...."

"Yeah," she said. "I remember that, too." She looked away.

It came to him after a moment that the statement had apparently killed the conversation. "Sorry," he said. "I think I said something I shouldn't have."

"I didn't know my father or mother anyway. Just my grandparents. When I was little, though, I used to dream, you know, that my father was out there somewhere, and that he'd come home one day. Then—I don't know, maybe when I was nine or ten—I figured out that dreams are for babies. I quit reading *The Velveteen Rabbit*, too. I got over it, though."

"I guess I know what you mean," he said. "Sooner or later you get over it."

"You mean losing the love of your life?"

"The love of my life? I'm not dead yet," he said. "But, yeah, something like that. What do you say we paint 'Hoptoad' on the side of the Boston Whaler?"

"We don't have paint."

"I've got a felt marker," he said. "Indelible ink." He stuck the base of his champagne glass under the river sand and picked up his book bag. "I brought some cartoons," he said. "I thought maybe I'd show you a couple. I mean, they're maybe not all that funny, but…"

"What if they *are* funny? What if you're wrong about it? What if you're wrong about all kinds of things? Like what if you're actually Mr. Wonderful but this Elaine woman couldn't see it? She made you miserable, and then you let yourself get into the habit of being miserable and turned yourself into a mope. You know why I brought you out here today?"

"Tell me," he said.

"That's what I'm doing. What I'm telling you is that we're done with Elaine. She just got written out of the script. Is that all right with you?"

"Absolutely," he said.

"Then show me one of your cartoons, and *I'll* tell you whether it's funny or not, and if I say it's funny, then it's funny. And quit looking like you're going to faint."

"I'm not going to *faint*," he said, staring at her. She actually looked angry. If he had a chance to draw the cartoon, it would be a picture of both of them wearing leopard-skin garments. She'd be wearing the Pippi braids and carrying a club, dragging him off toward a cave, and he'd have a lump on his head. Over the cave door it would read "Vena Vena Cava." It would be a heart-shaped door. He started laughing.

"What's so funny?" she asked.

"Nothing. I can't tell you." He laughed again.

"I'll hurt you," she said.

"Later," he said. "I'll tell you later, and then you can hurt me. Here..." He took his sketchbook out of his book bag and opened it at random, handing it to her. It was the cartoon of the lunatic doctors in the doorway.

"'That's the one,'" she read, apparently baffled. "I don't get it." She looked at him blankly.

His heart sank. "Well, I guess I wanted to imply that..."

"You're *so* easy," she said. "Okay, it's funny. It really is. What do you do with these, mail them out to magazines?"

"Sometimes, I guess."

"Sometimes? Like you did it once?"

"Maybe two or three times. Take a look at this." He flipped back a couple of pages to a drawing of a sheep floating through space. The caption read "To boldly go where no sheep has gone before." "What do you think?" he asked.

"Okay, this time I really don't get it. Is this one of your Martian things? The brothers upstairs, or whatever it was? The sheep upstairs?"

"No! Are you kidding? It's a line from *Star Trek*!"

"Sheep?"

"In *Star Trek* it was people—mankind. Look at this one." He turned the page. This time the sheep was climbing a pyramid. On the adjacent page the same sheep was swimming under the ocean. There was a jellyfish going past and a starfish on a rock.

"I'm not sure 'to boldly go' sounds right. I'd write, 'to go boldly.'"

"Right. Me, too. It's a split infinitive. But you *must* have seen *Star Trek* at least once or twice...."

"I don't think so. But I'm absolutely certain that if I *had* seen it I'd be laughing like crazy. I swear it."

"Don't swear it if you don't mean it," he said, giving her a hard look.

She nodded her head seriously. "I *do* mean it," she said. "Under those other circumstances I'd be laughing. Hey, here's one for you. You could draw a cartoon for it. What happened when the boardinghouse exploded?"

"I don't know," he said.

"Roomers were flying! That's pretty good, isn't it?"

"Yeah," he said. "You should be the cartoonist."

"Except I didn't make it up. It's about a hundred years old. I heard it from Miles."

"Okay, I'm going to show you my most recent."

"Not another drawing of a sheep?"

"No. This is an Attila the Hun gag. Check this out." He flipped to the back of the book, grinning despite himself. She looked at the sketch—a picture of a perfectly round, perfectly flat man with a tiny little helmet on, holding a bottle that said "Mead" on it. Next to him stood a woman who looked like a cinnamon roll. The caption read "Tortilla the Hun and his Honey Bun." He nodded at Donna. "Eh?" he said. "Is that funny, or what?"

For a moment she stared at him poker-faced, but she apparently couldn't keep it up, and she started laughing. Then she leaned forward and kissed him. He was silenced for a moment, and then realized that he was smiling stupidly at her, and that she knew she had struck him dumb. "We haven't had enough champagne yet to..."

"No. So it's not the liquor talking."

"Speaking of the liquor talking, did you know that Attila the Hun drank himself to death on his wedding night?"

"What a guy," she said. "I bet it made his bride happy, though. Hey! I bet he drank mead! That explains the bottle."

"And the 'honey bun' in a way. Sort of."

"I get it—mead, honey wine. That's *so* obscure..." she said doubtfully.

"Yeah, but that's all right. People don't have to get the whole thing."

"God knows that's true. Lots of people *never* get the whole thing. Why don't you put your sketchbook back into the bag? Your cartoons are really funny, by the way."

"Sure," he said. "Thanks." He got up and put the bag back into the Whaler. When he turned around he saw that her chair was empty and that she had spread a big beach towel down on the sand and was sitting on it.

"Either you pitch some woo at me or I'm going to pitch you into the river and steal your cartoons," she said. "It's your choice."

"Give me a moment to decide," he said.

ON THE PAYROLL

They ran the Whaler up to the dam, past the casinos and ferry docks, and then turned around and headed back downriver toward New Cyprus, catching up with and passing the New Cyprus ferry not far from home. His aunt was on board the ferry, with her back to them, and he saw Betty Jessup turn to say something to her. Nettie swung around and shaded her eyes, spotted the Whaler, and waved. He waved back. It was a solidly good thing, seeing Nettie out on the river.

There was a wind coming up, but it seemed to cool things, like a trade wind, and he realized that for ten cents he'd be happy simply staying on the river, stopping here and there to launch the lawn chairs, watching the stars come out over the hills, maybe, and returning to their cove in the shelter of the

Dead Mountains to sleep under the stars. Right now it sounded like the plan of a lifetime to him—a long lifetime. He looked at Donna, whose hair caught the sunshine and seemed to flare up. *Ideally a* really *long lifetime,* he thought.

A crowd of people in a speedboat blasted past them heading upriver toward the dam, towing two children on big, flashy, canvas-covered inner tubes. He waved at the people in the boat, and they waved back cheerfully, and he wished at that moment that he could wave at the whole wide world, but instead he waved at the children on the tubes, one of whom, a little boy of maybe five or six, let go with one hand to return the wave, but immediately flew off the tube and went cartwheeling away across the water. Calvin turned to watch, feeling like a criminal as the speedboat slowed down to rescue the victim. *Heck,* he thought, *every silver cloud...*

He watched New Cyprus approaching on the right. Donna swung the Whaler into the bay, cutting the engine way back, the boat sort of ghosting along over the smooth water. The fisherman was still out there, fifty yards downstream from where he'd been earlier, his line still slack. He apparently had all the patience in the world. He tilted his head back to take a drink of something, and just at that moment there was the gurgling roar of an approaching boat, which angled out away from the shore where it had apparently been hidden by cottonwoods—very near his uncle and aunt's house.

Calvin watched it swerve tightly around the end of the ferry dock and shoot downriver past the fisherman, passing so close that from Calvin's perspective it looked like they had run him right down. But then he saw that they hadn't. The fisherman stood up and shook his fist, and then grabbed on to the edge of the boat for balance as it rocked back and forth in the wake.

Drunks, Calvin thought, *out having a little fun,* but suddenly Donna gunned it, and they were shooting in toward Taber's dock at warp speed. She throttled down again at the last moment, backing water, and bumped softly against the dock, cutting the engine. "Tie it up!" she shouted, and headed up the dock at a run toward the house. The ferry came in behind them, moving strangely fast toward the dock on the island, and he had no sooner finished putting a couple of loops of line over the bollard than his cell phone rang, surprising him. He dug it out of his book bag and flipped it open, glancing at the long-distance number, which he didn't recognize. A man was already talking, although about what Calvin had no idea. Then he realized it was Warren Hosmer, calling out of the blue like God in the Old Testament. "Sorry?" Calvin asked. "I didn't hear that."

"I said they *got him.*"

"They got *who*?" Calvin thought about the man in the rowboat, but why would Hosmer...?

"*Lymon,*" Hosmer said. "*They got Lymon.* Are you listening now, or should I get out the bullhorn? Betty Jessup rang through to me twenty seconds ago. Nettie went into town and left Al resting out on the river, in one of those chairs they have. When the ferry was coming back down just now, Betty caught sight of a boat down there along the shore—must have been a jet boat, because it came right out of shallow water, moving fast. They snatched him from right out behind the house. It was a bold damn stroke. They headed back downriver toward Needles, and *I mean just now.* Betty saw the whole thing."

"Good God," Calvin said. "I saw it, too. What should *I* do? Donna went up to tell Miles."

"I don't know any Donna," Hosmer said. "So what you're saying conveys no meaning to my mind. Pipe down for a moment and listen to me. There's only one thing *to* do—*get him back*. They'll want the veil—maybe they already have it—but don't be fooled. That'll just be the start of it. What they really want is the whole nine yards, the whole ball of wax, the enchilada, and they mean to get it this time. They'll ask for a ransom, but they won't play ball once you throw it to them. They'll knock it right back at you and ask you to buy another round, right up to last call, because they're lying sacks of crap, every man jack of them. You hear what I'm saying? This is *match point* we're talking about. Do what you've got to do, Cal. You're on the payroll. Your time has come."

✠

What do you think, Calvin?" his aunt asked him after Taber said he was stumped. "What would you have us do?" They were sitting in the Temple Bar, the swamp cooler sounding loud in the silence.

"I've got no experience with this kind of thing," Calvin said. "I didn't even know it went on in the world."

"Well, it does," Taber told him. "All kinds of things go on in this part of the world. What did the boat look like?"

"It was blue or purple. Metal-flake, from the way the sun was shining off it."

"Yes, that's right," his aunt said. "Betty saw a name on the back. Looked like 'paint' or something."

"*Painted Lady,*" Calvin said. "I got the second word when they buzzed that fisherman. Maybe we can we find the name of the boat owner by tracking the name of the boat."

"A boat doesn't have to have a name," Taber said, "so there's no reason its name would be registered. We'd want the license number on the side, which we don't have. We can ask around easy enough. It's *got* to be a local, probably out of Needles. We have to find out why they took him—what they want."

"Obviously it's the veil," Calvin said. "That's what Hosmer told me, anyway. I don't know why they had to snatch Uncle Lymon, though, after Bob Postum offered me a bribe to deliver it out at the Gas'n'Go tomorrow. Why couldn't he wait a day?"

"Either he's upping the ante or he doesn't trust you to make that deal happen out at the Gas'n'Go, so he's giving you more incentive. I'd have thought Lamar Morris would be enough to throw at you, but apparently he wants to push it a little further. He figures you'll run, otherwise. They're in an all-fire hurry to get this thing done."

"How about George Fowler? Maybe he can do something."

"George is just one man out there in a little bitty substation. If he needs a deputy he calls down to Ludlow. We don't want to put in any calls down to Ludlow or anyplace else. And besides, this is bigger than that. We want to keep it in-house." He fell silent for a moment and then said, "How are you getting along, Nettie?"

"I'm doing well, Miles. Awfully well. Today was my first trip into town in I don't know how long. It's like a miracle. Prayer is what did it. That's what Al says."

Calvin glanced at Taber, who nodded heavily. "I've got to ask," Taber said to her. "Did Al tell you much about the veil?"

"Which veil would that be?" she asked.

"The one that Calvin brought out."

"Not a thing, although when I was under the weather my mind wasn't worth a nickel. Today's different, but like I said, I haven't felt like this in a couple of years. It's like a weight's been rolled away, and I've come out into the light."

"Good," Taber said. "That's good, Nettie."

"I praise God for it. What's this veil, though? Is that what they're after? That's why they took Al?" Her eyes narrowed, and it was clear to Calvin that she wanted an answer, and he decided to let Taber give it to her.

"Yes, it is. What Cal brought out here was the Veil of Veronica, which I believe you've heard of."

"I remember it, yes. I know the story well. They say it has healing powers. Al and I saw a carving in stone in Rosslyn Chapel, in Scotland, when we were out there in the nineteen sixties. We were traveling with Warren Hosmer and his wife, and I remember that he and Al made a connection concerning the veil with a man named MacLaine, but nothing came of it, as I recall. Al and Hosmer were always on the trail of something."

"Well, Hosmer got hold of the veil some time back. He's had it out in Orange City, and he sent it on to us when things started to heat up out there. Our old friend de Charney and his crowd want it, and they know we have it. I expect we'll hear a ransom demand, so we've got to figure out where it is."

"You just said you had it," she said. "Didn't you say that Calvin brought it out here?"

"Yes, I did," Taber said. "It was here in the Temple on that first night Cal arrived—Al brought it over with him—but now it's not here. At least it's not in the antechamber, where we put it."

She nodded slowly. "And you think Lymon took it over to the house? You think that's why I'm here right now. Why I'm better? He made use of the veil?"

"That's what I believe, Nettie. I think he wanted to use it to take up some of your burden. To take it on himself."

She sat for a moment thinking, staring straight out in front of her, as if putting two and two together. "Yes," she said finally. "He must have had it over to the house. I'm sure he did. Of course he did. That's explains the change." She began to cry silently, and Calvin looked away. "Did he take on the *cancer*?" she asked.

"I don't know, Nettie. We can't... "

"Yes, that's it. I don't even have to ask. He took on the cancer. I can feel it's gone. He used it to heal me. He was laid up pretty bad this morning. I shouldn't have left him alone. I should have known."

"You *couldn't* have known, Nettie. You didn't even know about the veil. You said so yourself. And what's done is done. The faster we sort this out, the more chance we've got to put things right. If they got hold of the veil when they kidnapped Al, we have to know."

She nodded. "Then let's take a look." She wearily got up out of the chair. Calvin wondered suddenly if she still wanted to thank God for the way she was feeling, but the question was unworthy, and he pushed it out of his mind.

"Cal," Taber said, "why don't you go on up to the house with Nettie and see if the veil's there. Bring it back down if it is.

I'm going to do some telephoning. We've got to be ready before that ransom call comes in."

Calvin and Nettie went out into the sunlight and crossed the footbridge. The afternoon had somehow turned into evening. His aunt stopped and looked out over the river, down toward Needles, as if she could see something on the water—the ghost of hope, perhaps. "He's a good man," she said, "but he's a God-blessed fool sometimes."

Calvin's cell phone rang again, and he flipped it open, ready to make his report to Hosmer. But it wasn't Hosmer. It was Bob Postum.

"Cal," he said heartily. "I just wondered whether we were still on for that little meeting tomorrow out on the highway. From where I stand, it looks like a better idea now than it did yesterday, and yesterday it looked pretty good. Pot's bigger now, too. Too high for a player like you to try to bluff. Like the man used to say on the news, Cal, 'See you at ten, see you then.'"

Calvin listened to nothing for a moment before flipping the phone shut.

THE MEETING OF THE ELDERS

They won't buy it," Whitey Sternbottom said. "A fake? Not a chance. They'd grab you, too, and then we'd have another person to spring. Except they'd probably just shoot you and dump your body in the lake out behind the Gas'n'Go. Lymon's got too much stature for them to kill him without any gain, but you don't, Cal—no insult intended."

"None taken," Calvin said. "But if it *really* looked like the original, how would they know for sure? They've never seen it. I'd deliver the box, wait till they opened it, walk out, and drive back toward Needles with the money in the trunk and Al in the front seat and give you a call on the cell phone. You could be waiting up the way to run interference if you had to."

"You'd never leave the parking lot," Taber said. "Forget

about any money. And what *about* Lymon? What if Lymon isn't there? What the hell did Postum say, that the *stakes* were higher? That doesn't mean they'll have Al along with them. That means they can do what they please."

"Okay," Calvin said, "then what if I took along a jar of kerosene and a lighter. If they don't have Uncle Lymon, or won't agree to let him go as a condition, then I threaten to dump kerosene over the box and burn the veil right there in the parking lot."

"Then they'll know for damn sure it's not the genuine article," Taber said. "We'd never do a thing like that."

"You wouldn't, but I would," Calvin said. "Why not? It's like burning an old flag or a bale of old money. It seems like a big deal, but once it's gone, it's gone—it's just ashes. And right now it's just a legend anyway, as far as anyone knows for sure, except us."

"Dust to dust," his aunt said.

"Exactly."

"Betty, what do you think?" Taber asked.

"Whitey's right," Betty Jessup said. "It's a fool's errand. Even if they thought they had the veil, they wouldn't let that money go. At best that pillowcase in the trunk will be stuffed with bundles of cut-up newspaper. Even if you asked to see the money before you handed the veil over—which anybody would—it wouldn't make any difference. You've got no leverage."

"So what? I won't ask to see it. I'd take the cut-up newspaper and drive away."

"You'd be lucky if you went anywhere," Whitey said. "Even if you were good enough to convince them it was the veil, they wouldn't tell you where they were holding Lymon. And your fancy analogy won't work. This isn't old money and it isn't a worn-out flag. It isn't any kind of symbol. It's the Veil of Veronica. And just to put it in perspective, this transaction is the *start* of things, not the end. You're thinking short term, but they won't be."

"Then if it goes bad, I'll make them take me along. Do they know Donna's a Knight?"

"Doesn't matter," Taber said. "Donna's not part of this equation."

"Of course not," Calvin said. "I wouldn't ask her to be part of it, although maybe someone *should* ask her. Someone asked me, and she's more competent than I am."

"*I'm* not going to ask her," Taber said. "I won't stop her if she's willing, but I won't ask her. And nobody asked you in so many words. Sounded to me like you made up your own mind. 'I think I'll stay,' is what you said."

"That's right, I did, and I thank you for the opportunity to say it." Calvin listened to the wind, rustling through the willows. Two nights ago he had been outside looking in.

"But it *was* a choice," Taber said. "You could have gone right on being uncommitted, with no skin off your nose, except maybe a little pride. Donna was committed from the get-go. She's already a Knight. And besides, I like that girl. I just don't want her in the vicinity."

"We're all put to the test, Miles," Nettie said. "If we never take the test, we don't know how we'll fare. It's like how we stand up to temptation. It's the only thing that shows what kind of mettle we've got. You know that. You preached that little sermon yourself more than once."

"Nettie's right," Betty Jessup said. "You and Lymon gave Calvin the opportunity to make his own mind up. We all did. We've been waiting for him to sign on ever since he rolled into town. Cal had the choice, and he up and did the right thing. So to answer your question, Cal, Bob Postum's crowd doesn't know Donna from Adam. There's no reason they should. She just recently moved back out to New Cyprus, and she's been a Knight for about a month."

"They shouldn't have known that Hosmer had the veil, either," Whitey said, "but they did."

Betty shrugged. "I think we ought to let Calvin say what's on his mind, and then if it sounds like anything at all, we'll call in Donna and ask her. Let the girl speak for herself."

"And remember one thing," Taber said. "They don't know Donna from Adam *unless* they saw her rescue Cal out there in the quarry. We *know* they saw her car."

"I don't think they saw *her*," Calvin told him. "They were behind us the whole time."

"What about today, out on the river, when you were coming back up on the Whaler?"

"We were pretty far upriver, and they headed the other way."

Taber remained silent now.

"She can drive *any* car," Whitey said to Taber. "She doesn't have to drive her own. We'll put her into that new Mustang Doc Hoyle bought. He won't argue about it."

"All right, Cal," Taber said finally, "what's the plan? And whatever it is, we've got to have an alternate take on the whole thing. We're going to give Donna a comfortable way out, and I'm going to encourage her to take it."

GAS'N'GO

Calvin passed the stone marker, heading out toward the highway in his pockmarked Dodge, the heat through the broken-out windows mixing with the cold air from the air conditioner. The wind was still blowing, now and then peppering the side of the car with sand, and the desert shrubs shuddered in the gusts. In the light of day, his Gas'n'Go plan seemed pitifully naïve for about a half dozen reasons, not the least of which was that it depended on Postum's wanting the veil so badly that he would play by some variety of rules—that he would be willing to barter Uncle Lymon for it. But why would he start that now? "Everything he says is a lie," Hosmer had told him, and so far everything Hosmer said was the truth.

By now Donna was somewhere down I-40 just west of Needles in Doc Hoyle's white Mustang. She had called Calvin a couple of minutes ago, and was twenty minutes behind him if he held it to sixty miles per hour. That would give him time to negotiate. She was his first line of defense—or rather retreat. A car full of Knights—further backup—was waiting beneath the bridge over the river right outside Needles. He only had to hold down the number two on his cell phone to send out the distress signal, and then they would move into action, whatever that meant. The whole thing looked likely to be a fine kettle of fish. He clanked down over the wash and up onto the empty highway, heading west.

The last few miles to the Gas'n'Go seemed to take no time at all, and he set the turn signal and slowed down, spotting the Postum-mobile in the parking lot as well as an old-model Chevy van, painted white and primer gray and with a two-by-four front bumper and no front plate. As far as he could see, no one sat in either one of the vehicles. He and Donna could outrun both of them easily in the Mustang if it came down to it, which he hoped to God it wouldn't.

He wondered suddenly if his uncle was being held in the back of the van, and he angled across the lot and pulled alongside it, then got out slowly, glancing in through the rear window. But there was a plywood partition like a bulkhead just inside the double doors, marked with a glued-on explosives warning—another Beamon truck, probably, and perfect for hiding a prisoner. He rapped against the side panel—the first notes of "Shave and a Haircut"—as he walked by, listening for an answering "two bits," but there was nothing. Could be Uncle Lymon was tied up....

He glanced in through the driver's side and noticed that the keys were in the ignition, and for one wild moment he considered climbing in, starting it up, and driving the hell out of there like Mr. Toad, leaving his beaten-up Dodge behind. It would be heroic if Uncle Lymon was in fact tied up back there, and sheer idiocy if he wasn't....

"Don't even think about it," a voice said, and he looked up to see his old friend the Bullhead City smoker regarding him from a few feet away.

"Think about what?" Calvin asked. The man had his hand in the pocket of a pair of khaki cargo pants. Plenty of room for a weapon.

"Whatever you were thinking about."

"I was thinking about getting some chili cheese fries and a soda," Calvin told him.

"Then you came to the right place. Bob says to go ahead and bring the box, if you've got it. And you better hope you've got it." Calvin returned to the car, got the box out of the trunk, and followed the man toward the door, studying his back. He was short and wiry, and Calvin was fifteen years younger, although the last time Calvin had been in a fight was in the third grade when a girl named Yolanda Kleemer had given him a bloody nose and ruined his life in elementary school. He wondered if Donna could fight like Yolanda Kleemer. He nearly laughed.

Shirley Fowler was cooking at the griddle when they walked in, frying up cheeseburgers, and at one of the two picnic tables sat Bob Postum and two other men, one of whom, unfortunately, was the tall, lanky man from the quarry, who wouldn't be a big Calvin Bryson fan after the merry chase the other day. The other was maybe sixty years old, stocky, and mostly bald. His nose had apparently been broken a few times and set by a drunk. He looked prodigiously unhappy at the moment—sad rather than angry. They were all sipping coffee out of foam cups.

"Cal!" Postum said, standing up and putting out his hand for a shake. "This here is Calvin Bryson," he said to the others. "Out here from L.A., where he's in the rare book business. I help him out now and then with some hard-to-find titles."

Calvin hesitated, but then he shook hands, even though he was fairly sure now that Bob Postum was some kind of grinning devil. *Not* shaking hands would mean starting things up in some way, and he wasn't ready for that yet. Best to avoid it altogether—play the game, wait for his opportunity. "I thought I'd join you," he said to Postum.

"Do we look like we're coming apart?" Postum asked, and then laughed. Maybe later Calvin would think it was funny. "Meet Pat Yorkmint and Stillwater Mifflin, Cal. They call him Stillwater because he runs deep. Isn't that right?" he asked. Mifflin nodded heavily. Postum's sense of humor was apparently lost on the man. "You already met Jefferson Davis here." He nodded at the small man. "Most people call him 'Defferson' on account of he's hard of hearing."

"Jesus H. Christ," the man muttered, and Postum laughed again and winked hard at Calvin.

"What'll you have?" Shirley asked him.

"Chili cheese fries," Calvin said to her. She nodded, loading the burgers onto buns that were laid out on wax paper in little pastel-colored plastic baskets.

"Anything to drink?"

"Grape soda, I guess."

"Soda's in the case," she said. "Opener's on a string at the end of the table."

He grabbed a cold grape Nehi, found the church key hanging from the string, and opened the bottle. He watched Shirley dip the wire basket of fries into the hot oil. She looked efficient and bored. There was no indication that anything was up, or that she recognized him, and he wondered how much Taber had told her, hoping that she knew enough to duck out the back if things got rough. The radio played the usual country-western music—a sad song about being a long way from home and family—and Calvin realized that Mifflin, the bald-headed man, was singing along with the song under his breath now, singing as if he meant it.

Shirley set the cheeseburgers on the table, each of them accompanied by a bag of chips and a wedge of pickle.

"These are *deli* pickles?" Mifflin asked, forgetting about the song and looking up sharply. "Cold process?"

"Yessir," Shirley said. "You cook a dill pickle and you ruin it, as far as I'm concerned."

"That's just how I feel," Mifflin said to Calvin, squinting his eyes to add emphasis. "Pickles are like people. When they come off the vine they're pretty much equal, and then they get screwed up along the way. A pickle don't know that, but a man does. You don't see a pickle with regrets."

Calvin nodded at him, at a complete loss for words.

"I like them big fat dill pickles they've got at the ballpark," the tall one said.

"You like big fat ugly women, too," the small man told him. "Because that's all you can get."

The tall man shrugged, as if there was no reason to argue. Calvin couldn't remember the man's name. Then he noticed that the wrapper of a peppermint patty lay next to his plate, and it came to him—Pat Yorkmint. What if it had been an Abazaba, he wondered, or Cup of Gold? Mifflin pointed what was left of his pickle at Calvin and said, "Now a dill pickle *chip* is whole 'nother matter, not to mention a gherkin. I like a good gherkin, although they're hard to find. One thing about your grocery store gherkin..."

"God *damn*!" the small man said, looking at Mifflin as if he'd just as soon kill him right then and there, but Postum gave him a hard look, which he seemed to take seriously. He sat back on the bench and shrugged, indicating he had nothing more to say.

For a long space there was no noise but the sound of rustling wax paper and chewing. "Pass the salt, Walt," Postum said at one point, and he salted his fries heavily and then squirted ketchup on them, set the ketchup down, and stabbed the fries around in the ketchup, getting them just right. The whole thing was distinctly surreal—time taken out of everyone's busy day to have a sit-down meal and a parlay, all very civilized, just like Julia Child recommended. Mifflin was a dainty eater, holding the burger with both hands, his pinky fingers extended, whereas Postum pretty much porked it down, mopping the ketchup out of his beard with his napkin. Calvin wanted to do something crazy—shout, break into song, sweep the cheeseburger baskets onto the floor. His anxiety level was climbing into the desperation zone. He looked out toward the parking lot. The dry wind gave him the jitters. A sheet metal sign blew back and forth on its hooks, and a crumpled newspaper flew out of the trash can and whirled away into the sky, bound for Oz. Donna was maybe five minutes out.

"Nothing like a good burger," Postum said, winking at Calvin.

"Amen to that, brother," Yorkmint put in.

Shirley brought his chili fries, poured more coffee into the foam cups, put the check on the table, set the coffeepot on its hot plate, and went into the back room, leaving them to it. Maybe she'd stay there, Calvin thought, or better yet, just go out the back, get into her car, and drive home to Essex.

"How does this work?" Calvin said as soon as she was out of sight.

"Pretty much like I told you," Postum said, wiping his hands with a napkin. "You in a rush here? Don't like your fries?"

"I've got a date," Calvin said, glancing out the window again and immediately wishing he hadn't.

"She picking you up outside? You seem to be eyeballing those gas pumps like you're expecting the Pep Boys to roll in."

The suggestion was so startling to him that it had to have shown in his face. "Figure of speech," he said.

"Figure of bullshit, I call it," the small man said senselessly. He looked at Calvin with strangely intense loathing.

"Go ahead and eat your fries before they get cold, Cal," Postum told him. "Chili fries aren't worth anything cold." He dug his wallet from his pocket, fished out a fifty-dollar bill, and slid the check and the fifty under the salt shaker. "Anyway, forget that date of yours. Have you got the *goods*, is the question. Deffermint, open up the box." He gestured at it, but it took a moment for the small man to realize that he was being spoken to. He put the last bite of his cheeseburger down and reached into his pocket, and Calvin braced himself, ready to tip the whole table over if he took out a pistol. The least Calvin could do was wreck their lunch for them. Then he could be shot in the back going out the door and die like a dog on the highway. . . .

The man came up with a little switchblade pocketknife, clicked it open, and slit the tape. Postum pulled back the flaps, reached inside, and drew out the veil, letting it fall open and staring at it carefully. Calvin waited for him. The reproduction was good—he'd say that much for it. He had sketched the face in charcoal on grocery bags until he got it right, and then reproduced it onto a thin piece of tattered muslin cut out of some weatherworn window curtains. After washing out excess charcoal and drying it, he had fixed the charcoal with a can of hairspray, and then hung it in the desert wind all night to get rid of the smell. The likeness was close enough to the original so that it would satisfy anyone who didn't have the original to compare it to. It didn't have the *effect* of the original—the power—but they wouldn't know that. Postum held it up again and looked through it. He shrugged.

"All right," he said, nodding heavily, "what're your terms?"

"What do you mean, 'what're my terms'?" Calvin asked.

"Well, the two of us talked about money, but I suppose you've got grandiose new ideas by now. I thought I'd give you a chance to renegotiate, but if it's just the money you're after, we're about through here."

"I want Al Lymon, obviously. I don't give a damn about the money. If it was just the money, I wouldn't be here at all."

"That's downright noble, Cal. It pains me to say I don't have Lymon with me, though. We left him back at the ranch. He's not for sale."

"You don't have the veil, either," Calvin said staring straight back at him.

"I'll be ding-donged," Postum said, breaking into a grin. "Is that right? Ain't this it?" He held up the veil and looked at it one more time, then put it back in the box. "You could have fooled me silly—taken my money and gone on your way. And now you tell me this is a *fraud*? What did I say to you about trying to bluff?"

"Yeah, it's a fraud," Calvin said truthfully. "The real veil is up the road a ways, safe. You deliver Lymon and it's yours. We figured he might not be here, so I'm authorized to negotiate, and I'm negotiating. That part isn't any bluff."

Postum stared at him for the space of thirty seconds, and then said, "Son, I just don't believe you. I think this *is* it. I think they sent in a boy to do a man's job. Sorry to have to say that. If there's negotiating to do, we'll get to it in due time."

"Think what you want, but..."

Out of the corner of his eye, Calvin saw a white car swing a U-turn into the lot and stop on the other side of the gas pumps. It was everything he could do not to look.

"That's gracious of you, allowing me to do my own thinking. What I *think* is I'll keep this one, is what I'll do. We'll let our...expert...authenticate it. That'd be your uncle. If it's a clunker, we'll shoot him in the head, cut him up, and feed him to the catfish. A school of them big fifty-pound bullheads are like hogs in a pen—they'll eat anything you give them and then crap out the teeth and bones somewhere downriver. They've got a digestive system that'd put an alligator to shame."

Yorkmint let out with a wolf whistle. "Look at that piece out there!" he said.

Calvin looked, since he'd been invited to, stopping himself from telling Yorkmint to watch his mouth. It was Donna all right, washing her windows, the Mustang pointing back east, toward Needles. She was paying a heap of attention to the job. She glanced toward the store, and worked away with the squeegee and towel again. Calvin realized that Shirley had come back into the store and was leaning against the counter.

"Apparently she's not going to buy any gas," Postum said to Shirley. "She's just going to use up a bunch of them expensive blue towels you've got out there."

"She's not the only one that does that," Shirley said. "Seems like half the people on the road drive in here just to clean off the bugs. It's just the cost of doing business."

"Stillwater, why don't you step on out there and inform the young lady that the polite thing is to buy *gasoline* to go along with the rest of the services. Check her oil while you're at it. Women have no idea of checking their own oil."

"Me?" the bald man asked. "She ain't doing no harm. Couple of towels is all it is...."

"Your name's Stillwater Mifflin, ain't it? Or am I mistaken?"

"You want me to go on *out* there...?"

"That's the idea. And hurry up. She's going after another handful. Them towels cost a nickel apiece. Bring her on back in here."

"There's no call to bother the girl," Shirley said.

But Mifflin got up tiredly and went outside. Calvin glanced at Postum, who looked back at him, smiling. The smoker had his hand in his pocket again, although he had put away the knife a couple of minutes ago, and there were no more boxes to cut open.

Move now, Calvin told himself, but he was frozen in place. Move *how?* It didn't take a high IQ to know that he was finished. With any luck, Donna could talk her way out of this and hit the road like they'd planned, put in a phone call to Taber, and then the Knights could save Calvin's weary carcass from death and decapitation.

"Take me along," Calvin said without thinking. "Me for my uncle. Even trade. You'll have the veil and a hostage both...."

"So now it *is* the veil? In that case I've already got the veil and *two* hostages, so let's just see how this plays out." Postum nodded out the window.

Calvin saw Donna look up in surprise at Mifflin, who was speaking to her. She took the gas nozzle out of its cradle and gestured, shaking her head, the wind blowing her ponytail out behind her. The man pointed at the "Pay First!" sign and then at the store, and Donna nodded and hung up the nozzle.

Don't come in, Calvin commanded, sending out the mental message, firing on all brain cylinders. *Don't come in.* But she was coming in, chatting away, followed by Mifflin, who was nodding sympathetically. The door opened, the bell jangled, and she spotted Shirley at the counter. "Didn't know I had to pay first," she said. Then she saw the rest of them sitting there and widened her eyes in a greeting, with no recognition in her face. She took a bill out of her pocket and handed it to Shirley, who punched up the appropriate amount on the pump. The register clanged open, Shirley put in the bill and slammed it shut, and Donna turned toward the door. Mifflin stood in front of it, unmoving.

"Excuse me," Donna said, as if she was dealing with an impolite bonehead, but it had no effect on him.

"Let the girl through the *door*," Shirley said. "Don't go fooling with my customers. I don't have enough of them as it is. That's just plain bad for business."

"Just you calm down," Postum said to her. "In fact, why don't you go on into the back room again for a bit? Yorkmint, you accompany granny, will you? See that she's not... uncomfortable."

"What's going on here?" Donna asked, brassing it out. "A robbery or something?"

This is it, Calvin thought. *Match point,* like Hosmer said. He stood up suddenly, his hands gripping the edge of the picnic table. But before he could move, Postum said, "Sit back down," and in that same instant the small man drew out the pistol and pointed it at him. Calvin sat back down.

Yorkmint got up and nodded at Shirley, gesturing toward the back room, but before he could take a step toward the counter, Shirley reached underneath, came up with a short-barreled shotgun, and leveled it at him. "I'll blow you to straight to Hell," she said evenly. "Can't miss with this riot gun. You know that." And then to the small man, she said, "Put the pistol on the counter, peewee. I got six shells in here. Plenty to go around." Calvin stared at the shotgun, his heart hammering and his mouth open. Shirley's face was set like concrete.

The small man looked at Postum, who shrugged and said, "Do like she says." He put the pistol on the counter, and Shirley picked it up and dropped it into the big front pocket of the apron she wore, and in that moment Mifflin moved forward and grabbed at Donna, but the move was slow and halfhearted, and she slammed her elbow into his windpipe, quick and hard, then backed off a step, spun around, and hammered the heel of her shoe into his ankle. A look of shocked pain came across his face, and he made gagging sounds and clutched at his throat. Calvin stood up fast again and threw the table over hard this time, and then in the same motion reached across and slugged the small man in the side of the head as the man tried to catch the table and heave it upright. He went over backward off his bench and the table fell on him.

Postum was already up and moving, dodging around the fallen table and saying, "Calm down, just *calm* down," and waving his hand at Shirley. The small man shook off the punch and stood up from the floor. He smiled at Calvin, who looked around for a weapon of some sort, spotted his own picnic bench, and picked it up with both hands, swinging it back behind him like a baseball bat. There was a shattering explosion then, and Calvin let the bench go on the backswing, ducking forward and putting his hands over his head, his ears ringing with the concussion of the blast, barely hearing the bench smash through the food racks behind him. Fragments of ceiling tile and neon lightbulb clattered down around him, and then water started leaking down from the swamp cooler.

"Next shot kills the fat man," Shirley yelled, pointing the shotgun straight at Postum.

Mifflin was bent over, wheezing and holding his neck, but still blocking the door.

"Out of the damn doorway," Shirley said to him, coming out from behind the counter and handing Donna the pistol from out of her apron.

Donna pointed it with both hands at the bald man, and he limped away, waving her off. "Christ!" he wheezed. "Give a man a chance!"

Shirley pushed open the door, gesturing Donna and Calvin outside, letting the door shut behind them. "Let's go," she shouted, and Calvin found himself running fast toward the Mustang. Then there was another shotgun blast, directly behind him, and Calvin threw himself to his hands and knees, rolling sideways into the front tire, gaping back at the Gas'n'Go where glass from the window and door was collapsing in a waterfall of fragments.

"Let's *go!*" Shirley shouted, turning back toward him and dropping the barrel of the shotgun toward the ground. She pushed him into the front seat when Donna threw the door open, and then hoisted herself into the back and rested the barrel on the doorframe, pointing it through the open window toward the building. No one came through the door. The Mustang tore out onto the highway, heading east, and Calvin started to breathe again.

"You did good," Shirley told him after a moment. "Nobody figured they'd ante up Al Lymon, but it was worth a try. You stood up to them like a Knight. We knew you would. Split your knuckle, didn't you?"

"I was scared to death," he said, looking at the blood on the back of his hand. "I think I still am." A big tumbleweed hopped across the road ahead, narrowly missing their bumper and rolling away into the limitless freedom of the desert.

"If you're going to pass out, breathe into a sack," Shirley told him. "If you've got one."

"Who *isn't* scared?" Donna asked, smiling at him as well as she could. "That big ape nearly had me."

It came to him that Donna could undoubtedly beat up Yolanda Kleemer. "Where'd you learn to do that?" he asked. "Beat people up?"

"Miles Taber. He used to be some kind of commando."

"He told me he taught literature at U.N.L.V."

"He did that, too," she said. "I was impressed by the way you took out the food racks with that bench. It reminded me of Carrie Nation, breaking up a bar, except it was Calvin Bryson, breaking up the Little Debbie snack cakes."

"There it goes!" Shirley said.

Calvin looked back through the rear window and saw a black plume of smoke billowing into the sky. "What the *hell*?" he asked.

"They've torched the store. I wish I'd have gotten that fifty off the table and cleaned out the till. You can bet Postum didn't let any money burn."

"Chickenshit bastards!" Calvin yelled back down the highway. He shook his fist. "Hey," he said, "my *car's* back there!"

"There're worse things to worry about," Shirley said, "although we'll get George to pick up what's left of it so they don't connect you to all this."

"That was a shocker when you came up with the shotgun," Calvin said. "I thought we were done for."

"Last thing I wanted to do was shoot anyone. The thing about a shotgun, though, is that it's a scary object, like a big, mean dog. It makes people pay attention, and then if you're lucky you don't have to use it. You just have to make them think you will."

Calvin looked at Donna, who glanced away out the side window, but not before he could see that she was crying. He remembered her talking to him about the store a couple of times over the past two days, about hanging out at the Gas'n'Go when she was growing up, the Hoptoad out back—all the memories literally up in smoke now. He patted her leg awkwardly.

"We can build a new one with the insurance, honey," Shirley said, and Donna nodded, wiping her eyes. "Unless I decide to retire out to New Cyprus on the proceeds."

"You're a Knight, *too*," Calvin said to her. "Of course."

"Got my forty-year pin last May," she said.

They drove on in silence. Calvin watched through the rear window as a car zoomed up behind them—an impatient Mercedes-Benz that passed them doing ninety. There was another car in the distance, which might have been the van or Postum's pickup, but it stayed a mile back for the time it took them to drive to the outskirts of Needles, where a fire truck passed them heading west.

"That's all the excitement for today," Shirley said. "They'll take the veil back and show it to Lymon, which means he's still alive. He won't be fooled for more than about sixty seconds, although maybe he can convince them somehow. Next time Bob Postum comes calling, though, he's going to be loaded for bear." They slowed down, hitting Needles traffic. "Pull off here, honey," she said to Donna, "and drive down to the water, out there on the other side of the bridge. That'll be them in the Jimmy, with the boat trailer on the back."

Donna slowed down to a crawl as they left the asphalt, cutting the engine and rolling into the shade, hidden from the highway. Calvin realized that his hands were still shaking, and he sat on them to keep them still.

BEAMON'S YARD

We board over the stern," Taber had told them. Calvin rolled the words around in his mind as they slipped downriver aboard the New Cyprus fireboat, a twenty-five-foot pontoon boat with a shallow draft, a long aluminum canopy, and water cannons fore and aft. There was a sliver of moon in the sky, the night clear and balmy. Taber hadn't been hesitant about any of it, and that was reassuring. "No talking, no calling out, no one left behind, especially not Al Lymon. We slip the mooring lines and tow her out into the stream. If Al's not aboard, we set her adrift."

Calvin sat at the water cannon in the bow. "Control that cannon," Taber had told him half a dozen times. "Don't blast our own people unless there's no other way to stop trouble. It's not a damned squirt gun, but it won't kill anyone, either." Calvin reminded himself of the advice now, and then he reminded himself that he would have to keep focused here—more focused than he had been yesterday at the Gas'n'Go. Today he had only one job to do—gunner—and he meant to do it well. The river was smooth and glassy in the moonlight, and the wind had died down aside from occasional gusts that swept across from the Arizona shore.

They had run through the details of the boarding yesterday, right there under the bridge above Needles, sitting around a couple of folding tables set up in the shade of the old bridge and eating cold fried chicken and potato salad, while two Knights had gone downriver in a little outboard to take a look at the setup behind Beamon's yard. What they had found was de Charney's houseboat tied up to the dock, with someone apparently living on board—maybe Al Lymon, maybe not. Carrying what was apparently the cardboard carton that held the veil, Bob Postum had come through the back gate of Beamon's storage yard, stepped aboard the houseboat, gone into the cabin, and come out again ten minutes later, heading back up the dock.

It was nearly three in the morning now—fifteen sleepless hours later, although Calvin was anything but sleepy—and there wasn't another living soul on the river aside from them. They had dropped Donna and Shirley off ten minutes ago at a spot on the river where Taber's International Harvester had been hidden, and the two of them had driven away up the highway toward a bend in the river a mile beyond Needles—a little beach where a person could climb out of the water after drifting clear of town. So if any of the Knights went over the side, and were swept away in the current, they only had to tread water until they sighted the truck on shore and then do a little swimming.

The big Chevy engine made a low, gurgling sound, with just enough speed on it to navigate, but still it sounded loud in the desert stillness. On the other hand, there was nothing in the sound that would give them away. They might be any group of houseboaters running down to Havasu in the cool of early morning—except for the absence of lights and the water cannon mounted at the bow and stern.

Powered by the 454-cubic-inch engine, the cannon had a fifty-yard range, able to blast a heavy stream over the tops of the riverside houses and into New Cyprus proper. Firing it didn't take a lot of study. The cannon swiveled up, down, and sideways, and had a piece of pipe welded to the shutoff valve so that a person could make small adjustments quickly and could close it off in an instant. After dark last night Calvin had spent a half hour firing the cannon while they ran the boat up and down the river—a common enough drill for the New Cyprus Volunteer Fire Department. He was sure now that he could knock down anyone within range. With any luck he would get a chance to clean the leftover ketchup out of Postum's beard.

Calvin spotted the shadowy outline of a coyote on the California shore, drinking at the edge of the river, and a moment later an owl flew past so close that he heard the whoosh of its wings. The sky was endlessly deep and starry, reminding him of walking home from the steakhouse the night before last with Donna. He saw the lights of Needles ahead on the starboard side now—not many lights yet, just streetlights and all-night diners and the three a.m. lights of insomniacs and insanely early risers.

They swept nearer as he watched, and then the dance of reflected stars in the river vanished and the boat fell into shadow crossing under the bridge. Then they were out in the moonlight and starlight again and Taber was hugging the California shore, moving just a fraction faster than the current. There were houses along the river now, and vacant lots that would grow houses in the coming years. He spotted a big corrugated-steel building ahead, with a tall fence around it strung with barbed wire and with an inlet dug into the bank and a long dock running out from a gate in the fence. De Charney's pontoon houseboat lay moored fore and aft along the dock, dark and silent, a heavy electrical cord snaking away from a portable air conditioner running in one of the cabin windows.

The question was simple: who was living on board? De Charney himself, or Al Lymon, or both? It made sense that it was Lymon, Calvin thought, since they could keep him on the move that way.

Whatever the answer, they were playing it the same way— grapple on at the stern, the boarding party away to cast off the mooring lines, the engines throttling up to power the cannon. Whoever was in the cabin would know they'd been boarded, but by the time they'd woken up and come outside they'd already be towed out into midstream, and Calvin would wash them straight off the deck and into the drink.

The fireboat shuddered, slowed, and then the engine reversed and they bumped alongside the dock and tied on. Two Knights stepped onto the dock, one of them carrying a big pair of bolt cutters, the other a heavy steel flashlight as long as his forearm. They bent over the mooring lines, working hurriedly in the light of a mercury vapor lamp on one of the high fence posts. The big engine on the fireboat geared up, powering the water pumps, and the night was suddenly churning with noise. A light came on in the cabin and then went out again, and then an alarm bell sounded some ways away—in the warehouse, probably—a wake-up call just barely audible to Calvin over the roar of the engine.

He bent over the water cannon, listening to the pumps winding up beneath him. The boarders were beyond the edge of the cabin now, working at a chain with the bolt cutters, the two of them leaning into it. He levered the gun around and shot a tentative blast out into the river, drawing a big squiggle with it, shutting it off and on—plenty of pressure to sweep the decks clear. The engines backed off slightly, and then, with a suddenness that was disorienting, spotlights blazed, blinding him, and he threw up his forearm to shade his face. More lights came on in the yard, dogs started to bark, and there was the heavy clank of a steel gate slamming open.

He could only half see the boarders now. They stood up straight and hurried back across the deck, and one of them leapt aboard and shouted, "Go!" just as the second man, carrying the bolt cutters, tripped and went down hard on the deck of de Charney's boat. Two big Rottweilers came flying out of the darkness from the direction of the yard, bounded across the deck, and leapt at the back of the fallen Knight, who was only halfway to his feet. He swung around now and tried to ward the dogs off with the bolt cutters, but was slammed over backwards, covering his face with his arms and curling up.

Calvin depressed the lever of the water cannon, swiveling the barrel too high across the deck, the water blasting out a cabin window and blowing off the corner of the roof with shocking force before he could back it off and get it trained on the dogs, which were spun entirely around by the force of the deluge. One of them was swept beneath the railing into the river, and Calvin saw the black, furiously barking shadow floating away downstream in the moonlight. The other dog was up again instantly, and it made another silent, determined rush at the Knight on the deck, who had been pinned against a railing post by the water and was just pushing himself to his feet again, stumbling forward and trying to make it to the fireboat, his pant leg torn and his leg bloody.

Calvin waited a split second, until he could train the cannon behind the man, and then swept the dog backward again, just catching its hindquarters the moment before it leapt. It disappeared behind flying water, but when Calvin shut the flow down it was scrambling to its feet again, although it must have been half drowned by now, and it stumbled sideways into someone who had come through the open gate of the yard and had just now stepped aboard. Calvin saw that it was Mifflin, the bald man from the Gas'n'Go.

The dog turned on Mifflin wildly, knocking him sideways into the cabin wall, then falling back and lunging forward again, growling furiously. There was a popping sound, and for a moment Calvin wondered what it was, but then he saw the pistol in Mifflin's hand just as the man was knocked over sideways along the wall with the dog sprawled down across him.

Now two different voices were shouting "Go!" and Taber

had the engine in reverse, but the boat was sitting still, straining at something that had them moored to the dock. Then the air-conditioning unit toppled backward out of its window and hit the deck with a heavy crash. The tethered boats lurched into motion, and the air conditioner slid backward, but caught on the low rung of the railing, jamming them to a stop again.

Mifflin was on his feet now, steadying himself against the cabin wall. Calvin saw the big pistol in his hand and tried to make himself small, swiveling the cannon, cranking the lever forward and blasting away wildly, sweeping it back and forth. When he shut it down ten seconds later Mifflin was simply gone, the body of the dog was jammed under the lower rung of the railing in the stern, the cabin door had been blown inward, and an awning set up aft was knocked sideways, the aluminum struts tilting out over the railing and the wet canvas lying on the top of the water, tugged downriver on the current.

"Hold your fire!" Taber shouted at him, gesturing furiously, and in the same instant the boat gave a big lurch and shot out into the river, towing the other craft. The heavy electrical cord that had stubbornly been holding them had torn away from the pinned air conditioner, and it danced on top of the river alongside the dock, throwing sparks. The lights at the rear of Beamon's yard and on the dock blinked out and everything was dark again.

"Watch for that shit-bird with the pistol," Taber shouted, and Calvin scanned the deck of the pontoon boat and the river, looking for Mifflin, ready to blast him to kingdom come. He was nowhere to be seen, though, and already they were out in midstream, a hundred feet below the dock and moving downriver fast. They anchored both boats in a little inlet on the deserted Arizona side. The engine throttled back, and Calvin got up from his seat and stepped across to the other deck, anxious to finish things.

He approached the blasted-open door of the big cabin cautiously. Inside there was a flooded hallway with an inner door leading into a flooded bathroom and another into a small galley. A third door apparently led into the living quarters. Calvin pushed it open, looked into the darkness, and stepped inside. The interior was silent, but there was the smell of a freshly lit cigarette. He spotted the glow of the ash and nearly stepped straight back out again, but Taber stood right behind him and immediately reached past him and found the light switch. Calvin was startled to see a woman sitting at a table, looking at nothing, the cigarette between her fingers. On the bed lay an old man, his eyes half open and staring toward the ceiling. It wasn't Al Lymon.

"He's dead," the woman said tonelessly, gesturing with the cigarette at the man on the bed. She looked weary—not just exhausted, but worn down under years of trouble. The dead man looked like waxwork, and he might easily have been a hundred years old. On a bedside table next to him the fraudulent veil lay in a heap.

"The man on the bed is Geoffery de Charney," Taber said to Calvin in a low voice.

"Bob Postum smothered him with a pillow," the woman said. "He would have killed me, too, if I meant anything to him, but I haven't meant anything to him for forty years. Killing Geoff was pointless, because he was almost gone from congestive heart failure. But Bob was in a hurry to assume the throne."

It's Salome, Calvin thought, the old man's niece, who had asked for the head of John Nazarite half a century ago. She had to be seventy years old. The dancer in her had long since disappeared, and she looked like someone's grandmother now. She'd be a hell of a lot better off, Calvin thought, if she *were* someone's grandmother instead of what she had become playing out her part in a dead man's empty schemes. Her name came to him suddenly. "Paige Whitney, isn't it?"

She nodded at him. "And you must be the nephew from out of town who was carrying salvation in a cardboard box. I'm pleased to make your acquaintance, but so far I haven't seen too much salvation."

"We're looking for my uncle. That's what all this is about."

"He's not here. I don't know where he is. If I did, I'd tell you. Happily. He *was* here, but they took him off a few hours ago. Bob was going to force him to use the veil to save Geoff, but he didn't need force. Your uncle was willing enough, even to save a man who didn't merit being saved. Then it didn't matter, because it wasn't really the veil, which your uncle figured out as soon as he held it in his hands. I think he was willing because he was dying himself. I'm sorry to tell you that, honey. He didn't look good."

"I'm not sure that's why he was willing to save him. It's the other way around—he's dying because he was willing to use the veil that way."

"Six of one and a half dozen of the other," she said. "I know I wouldn't have done it. And I loved Geoff, too, in my way. But he was ready to die. I think your uncle knew that. Bob just wanted to authenticate the veil. He would have killed Geoff one way or another, once he was sure of the veil. With Geoff and Al Lymon both out of the way..." She shrugged and stubbed the cigarette out in an ashtray and looked out the cabin window, into the darkness outside.

"I'm going back to Beamon's yard," Calvin said to Taber. "It makes sense Lymon is there."

"We'll head back upriver and tie on again at the dock. What about you?" he asked the woman.

"I'm fine," she said. "Don't worry about me. I've got a car in the lot across the street from Beamon's. I'll just wait here with Geoff a moment longer, though, and do the right thing by him." She lit another cigarette and looked out the window again as Taber and Calvin went out, closing the door behind them. There was light in the east now, a purple glow above black hills, and the stars were fading. The wind seemed to be coming up again with the sun.

"What'll we do about the old man?" Calvin asked.

"Nothing. Let the cops in Needles work it out when they find him. We'll get Shirley to drive the Harvester down here to pick you up. There's room for Al to lie down in the back, if you find him. Best you're all out of here before real daylight. I don't know when the first shift comes on, but it's probably early, so don't waste any time. If Al's not there, you'd best head back to New Cyprus."

They pulled in the anchors, started the engine, and crossed the river. Calvin went back aboard de Charney's boat along with Whitey Sternbottom, and they unhitched it from the fireboat, cut away the canvas awning that was still trailing in the water, started the engine, and ran the boat back into the dock, tying on again fore and aft. The fireboat came in afterward, and Whitey stepped back aboard, waving at Calvin as they took off. Calvin paused for a moment to watch them go, looking at the dark outline of the Dead Mountains in the distance. In a half hour or so the peaks would be lit up and golden, and then the day would set in again.

As the thought came into his mind, there was a sudden orange glow low in the sky over the mountains, and then the sound of a muffled explosion, very distant, and then a second glow, flashing and fading, and a second muffled boom. Calvin heard the engine on the fireboat wind up, and the boat slewed sideways and shot away forward, back toward New Cyprus. Calvin turned and sprinted up the dock, up onto the shore, and in through the open chain-link gate into Beamon's yard.

THE RESCUE

The moon was gone now, and it was darker than it had been despite the predawn glow in the east. There were half a dozen stake-bed trucks parked in the yard and other pieces of light equipment along with stacks of plywood, big rectangles of sheet iron, piles of sand and gravel, and pallets of bagged cement. Beyond the pallets stood a boat trailer with a boat on it, the hitch balanced on a slice of tree stump. The boat was the *Painted Lady*, not that it made any difference now.

Calvin moved along warily at first but rapidly came to the conclusion that there was nothing to see out here. It made sense that his uncle would be inside the warehouse somewhere, either tied up or in a locked room. A big load-in door to the interior stood open—revealing a black rectangle of shadowy darkness thirty feet in front of him. Inside, it was pitch-dark, and he had to wait what seemed like an interminable time for his eyes to adjust. He listened hard, but he could hear no sound at all aside from his own breathing. Shadows slowly appeared out of the darkness, and he saw that he was in a large warehouse with a high ceiling. There were skylights, although they didn't help much yet, and there were more pallets and machinery—concrete saws and wheelbarrows and jackhammers and small skip-loader tractors with backhoes. Across the room, against a far wall, steel shelves were neatly stacked with crates and hard hats and water jugs and power tools.

He was able to see enough now to make his way across the floor and into an open hallway. There were doors going off on either side—two restroom doors and a half dozen small offices with glass windows and open louvered blinds, the offices apparently empty. There was a windowless steel door, however, with a hasp hastily screwed onto it, fastened with a heavy lock. Calvin listened hard at the door and heard what sounded like a cough behind it, and the sound of shuffling. He knocked sharply, and heard a voice, too low or feeble for him to make out any words. Who else could it be, though?

"It's me," he said. "Cal. Hang on!"

He grabbed the lock and yanked on it, nearly tearing the skin off his hand, and then turned and jogged back out into the open warehouse, spotted pry bars and claw hammers hanging from the shelves, decided on a pry bar, and grabbed a big one. No time for half measures here. He stopped, hearing a horn toot outside, just a fragment of a honk—Shirley and Donna; it had to be, and right on time. He jogged back down the hallway, past the locked door to the front of the warehouse, where the dead bolt on the big entry door had a simple latch on the inside, thank God. When he opened the door a crack and peered out, they were already out of the Harvester, which sat facing the street, the rear cargo door open with the dome light on so they could load Lymon up and get out.

"I think I found him," Calvin said, turning away and leading the two of them back down the hall. He jammed the end of the pry bar under the hasp, banging on it a couple of times to get some leverage, and then leaned into it, the screw heads snapping off and the lock and hasp breaking away. He opened the door onto a large room, twenty feet deep or so, and maybe twenty-five feet wide. In the dim light he could see three large safes, all standing open. Clothing racks hung along the wall—long lengths of iron pipe hanging from the ceiling. The racks were mostly empty, aside from what appeared to be a few theater costumes—some chain mail and tunics, but mainly white robes and burnooses and red sashes, as if for a production of *Arabian Nights*.

Lymon lay on his back on a foam pad on the floor. There was a water bottle next to him. He looked at Calvin with a fixed expression on his face, as if he was working hard to keep any kind of composure at all.

"Good to see you," he said. His voice sounded weak. The change in him was shocking, as if Nettie's sickness had swept through him like a tidal wave, simply crushing him.

"We're glad to see you," Calvin told him.

"You shouldn't have wasted your time. I can't help you now.

I'm like that fellow who apologized because he was taking too long to die."

"To hell with that," Calvin said. "Let's get you out of here. There were a couple of explosions up in the hills just about ten minutes ago, probably in the quarry."

"We saw it, too," Shirley said.

"They took weapons out of the safes," Lymon told them, trying to push himself up onto his elbows, but he was evidently too weak, and he lay back down. "Costumes, too. They mean to take out the relics and everything else."

"How many of them are there?" Calvin asked. "Besides Bob Postum? It would take an army."

"Can't say. But if they didn't have an army, or something like it, they wouldn't have started it up. You three go on, but not over the hill if they're already up there. Go back up the river."

"And tell Nettie we left you behind?" Shirley said.

"We'll *all* go up the river," Donna said. "Let's get him down to de Charney's boat. The ignition key's got to be on board somewhere."

"The old man's in it, dead," Calvin said.

"Then he won't care," Shirley put in. "If he starts to argue we'll dump him in the river."

Calvin put his hands under his uncle's arms and tried to lift him, but Lymon let out a gasp of pain, and it seemed to Calvin as if he were pulling him to pieces. Dragging him out of the warehouse by his boot heels wasn't going to fly. "Give me half a second," Calvin said, and he hurried out of the room and down the hallway to the warehouse again, where he grabbed a high-sided wheelbarrow. He tipped it over onto its side when turning it around, righted it again, and then forced himself to slow down and take it easy.

"In you go," he said, backing the wheelbarrow into the room. Together, pulling and pushing, they managed to haul Lymon up between the handles. He slumped backward, sitting down in a heap on the foam pad from the floor and resting with his hands in his lap, his head back and eyes closed.

"It's been a long time," he said weakly, "since I've been hauled home in a wheelbarrow." He tried to laugh but couldn't manage it.

Calvin had the unshakable feeling that he had been running around in the dark warehouse for half an hour, and that the sun was rising like a helium balloon in the sky outside. He kept the wheelbarrow low, so that it wouldn't spill, and turned sharply into the hallway, heading down toward the warehouse and to the river. Lymon now appeared to be unconscious, breathing heavily and erratically.

It was lighter in the warehouse—the gray dawn showing through the skylights, and through the open door ahead Calvin could make out the materials piled in the yard. Then they were out among the pallets and machinery, under the windy morning sky, heading for the open gate that led out to the dock. Calvin thought about the racks of costumes in the locked room. What was that all about? Somehow he couldn't imagine Bob Postum playing the lead in *Scheherazade*....

He stopped abruptly when someone stepped in through the gates and held up a pistol, not pointing it at them, but letting them see it—the same pistol that Calvin had seen earlier that morning. It was Mifflin, his clothes wet with river water, the hair on the sides of his head standing straight out. He held up his free hand, like a traffic cop. "You folks hold it," he said. "Just stay right there."

Calvin wondered whether it mattered that the pistol had gotten soaked. What he knew about pistols would fill half a postcard. Shirley and Donna, he noticed, had stopped dead, and both of them knew more than he did.

"At ease with the wheelbarrow, son," Mifflin said to Calvin. "We aren't going anywhere till we think this through." Donna moved across to stand next to Shirley, and Mifflin edged back a step. "You don't come anywhere near me, Red. I don't like to be crowded by jujitsu queens, and I don't intend to shoot anybody if I can help it. We'll all move back inside now."

"My uncle's sick," Calvin said. "He needs a doctor and a hospital."

"You're right about that," Mifflin told him. "If you had a siren on that wheelbarrow, you could run him right on down the highway into Needles. Move on inside now, like I said."

Lymon was still unconscious, and had slumped sideways down into the wheelbarrow. Calvin lifted the handles and started to make a wide turn, in order to follow Shirley, when out of the corner of his eye he saw a black dog run in through the gate, a moving shadow against the early morning twilight, leaping silently at Mifflin's back. Mifflin shouted in surprise, stumbling forward, the dog clamping onto his arm and bearing him over onto the ground.

Mifflin threw himself back and forth, shrieking, "Hey, hey!" in a falsetto voice, audible above the sound of deep muffled growling. He still held the pistol in his right hand, trying to keep from beating it on the concrete floor of the yard. Calvin started forward but stopped dead when Mifflin quit fighting and jammed the gun against the dog's side and pulled the trigger. There was the sound of the pistol going off, muffled, but loud enough, and the dog lay dead on the ground.

Mifflin pushed himself to his knees, still holding the pistol, his left arm turned outward. He stared at his mangled hand and forearm, blood running down onto his khaki pants, and then he stood up shakily, getting his bearings. Calvin sprinted forward, pushing the wheelbarrow at a dead run toward Mifflin, who looked at him incredulously from fifteen feet away. He felt the wheelbarrow slam solidly into him at mid-thigh, knocking him backward, the wheel bouncing up and over Mifflin's body and down again onto the concrete. Calvin fought to keep it upright, but tripped over Mifflin, letting go of the wheelbarrow handles and falling heavily. He caught himself with his hands and got back up fast—fast enough to see the wheelbarrow teeter along for another five feet or so before it hit a head-high pile of sand and went over sideways.

"I got Lymon!" Shirley yelled, and Calvin sprang to his feet and looked for the pistol, which lay on the concrete near a pallet of fence block. Mifflin was already up and lurching toward it. Calvin took three running steps and threw himself forward, hitting him in the back of the knees with his shoulder, the two of them going down in a heap, Mifflin grunting with pain. Calvin scrambled up again, just as Donna was snatching up the fallen pistol.

Mifflin was finished, and evidently he knew it. He didn't try to get up, but held his bleeding arm to his chest and waved Calvin away. "*Okay*, for Pete's sake!" he said. "Dog*gone* it! I want to *talk*, is all!"

Calvin felt most of the fight leak out of him, and for some reason he recalled Mifflin's going on about pickles yesterday at the Gas'n'Go, and the way he had seemed polite and deferential when he'd gone out unhappily to lure Donna inside the store. What door had the man stepped through years ago that had led him, like Paige Whitney, to this strange place on the river?

"Gimme a hand here," Shirley called, and Calvin hurried across to the sand pile where Lymon had spilled about halfway out of the wheelbarrow. The sand had stopped him, and he was lying on his side, apparently oblivious. Calvin managed to boost him back into the wheelbarrow and to lift it upright by heaving upward on the down side of it while Shirley pulled back on the top side. He beat sand off the edge of the foam pad and dusted it from his uncle's cheek.

"What now?" he asked Shirley breathlessly.

"Your call," she said.

Mifflin's shirt was torn down the front, and his arm was still oozing blood. He shivered suddenly, and looked at the dead dog. "*God*, I hate to hurt an animal."

"What goes around comes around," Shirley said.

"It's coming around fast, too," Mifflin said. "First shift's on at seven. You three are burning daylight."

"Let's tie him up and get out of here," Donna said.

"Can I put in a quick word?" Mifflin asked. "I'd like to negotiate."

"What do you have?" Calvin asked him.

"I've got a place up in Idaho. Up on a lake. Three-bedroom log cabin with a Franklin stove. Big porch close enough to the water to fish off of. My daughter's up there along with her two kids. Her no-good husband left them a couple of years back. So here's what I've got to offer. I tell you what I know, and you let me walk out of here. I mean to take some tools for my trouble and head on up to Idaho. And I'll tell you right up front that Bob keeps a couple of bundles of hundreds tied up with rubber bands hidden in his desk. I'm fixing to take the money, too, if you folks don't. I'll show you where it is if you want it."

"We don't," Calvin said.

"I understand that. I'm just telling you so that you know I'm on the up-and-up. I don't have no quarrel with you folks, and I swear to you on the grave of my dead mother that I wouldn't have let them torch your store yesterday, Grand-maw, but I couldn't do nothing to stop it. That was pure Bob Postum all the way. He'll do the mean thing just because it's mean, and he'll make a joke about it afterward. He killed Lamar Morris at the bookstore for no reason at all—or at least that's what Slim told me. I've been fed up with this outfit since he put his big plans into motion six months ago. So if I got nothing to say that interests you, then tie me up, although I'd kind of like to wash out this dog bite with peroxide first."

Lymon groaned in the wheelbarrow. Calvin realized that it was real daylight now. He could see the tops of the Dead Mountains glowing in the first light. The breeze blew across the lot, stirring up dust. It had a barnyard smell to it, as if there were animals stabled nearby.

"Get on with it," he said to Mifflin.

"All right, son, I will. Truth is, they're going in through the passage. They traced it out with sonar. They grabbed your uncle as a diversion, and you Knights came right on out here just like Bob figured you would."

"How many men are there?"

"Fifty. Armed. Desert rats and drifters from Beaumont to Panamint Flats. 'Extras,' Bob calls them. Some of them headed up into the hills last night, and some upriver."

"And they're loyal to Bob Postum?" Shirley asked. "I can't make any sense out of that."

"They're loyal to a share of those silver ingots that came out of the Essex smelter back in the day."

"*What* silver ingots?" Calvin asked.

Mifflin stared at him. "Well," he said, "that's the rumor anyway. But you've only been in town for a couple of days, so maybe you haven't heard it yet. Lamar Morris's daddy wrote a piece on it, but the Knights paid him off for it and then burned all the copies of his little book, leastways all except one, which Bob's got. That's how I know about it. I've seen it. Bob uses it as a recruiting tool, you might say. He's got a box full of those Essex smelter ingots, too, mined in New Cyprus in the thirties. They say Bob took them off of James Morris, Lamar's father, when he killed the man. A box full of silver ingots makes for a good-looking rumor."

"What else?" Calvin said.

"They'll only use the guns if they *have* to, because it tends to make a lot of noise, and it don't resemble the Crusades a whole lot. It runs counter to the movie scam. Everyone knows you Knights beat your swords into ploughshares, which puts you one down if push comes to shove. Bob thinks you'll hesitate, because you've got scruples. He doesn't have any scruples at all."

"The movie scam..." Calvin said, abruptly remembering the script stuck into the box full of books. Robert P. Wolverhampton, LL.D.—*Bob Postum*. Of course. He thought about the script's multiple endings and wondered whether Postum had meant them as a *choice*. Sending the script with Morris's books was like leaving the trunk of the Dodge open after he had stolen the veil. Postum saw all of this as fate playing itself out, the whole thing scripted. *Pride goeth,* Calvin thought, repeating his uncle's sentiment.

"The kicker," Mifflin said, "is what Bob likes to call his siege engines—two big catapults. He means to bombard New Cyprus from the heights."

"And the costumes...?" Calvin asked. "That's for what—a film?"

"It's cover," Shirley told him. "We've got them, too. No one in the world is going to think there's real trouble with everyone dressed up like the Crusades. They can keep it up all day and night."

"That's right," Mifflin said. "They plan to have some fellows with camera equipment out on a barge, keeping tourists away and passing out flyers saying it's a film shoot. That corralled-in area you see over there?" He pointed away across the yard. "That's for the camels—or was. Bob rented a couple of dozen of them from a big outfit that supplies the Hollywood studios. He's going to run twenty-five armed men down the trail from the quarry on camels. Then while everything's breaking loose topside, he means to take the silver and what-all else back up the passage and put the Knights right out of business. Once he gets set up on the heights, there's not a lot you can do to stop him. And Bob figures that the Knights won't call in the authorities. There's a lot of history out here that doesn't bear scrutiny."

There was the sound of a semitruck rumbling past out on the highway. Calvin realized that Donna and Shirley were watching him. "Good luck in Idaho," he said to Mifflin, who nodded his thanks and turned around to walk away, but then stopped abruptly.

"One more thing," he said. "You-all have some kind of rat among the Knights. Bob's got ahold of someone. I don't know who it is, but I heard Bob bracing him in the office late last night. The man was pretty liquored up, it seemed to me, and Bob wasn't happy about it, and wanted to know how he expected to do any driving. I was on my way out to get a bite to eat down at Norm's, and when I got back they'd cleared out, although Bob's truck was still here. It's out there now. You folks had better watch who you trust."

He turned around and went on his way again, disappearing into the warehouse.

CLEARING FOR ACTION

Geoffrey de Charney's houseboat wasn't moored at the dock any longer. It lay in mid-river, a hundred yards down, swept along by the current, the cabin flaming like a funeral pyre despite the drowning Calvin had given it with the water cannon. Someone—it must have been Paige Whitney—had doused it with gasoline, because it was burning like it was built of pine boards. A chemical reek of black smoke poured into the sky where it was pulled to pieces by the wind and blown out over the desert. The boat swung around sideways, and the bow was close enough to the California shore to ground itself for a moment before the current pulled the bow free again and the boat drifted around a bend in the river and disappeared from sight.

"There goes our ride," Shirley said.

"No, it doesn't," Donna said, turning around and unlatching the gate again. Calvin set the wheelbarrow down and hurried after her, and together they lifted the hitch end of the *Painted Lady*'s trailer. Calvin was faintly surprised at how easy it was to turn it and roll it out through the gate. They angled it past the edge of the dock and down to the steep beach where it started to pick up momentum. Calvin held on, following it right into the shockingly cold water until the trailer was submerged to the top of the tires. "The key's here somewhere," Donna said, climbing on board. "Cast it loose."

Calvin unhitched the boat, pushed it deeper into the river, and let it go, setting Donna adrift and then slogging back up onto the beach where he stood at the water's edge.

If she couldn't get it started, she'd have to swim for it and let the boat go. In that case, he thought, they'd put Lymon in the Harvester and call Taber on the cell phone and arrange for a boat to pick them up down at the bridge. He could see Donna rummaging behind the seats now, lifting cushions and running her hand up under the dash. The *Painted Lady* was thirty feet from shore, the current sweeping it away. The river ran green and flat, with swirls glinting in the early sunlight, and away downriver smoke still rose from the burning houseboat.

Jump, Calvin thought, and he walked backward up the gravel beach in his wet shoes, signaling to Shirley and pointing toward where the Harvester sat at the edge of Beamon's yard. Shirley nodded and started back along the dock, but just then Donna sat down in the pilot's seat, and Calvin heard the engine turn over and roar to life, and within seconds she whipped the boat around in a tight, bubbling circle and ran it upriver to the dock.

It took both Calvin and Shirley to lever the wheelbarrow sideways and roll Lymon down onto the cushions on the long bench seat. He grunted, opening his eyes and staring, and then closing them again, moaning a little bit. Calvin wondered whether he knew what was going on, or whether he was already mostly gone, drifting out across his own river. But there was no time to chat. Calvin pushed the empty wheelbarrow off the edge of the dock and then climbed into the *Painted Lady* and hunkered down in the passenger seat next to Donna. She kept the speed down for Lymon's sake, but even so the trip seemed to take a quarter of the time that it had taken this morning on the fireboat. The wind blew warm and dry, and he could smell the river and the desert, and there was already some warmth in the morning. The sheer wall of the Dead Mountains loomed up on the port side, and he could see New Cyprus now in the distance, lit up by the rising sun. There was another barge-like boat on the river up ahead, probably moored off the island. "What's that?" he shouted.

"Film crew's my guess," Shirley shouted back at him.

And just then Calvin spotted a clump of cottonwoods on the Nevada side where there was a little camp set up in a clearing, with canvas awnings and catering tables and men milling around. There were a couple of boats tied up to willows, fast-looking outboards maybe sixteen feet long. Two men sat in one of them, and one of the men waved in their direction, then did a double take and stood up, shouting at his partner, who went to work on the line that tethered them to the willows. It was Pat Yorkmint and the small man—Defferson. Obviously Yorkmint had recognized the *Painted Lady* before he realized who was in it. The big boat angled out into the river in a wide arc as if to cut them off, although it was unclear how they meant to do it without simply ramming them.

"They're after us!" he shouted at Donna, just as Defferson answered Calvin's question by half standing up and leveling a rifle across the windscreen. "Down!" Calvin shouted to Shirley, but she had already seen the rifle and had slid off the seat onto the deck. The pursuing boat hit their wake and Defferson sat down hard, lurching sideways, the barrel of the rifle apparently cracking Yorkmint on the side of the head. Their boat slewed atop the water as he let go of the wheel and grabbed his ear.

Donna glanced back and yelled, "Hold on!" and Calvin was slammed back against the cushions as the boat shot forward, the bow rising up out of the water, the long, smooth jet stream shooting away behind them as Donna ran them dangerously close to shore, the willows whipping past so close that Calvin could have grabbed a branch. He looked over the side, horrified to see that they were skimming along in what appeared to be less than a foot of water. The big outboard kept well out into the river as Defferson scrambled to his knees and tried to get some kind of steady aim over the seats.

There was the crack of a gunshot, and then another, but Calvin didn't look back, because the *Painted Lady* swerved out into mid-river again and bore straight down on the camera boat. He braced himself against the dash, his feet pinned to the floorboards. The outboard behind them was gaining fast, although the rifle had disappeared now that the camera boat was dead in front of them. Donna's hair blew straight back out behind her, and she had a wild, happy look on her face, as if she had lost her mind.

"Shit!" Calvin yelled, watching the sudden panicked scramble on the camera boat when they figured out Donna was serious. He braced for the collision, glancing back at his uncle. Somewhere along the line Shirley had slipped an orange life preserver around him, and she had one arm across his chest, holding on to him. The gap between the boats closed as two people dove off the camera boat into the river and swam hard toward the opposite shore. The camera boat itself heaved around in reverse suddenly, camera gear toppling, the pilot trying desperately to get out of the way as the *Painted Lady* shot past, skimming the bow within inches. Calvin locked eyes for a split second with a terrified man who couldn't have been more than two feet away, and then they were decelerating, angling in toward the Temple Bar. The boat pursuing them turned wide toward the Arizona shore, and Calvin watched as it slowed down to pick up the men in the water. A sandbag fortification had been thrown up along the river side of the island, head high, atop a long rampart of sand and rock that hid most of the Temple from view.

Several small Bobcat tractors were pushing more sand and rock around, and twenty or so men were heaving sandbags, fire-brigade-style, off the flatbeds of a line of Pullman carts heading over the bridge, incoming carts alternating with empty carts going back after more sandbags. The *Painted Lady* swept past underneath the bridge, aiming toward Taber's dock, where a half dozen people waited for them.

I t was your call," Taber said to Calvin. "It's damn well sure we won't see Mifflin again this side of Hell. He won't come back out here, not with Postum's money in his pocket. If you'd have left him tied up in Beamon's yard he probably *would* be here. As far as I'm concerned, we'd be a long chalk better off if they *all* ran off to Idaho to take care of their family. What he told you was right on the nose, although we already knew some of it because of that script Postum so kindly sent to us. He over-reached himself there."

They walked along one of the dimly lit passages, the air smelling of cool, dry stone. Taber had something that he wanted Calvin to see, now that Calvin was a Knight—what Taber referred to as the *Mint*.

"So it's true that this was a silver mine, like Mifflin said?" Calvin asked. "I thought they used the tracks to run carloads of cut stone down from the quarry."

"They did, among other things. The Knights found the silver ore when they were tunneling out the passage up to the quarry, and from that time on they killed two birds with one stone. Blankfort said it was divine intervention, and I wouldn't argue with the man. That little bit of intervention assayed out at over three thousand dollars a ton. Most of the mines out in this part of the desert played out pretty quickly. Someone would find silver ore, there'd be a lot of excitement, and then after a couple of months or a year it would dry up. What the Knights found here was different, though."

"Wasn't there some kind of silver rush?" Calvin asked. "Like with the other strikes out here?"

"Not much of a rush, not like when they found the Comstock Lode or the Panamint strike. Silver fever had faded out forty years earlier. And New Cyprus was what you might call a closed society. There was no way for a man to stay ten minutes if he wasn't wanted, and if you weren't a Knight, you weren't wanted. James Morris started poking around, taking photos and asking questions down at the smelter. When he wrote his pamphlet, he got so much right by guesswork that the Knights bought out the stock and swore him to secrecy. He didn't have to work for a living after that, and neither did Lamar, when he came along. That bookstore of theirs has always been a hobby."

"And all of this led to his being murdered?"

"Years later. He was honorable enough to keep the secret, and he told the wrong people to go to hell."

Two men appeared farther up the tunnel, stepping out of yet another passage and into the glow of one of the hanging bulbs. They were apparently flesh and blood. When they drew near, Calvin recognized one of them as Jake Purcel, who had been one of the two boarders this morning—the one who hadn't been mauled by the dog. "All set up," Purcel said.

"No problems, then?" Taber asked.

"Pretty much cut and dried, given that we're right about where they'll set up. One funny thing, though, was that someone chalked the wall on up the way."

"Chalked it?"

"Like they were marking it—back where the passages branch off into town. It looked like maybe someone came in from that direction and wanted to find the right turning on the way back. It's hard to say when it was done, though. Might have been a month ago."

"Could you follow the marks?"

"No, it was just the one mark as far as we could see. Just enough to navigate the passage where it gets complicated there."

The two men headed away down the passage again, leaving Calvin and Taber alone. "So what does that mean?" Calvin asked. "Who would have chalked the passage?"

A tunnel opened on the right, and Taber headed down it, going steeply downhill now. "Could be a Knight," Taber said. "Could be a skunk. One mark's not enough to go on, though. It'd take hours to search the tunnels, and we don't have hours."

"How about the cameras?"

"That's our best bet, although aside from in the catacombs and the mint, we don't have much surveillance. Some places it's taboo."

Taber stopped now, and within the silence of the dead air, Calvin could hear what sounded like rushing water, although it might as easily have been the sound of blood in his own veins. In front of them stood a door built of rough-hewn cypress beams, which began to be hauled upward now, although Calvin hadn't seen Taber do anything to make it happen. The door was counterweighted with solid globes of what must have been silver, and as it rose out of sight above it revealed a dim cavern, apparently sizable, although the ceiling was only a couple of feet overhead. There was the smell of river water and wet stone now, and a metallic smell, like old coins in a sack. The sound of water was more pronounced, and he realized that they must be very near the river itself, perhaps in the upper reaches of New Cyprus or beyond, where the river swept deep and fast along the cliffs of the Dead Mountains.

Nearly lost in the twilight, in the downward-sloping end of the room, lay a pool of water that appeared to have leaked beneath three other wooden doors, their heavy, water-darkened planks cleated with silver bands and fitted into square-cut holes in the stone wall, as if the doors shut out the river itself. Lamplight glinted on flecks of quartzite and on jagged veins of silver that appeared and disappeared in the hewn granite walls of the cavern. On the stone floor, and stacked on stone tables cut into the walls, stood wooden casks and crates, some fixed with lids, some open, revealing thousands of silver coins of varying sizes. Broken casks on the floor had spilled coins into silver deltas that flowed out around pyramids of ingots the size of decks of playing cards. Other pyramids were built out of what might have been globular, two-pound fishing weights if the metal had been lead rather than silver. Farther back in the recesses of the cavern, bar silver lay in piles four or five feet high, stacked back and forth like bricks on a pallet, the stacks making a wall that partially screened further casks of coin and heaps of ingots and silver bricks that would have been almost too heavy to lift.

Bob Postum suddenly made perfect sense to Calvin. Simple greed explained him—it was the only sort of "belief" that he needed. That hadn't been clear when Calvin was talking to Mifflin that morning, but it was clear as a bell now that he saw the silver lying before him like moonlit dunes.

"The coin is stamped with the Knight's crest," Taber said, stepping into the cavern and motioning Calvin in after him. "You'll see it advertised in coin collectors' catalogues now and then. A coin fetches a pretty good price, too, although if all of this were dumped onto the market it wouldn't be worth more than the weight of the silver. How much weight do we have here? I have no earthly idea. We move some pallets of these bricks to a man out in Vegas now and then, which keeps us in chips, but in my years here I can't tell that the pile has gone down much at all. And there's more silver in the mines. Who knows how much? Bob Postum's got no idea what he's going to find. It'll be a *hell* of a memorable moment for him when he walks in through this door."

Calvin followed him back out into the passage again, glancing upward toward the high ceiling, where he saw a pinpoint of light glowing off a small circle of glass—another camera lens. "So we're just leaving the door open like this?" Calvin asked.

"Like a dare," Taber said.

ALONG THE RIVER

Calvin stood in the shade at the foot of Taber's dock, where he looked out over the river through a pair of binoculars. The camera boat was securely anchored from all four corners now, and aside from what looked like legitimate film-shoot activity, the day was quiet and waiting. On the water they had put out a line of fat red buoys, routing pleasure boats along the Arizona side and cordoning off New Cyprus from the rest of the world, and there was a man in uniform on the ferry dock, evidently a sheriff, now and then shouting things and gesturing. When the trouble started, according to what Taber had told him earlier, they'd shut the river down entirely, opening it back up now and then to let boats through and then closing it again. That is, if the battle lasted long enough to make that necessary.

Lasted long enough. Calvin wondered what it meant, exactly. There was a cold-blooded quality to this whole thing that Calvin couldn't quite get his mind around. And what about himself? Was he willing to kill people over a cache of religious relics and a heap of silver? Maybe more to the point—was he willing to kill people who were willing to kill his friends in order to take the loot? That was another story, way more complicated, but with a more evident answer.

He watched the ferry take off from the dock with Betty Jessup at the helm, running a load of children and their mothers out through the buoys and up to the Colorado Belle in Laughlin where they would wait out the battle. Anyone could leave who wanted to leave, although from the Knights' point of view, mothers with children didn't have a choice.

A sheriff's boat had come in alongside the camera boat a few minutes ago, and had chatted with the uniformed man on the dock, and then had gone away again after the crew in the water had shifted buoys and signed paperwork. Through his binoculars Calvin could see the crew eating box lunches. He wondered how many of them were innocent—actual union slobs or film student interns making a few extra dollars at a weekend shoot. Across the river there were more cameras on scaffolding, all of it thrown up in the past couple of hours.

The Boston Whaler, Calvin noticed, was hauled up onto the beach, but the fireboat was moored to the end of Taber's dock. It had taken him a moment to recognize it, since it was decked out on the starboard side like some kind of Moorish galley, with a fake mast and square-rigged sail and a dozen oars thrusting out through a plywood gunwale. There were little curlicue cutouts fore and aft like fancy bowsprits. The water cannons weren't in any way hindered, however, and they had a clear aim out over the river and the town both. Another water cannon had been towed in on a raft built of railroad ties, and two men were busy mooring it to the ferry dock. There was a fourth set up below the footbridge.

Calvin could see men milling around up on the hill, where there were pieces of dismantled wooden equipment, what Mifflin had referred to as Postum's "siege engines." Even with the binoculars it was hard to make sense of it, although almost certainly they were built of wood in some authentic, old-fashioned manner. The assembly was already under way—two skeletal-looking frameworks, one set up on the turnout itself, and one back up behind it on higher ground. The Dead Mountains were full of projectiles, there was no doubt about that.

"What do you think?" someone said to Calvin, and he turned around to find Taber standing there, dressed in a Hawaiian shirt, although only the collar was showing. The rest of it was hidden by the Knights' tunic with the embroidered red cross. He had on a straw hat that looked new, with a garish silk band patterned with red hibiscus on a gold background.

"Nice hat," Calvin said.

"I knew you'd be jealous of it. I bought this in one of those upscale shops at Caesar's Palace, must have been fifteen years ago. I've been waiting for an occasion to wear it. A man might as well go out in style."

"I hope you mean out on the town."

"Sure. Why not? The last ditch, if it comes down to it."

"Is that a *sheriff* out on the ferry dock?" Calvin asked. "I keep hearing about how we're keeping the authorities out of this."

"That's George Fowler," Taber said. "I'll introduce the two of you later on. He's our liaison. That's one of the ways we're keeping the authorities out of this. What do you think of those devices up on the hill?"

Calvin turned his attention from the doings on the river and looked up into the Dead Mountains again through the binoculars. "I've never seen a real catapult before," he said.

"Technically it's called a *trebuchet*, widely in use during the Crusades," Taber told him. "They brought them out of China, out along the Silk Road. It was a heck of an engineering feat, with a big old ballast box pulling down on a lever as long as the mast of a ship. There's a sling at the end of the lever, and it's got a mean whip when it comes over the top. It takes a lot of men to raise the ballast box, but Postum's probably figured out some mechanical means to get the job done. He used to be an engineer—apparently a good one. It's a shame he went crooked, but he's bent so far out of shape now that they're going to have to dig his grave with a corkscrew."

"How accurate are those machines?"

"Not very. I saw one of those two there in action once. They had a pumpkin-throwing contest out in Oatman. Half a dozen teams built catapults, but most of them were designed on the Roman model, big enough to toss a pumpkin the size of your head a couple of hundred yards. The Beamon's crew set up a trebuchet and threw a three-hundred-pound blue-ribbon pumpkin half a mile. They can find the range if they work at it, but they can't aim it at anything, which actually makes it a little more worrisome."

"Yeah, I should say it does. What about those camera people, out on the raft? Aren't they in trouble when Postum's finding his range?"

"God knows what he told them, but human expendability is part of his way of doing business. You can bet he promised them a big payday." They watched the hills for another moment in silence, and then Taber said, "Do you mind a little chitchat? I'm worried about something."

"Sure," Calvin said.

"I talked to Doc Hoyle about the Lymons, and he says he never saw anything like it. Al simply took the cancer away from Nettie."

"I guess it doesn't surprise me that he'd do that," Calvin said.

"Well, it does and it doesn't. But maybe Lymon should have asked Nettie before he went ahead and hijacked her illness. The thing is, I'm pretty sure Nettie got her hands on the veil some time after you finished the sketch, but I'm not sure what she's up to with it. She won't talk to me. That veil doesn't belong to Al Lymon or to Nettie or to the Knights, either. Lymon's using the veil to take on Nettie's cancer looks like what we'd call a selfless act, but it wasn't. If Lymon had been in a selfless mood, he'd have left the veil where it belonged."

"*Nettie* doesn't see it as selfish, though?"

"She sees a man who's killed himself to save a life that was already forfeit. Now she's alive and her husband's on his deathbed instead of being out here with us where he's supposed to be, and on top of that she's got to watch him die and then be left alone. Seems to her that it's sort of a mixed blessing."

"What do you want me to do?" Calvin asked. "Tell her that two wrongs don't make a right?"

"Well...do what you *can* do. Make her see reason."

"Sure," Calvin said. "Okay. I'll reason with her."

"Good. And bring back the veil. It's not a means to an end. It can't be left in private hands, and I don't care whose."

PHARAOH'S ARMY

Calvin ran into a nervous little man in the driveway of the Lymons' house. He wore a straw fedora and a white linen shirt and slacks, and he carried a medical bag. "You must be the nephew from out on the coast," the man said to him.

"That's right. I'm Calvin Bryson. You're Doc Hoyle, I guess. How's Lymon?"

"Not good, son. He was conscious enough to refuse the offer of a morphine drip. I could have done that much for him, but I let him make the call. If it were me, I'd take the morphine."

"So he's got cancer? There's no doubt about it?"

"Not in my mind," Hoyle said. "This...*transference*, or whatever we want to call it, would qualify as some kind of miracle, except a man's going to die because of it. That's not the standard result of a miracle. And then there's Nettie. She could go to work up in the quarry tomorrow, if she had a mind to." He shook his head, then shut his eyes and rubbed his temples. "I'm in a small hurry," he said. "I've got to look in on a couple more folks."

Calvin watched the man go away down the drive. The door of the cellar shelter in the carport wall was standing partway open, so he looked in. His aunt sat next to the bed where his uncle lay on his back, apparently asleep. A wheelchair stood nearby, and he could see a bathroom beyond, and a little kitchenette and shelf full of books and puzzles to while away the time. Nettie saw Calvin standing in the doorway and nodded, and he came down the steps into the cool of the interior, pulling the door shut behind him.

"Take a seat," she told him, and he sat down on the edge of his uncle's bed.

Lymon opened his eyes, nodded faintly, and then closed them again. He fumbled his hand on top of Calvin's. His breathing was labored, and after every third or fourth breath it caught in his throat.

"Sorry I dumped you into the sand pile this morning," Calvin said to him.

His uncle squeezed his hand, but that was his entire response, and after a moment Calvin realized that he was asleep again or else had slipped out of consciousness. His mouth was open, and from time to time his aunt mopped it with a tiny sponge on a stick that she dipped into a jar of clear liquid. The two of them sat silently in the dim light. Calvin looked around the big room, at the stone ceiling and cypress posts that supported it. Beyond a set of downward-sloping stone stairs ending against the far wall there was another wooden door, double-barred with heavy six-inch planks about three inches thick, set into flatiron hooks. There must be a room on the other side, Calvin thought. Or more likely another passage of some sort, given that it was barred on this side. This whole side of the river was a warren of passages. One well-placed rock from that trebuchet and the whole place would probably collapse in a cloud of dust.

"We'll let him rest," his aunt whispered. Calvin got up and followed her outside, where they sat down in the lawn chairs, looking out on the river and all the activity, just as they had on the evening he arrived, although the view was different now. He remembered how awkward he had felt trying to talk to her. Now she understood everything too well. And clearly she was deeply unhappy, and that didn't help.

"I've been over talking to Miles," he said finally.

"I know you have," she said. "I saw you two out there on the dock. I know why he sent you over. He wants you to talk sense into me about that veil. But I don't know that there's any such thing as *sense* in this case, so I might as well make my own sense out of it, and you can tell him I said so. Anyway, he already had Doc Hoyle try to weasel it out of me, but I didn't budge."

"Doc Hoyle told you that Miles sent him down here after the veil?"

"He promised Miles that he'd fetch it back to him, but I sent him off empty-handed."

"Good for you. Did you tell him you had it, though?"

"I didn't see much reason to tell him anything, but I didn't lie to him. I didn't tell him I didn't have it."

"So you've made up your mind about it?"

"My mind is pretty much settled, but you might as well have your say. I don't suppose I can stop you anyway."

"Okay. What I want to say is that I don't pretend to understand what went through Uncle Lymon's head when he took the cancer on himself, but I know what was in his heart."

"Any fool can figure out what was in his heart," she said, suddenly getting angry. "But that's where he should have kept it. Why in God's good name did he have to carry through with it? I take that back. I don't think he did it in God's good name. I think he did it in Al Lymon's good name, because he's so bullheaded. Once Al gets an idea into his mind, he can't let go of it. He can't see it any way but his own. There's something too self-righteous in what he did."

"I don't think that's fair," Calvin said. "And when it comes down to it, most of us like our own ideas pretty well."

"Lord knows that's true, but it doesn't make it right. We can be sure of the truth and not be so ever-loving sure of ourselves. What on earth *possessed* him to think I'd want to be alone like this? And he did it to me when I didn't know what was being done. That's just not right. I made my peace with Al and I made my peace with the world and with God. God dealt me a hand and I played it out the best I knew how. Whatever regrets I had left over were long gone out of my mind. And now I don't have any peace at *all* to speak of, but instead I've got a parcel of new regrets and I've got to bury my husband. If he weren't so sick, I'd tell him just what I think. But now I can't. He got in the last word."

"But you *know* he did it out of love," Calvin said, his words sounding lame and inadequate even though he meant what he said. "He *couldn't* talk it through with you first. You know that. He saw his chance and he took it, come what may."

"He should have thought it out more than halfway. He thought through *his* half, but he didn't think through mine."

"It's not the kind of thing you can reason out. I've only known Donna for about three days, but I think I'd jump into the river to save her if she fell in. I hope I would."

"That isn't the same thing," she said. "Not at all. This isn't that kind of river. He knew he wasn't going to make it back to shore. He knew he couldn't swim, and I'd have to go on alone. I don't *want* to be alone—not under these circumstances. Why couldn't he see that?"

"He didn't want to be alone, either."

"And he took good care to see that he wouldn't be. That's just my point."

"You shouldn't look at it that way. That's not why he did it."

Her anger had apparently carried her about as far as it was going to, and she began to cry. Calvin felt like a complete creep, shoving his oar in where it wasn't appreciated, stirring up the water without making any headway. "I don't mean to sound like I'm sure about anything," he said. "Especially not about what I would or wouldn't do. I just—"

"Give me a second," she said, wiping her eyes. "You're as bad as Al." She shook her head. "Maybe I haven't played out my hand yet, like I thought. If Al couldn't stand to see me go on to the next place alone, then I'm willing to play it the same way."

For a few minutes neither of them spoke, but sat watching the river. He wondered what she meant by what she'd said, that she'd "play it the same way." But he couldn't ask her. She would go her own way whether he wanted her to or not. It was enough that she thought she had a part in things again. The veil would have to look out for itself.

No sooner had the thought come into his head than he saw what looked like a small speck in the sky overhead, a bird, maybe. It grew, though, as it fell to earth, metamorphosing into a huge stone, turning end over end and smashing down silently beyond a gap in the willows out beyond the river. A dust cloud rose in the air, blowing away on the Arizona wind, and the bells began to ring in the church belfry down by the old riverbed.

"I guess I'd better get on back over to talk to Miles," he said, standing up. "Why don't you head down into the shelter with Uncle Lymon, just in case they get lucky with one of these stones."

"I will. And you tell Miles to settle down. I'll be all right. I'll take good care of Al just like I always have. And I'll take care of that veil, too. That's what this is about, you know. It's not about the silver, and it's not about the real estate. It never has been. There're some things, like a person's soul, you might say, that just shouldn't reside on earth."

Another stone thumped down into the field while he was cutting back through town toward Taber's place. He turned up between two houses and onto Main Street near the Cozy Diner, listening to the tolling of the church bells. What had Nettie meant by saying she would "take care of" the veil? He wondered whether he should relay the cryptic remark to Taber out of loyalty to the Knights or keep it to himself out of loyalty to his aunt.

There were a dozen crusaders milling in the street, wearing white tunics over chain mail and the familiar red cross over the heart. They were looking out across the old riverbed, up toward the hills, where a dust cloud rose out of the shadows and into the sunlight. He saw Downriver Du Pont and his wife in the group, along with Whitey Sternbottom, who waved him over.

"It's those camel riders," Whitey said. "They started down out of the hills just about the time they let loose with that first rock. One of them's a distraction from the other, or both of them from some third thing. It's hard to say what they're up to. Watch along that cut—up top in the hillside there."

Calvin watched, and within moments saw a line of a few dozen men on camels ride out of the rocks along the edge of the steep precipice, the sun beaming on their white burnooses. The bells abruptly stopped tolling, and he heard a wild yipping and howling that carried down toward New Cyprus on the now-still air as the men worked their camels downward, looking like toy figures from this distance, skidding and sliding and hopping along, switchbacking their way slowly. In a moment they disappeared again, and all Calvin could see was dust.

He wondered what this meant. Bloodshed? Rifles and artillery? The Knights apparently carried no weapons at all. Calvin half expected to see pikes and halberds, or at least a shield or two, but they were empty-handed. Perhaps it was just as well, because it made it that much less likely that the riders would find any need to shoot the place up. Certainly that was a relief, at least for the moment. Either that or he was hopelessly naïve.

"What do we intend to do?" Calvin asked. "Throw rocks? Make ugly faces?"

"Something like that," Whitey said. "We wait till they're coming down into the riverbed. Then we fall back and take shelter behind the old levee there to see what happens. Could be they don't try anything at all here, but head on down the riverbed and try to get through the park to the bridge. In that case we're strictly the rear guard. We'll follow them down and tackle them in the park, because by then the bridge will be history."

"We're going to blow up the bridge?"

"Just the middle span, or so we hope, and only if we have to. If we're lucky, though, we'll get a little help from the river itself before all of that comes to pass. This section's been dry a long time."

Calvin blinked at him. "It doesn't look much like rain."

"You never know. Water does some funny things out here in the desert. I've seen a flash flood cut a gorge in a hillside twenty feet deep, and a half hour earlier it was picnic weather." He winked at Calvin, as if they were both in on a joke, and then nodded up toward town. "Here comes Donna," he said. "She's been up in the belfry sounding the alarm. Everybody's underground now, unless they've got something better to do."

Calvin watched her coming down between the Cozy Diner and the church. She smiled at him and waved. A third stone passed silently overhead now, flung out of the now-invisible trebuchet, and a dozen heads turned to watch it drop down toward the river.

"Postum hasn't gotten serious yet," Donna said to him.

"Maybe it's an effort to promote a negotiated settlement."

"It'll fail," she said. "And then we'll see."

Whitey motioned them forward along a low stone wall that edged the churchyard and out into the full sunlight on a sort of levee of piled boulders that ran along the old riverbank. The men and women spread out along the top as if they meant to hold their ground. There were still some muddy areas above the opposite shore in the shadows against the hillside where water had run down in the storm a couple of nights back, but the river-bed itself was baked white, scattered with bare-looking grease-wood and sagebrush.

"Have you been to the Lymons'?" Donna asked him.

"Just came from there. Nettie's got something on her mind, but I don't know what. Where's Shirley?"

"At the Temple, which is where I'm supposed to go when this is through. I'll look in on the Lymons on the way, though."

"Thanks."

They stood silently for a moment, and then Donna looked at him and smiled. It occurred to him that in a few minutes she'd be gone again....

"I want to say thank you for picking up that oilcan," he said, getting off to a vague and metaphoric start. "I mean..."

"I know what you mean. Don't just stand there looking all moony," she said. "Show me."

"Okay, I will." He kissed her then, smiled at her, and kissed her a second time. Someone clapped nearby, and someone else said something that was probably witty, but he didn't catch the words. He traced the scar on her face with his finger and said, "Sorry I pushed you into that picnic table. Obviously I was out of my mind."

"Obviously," she said. "But how do I know you're sane now?"

He reached behind his neck and pulled his tiki off over his head. Donna bowed slightly, and he slipped it over her head, pulling her ponytail up through the cord. "Being of sound mind," he said, "I bequeath you this tiki as a token of my undying love."

"Nobody's ever said anything *nearly* that romantic to me," she told him, tucking it inside her shirt.

"The Order of the Tiki is an exclusive club. Now there're two of us in it."

"Good," she said. "We'll keep it that way."

She kissed him and started to say something more, but just then Whitey shouted, "Here they come!" as the first of the camel riders edged out into the sunlight, reining up his camel, the others following, one by one out of the narrow gorge, massing in the open river bottom. It was the strangest thing Calvin had ever witnessed—robed men on camels fresh from the Arabian Desert or Barnum & Bailey. The riders had rifles slung across their saddle pommels, although so far no one was making any move to use them. Calvin could smell the camels now, a heavy, musky odor, and could hear them snorting. Many of the riders were awkward, clearly novices, and they fought simply to maneuver the edgy camels.

The ground shook then, a quick side-to-side, sliding tremor and a noise that might have been a distant muffled explosion or might have been the sound of the earth moving beneath them. Calvin braced himself, waiting for it to worsen. "Earthquake?" he said needlessly to Donna.

The camels were still coming down out of the gorge, and there were fifteen or sixteen in the riverbed, turning and bumping into each other nervously, as if trying to knock their riders off.

"Listen," Donna said, and pointed up the river. There was a rumbling noise now, which grew steadily in volume. Several of the camels bolted helter-skelter down the river, their riders futilely trying to rein them in, two or three falling off into the sand and rock as the camels galloped up onto higher ground. Several others turned back toward the hillside, jostling each other. More riders fell off, their weapons clattering on the stones, the other riders trying to control the camels, which cantered back and forth and sideways.

"Back up!" Whitey yelled, shading his eyes from the sun with one hand and pointing up the river with the other. "Here she comes!"

Donna tugged on Calvin's arm, scrambling up onto higher ground. The air was full of an immense roaring sound now, generated by a head-high wall of green water surging around the nearby bend in what had been the dry riverbed, moving like an express train, sweeping up boulders and dead brush, foaming and roiling. There was a pontoon houseboat, apparently empty, careening madly along on top of the rushing water, followed by a wooden shed tilted over onto its side.

The tide bore down on what was left of the camels and riders, the camels snorting and shrieking in a mad panic as the wall of water surged through, running swift and deep, tumbling boulders and flattening brush, and for the space of a long minute the Colorado flowed deep and green through its old bed.

Then it began to diminish, the high side emptying, until it became a rivulet. Within a few minutes there were simply a few pools of water shining in the sunlight and draining away into the earth. The air was perfectly silent, as if the raging water had deadened it.

"Moses couldn't have worked it better," someone said in a low voice.

Calvin heard a weird ringing noise now. *What the hell?* he wondered, and then realized that it was his cell phone. He hauled it out of his pocket and flipped it open.

"What do you have for me?" a voice said.

"*Have* for you?"

"Miles tells me you approached Nettie about the veil."

It was Cousin Hosmer. Calvin nearly burst into laughter. "I was a complete failure," he said. "I think maybe she doesn't have it."

"You've got the IQ of a snipe. Of course she has it."

"She told me not to worry about it."

"Why *should* you worry about it? Your worries are beside the point. Give her another try. Don't take no for an answer. Where the hell are you now?"

"I'm down by the old riverbed. Postum's men tried to launch an attack on camelback. They rode down out of the hills, and when they were in the middle of the old dry bed, the river turned out of her banks and drowned them, or *maybe* they drowned. I don't know. Most of them got washed away."

There was dead silence on the other end of the phone—the first time Calvin could remember having said anything that took the wind out of Hosmer's sails. "You're telling me you *saw* this?" the old man asked.

"With my own eyes. I wouldn't have believed it otherwise. There was an earthquake, and then a wall of water came down the river in a flood. Swept the pharaoh's army clean away. The timing was perfect."

"I'll be damned," the old man said. "I wish to hell I'd seen it. That kind of thing can make a believer out of you."

"You've got that right. Anyway, I'm not going to bother Aunt Nettie anymore. If you want to argue with her about the veil you should give her a ring. Be ready, though. She's in a mood to say what she thinks."

Calvin flipped his phone shut. "I'm running late," he said to Donna.

"Take care of yourself," she said, kissing him one last time. "It's going to get worse before it gets better."

FINDING THE RANGE

From the vantage point of Taber's dock Calvin could see the two catapults set up. They appeared to be spindly things— long levers bent across a fulcrum, with a heavy weight attached to the shorter, lower end. As he watched, the weighted end raised slowly skyward. The ballast, whatever it was—iron, probably— looked to be the size of a man, maybe larger. What would such a thing weigh? Half a ton? It hung there suspended for a time while they loaded the missile into the sling at the other end, and then with a movement that was nearly too quick to follow, the ballast fell and the sling shot forward, and the missile was air- borne. It flew upward until it was miniaturized, like a high fly ball over a baseball diamond, and then it plummeted down- ward, spiraling lazily, growing in size. Calvin watched it with a sense of wonder until he realized that it would fall on this side of the river—way too close for comfort, and he moved back up the dock, watching it land in the middle of the bay, sending a geyser of water into the air. If they were looking for the range, they had found it.

Taber approached, wearing a pocket watch with a big chain, contrary to usual New Cyprus policy. "Railroad chronometer," he said to Calvin. "Swedish model. We've got a two-piece set of them. We take them out when we need to, like right now. I'll give you a little display of its accuracy in a moment. You'll get a kick out of it. We've got about two and a half minutes, which should do it, since it takes them about that long to launch those damned stones."

"Two and a half minutes till what?" Calvin asked.

"Till the display, like I was telling you. What did you make of the river turning out of its bed like that?"

"You saw it?"

"Oh, yes. Might have been the earthquake that did it. The camera crew bottomed out. The river ran dry. Then just like that it was flowing again. Washed right over the damned camera boat. Cleared the deck. She's still moored out there, but there's no one left on board, although they've still got the cameras rolling on those towers they built on the far shore." He laughed out loud, and then looked at his watch. "One minute, thirty seconds now," he said. "Bob Postum is wowing them with those two trebuchets, so we want to have our turn. Now if you look hard down toward the base of that lower machine," he said, "you can see that they've got a Humvee parked there on the turnout. That's what they're using to winch that ballast box up. Look there! They're connecting her to the winch."

Calvin watched through the binoculars, spotting the small figure of Bob Postum standing behind the trebuchet with his arms crossed. Calvin wondered whether a marksman with a high-powered rifle couldn't simply shoot the man dead right there on the mountainside and end this whole thing before someone else was hurt—someone besides Postum.

"There's some power in those Humvees," Taber said appreciatively. "Fifteen seconds! Here we go! Ten, nine, eight—watch it now! Don't look away! Two, one!"

For a moment nothing changed. The ballast box rose a couple of more feet, nearly to the top, while the sling-end dipped. But then the ground shook, as if from another small earthquake, and the hillside twenty feet below the trebuchet blew outward in a silent cloud of rock and dust. A second later there was the muffled sound of the explosion, and then the roar of the avalanche.

Calvin could see men falling to the ground and others scrambling up the hill to safer ground. The Humvee lurched forward, still winched to the trebuchet, the driver evidently trying to put some distance between him and the hillside. The rocking ballast jerked the trebuchet sideways, though, and the entire machine slammed down onto the top of the Humvee, burying it in a tangle of wooden spars.

The edge of the cliff appeared to be crawling now, collapsing in on itself, the Humvee and the trebuchet sliding with it, picking up speed until what looked to be several acres of hillside avalanched downward in a second cloud of rock and dust. When the wind whirled the dust away, it was evident that the turnout was gone, the road destroyed. The second trebuchet still stood in place, although it was canted forward and had slipped around sideways. Calvin watched it, willing it to fall, but very quickly a couple of men were tying lines to it, setting up to drag it away from the brink.

"There's the driver," Taber said, pointing, and Calvin saw a man crawling up the hillside, moving like a big, slow lizard. Somehow he had jumped or fallen out of the Humvee. A tire-size rock suddenly let loose above his head and bounded downward, right over him, starting another small avalanche. He held on for a moment and then started crawling again.

"Hell," Taber muttered.

"What?" Calvin asked. "Did we want him dead?"

"No, we want that second trebuchet."

"Leastways they can't drive down into town now," Calvin said.

"And we can't drive out. But you can bet they'll quit playing around now. They made their point and now we've made ours, although it fell a little short. They'll try harder with that second machine."

The remaining trebuchet lurched sideways, seeming to square itself with the hillside as they dragged it upward and away from the precipice, towing it with a vehicle that was hidden from view. And in a moment it was apparently on solid ground again, and they were pounding away at the corners of the base with sledgehammers—knocking in wedges, probably, to steady and level it.

"This is it," Taber said. "Let's go inside."

Calvin and Taber went back up the dock and in through a big wooden sliding door. Taber's house was the same vintage as the Lymons' house, although it had a better view downriver, and it looked down on the Temple Bar, so that they could see over the ramparts now at the men still working, going in and out across the bridge. There were heavy steel shutters over the Temple windows, and the wooden door had been barricaded with a steel panel.

The television set was turned on in the living room, and sitting on the coffee table lay what looked like a small, theater light board, with a dozen faders and glowing red lights. Calvin realized that the television screen was actually a monitor. At the moment there was a moving picture of the interior of the mint, scanning the hoard of coins, then focusing on the door in the passage. The door still stood open, which still seemed to Calvin to be strange under the circumstances. The camera image winked out, revealing the lamplit passage, looking uphill. It was dark farther up, but he could see the tail end of the rail line set into the stone floor. The image was replaced by a picture of the doors in the far wall of the mint—the riverside doors. Then the mounds of coins reappeared, the open door, and the passage again, except that now, way off in the distance, there were three bobbing, firefly specks of light. "Here they come," Taber said.

Shadowy figures appeared in the passage, moving downhill into the lamplight—three men wearing helmets with lamps, two of them walking ahead, holding shotguns. Calvin recognized Defferson and Yorkmint. The third man was Bob Postum, with the brim of his helmet pulled down to shade his eyes. Postum had gotten down the passage fairly quickly, given that he had been up top a few minutes ago. They hesitated outside the open door, looking into the room, the shotguns ready.

"Go on in," Taber murmured, his hands hovering over the switches in front of him. "Help yourself. Fill your pockets."

After a moment they stepped forward warily, swiveling the shotguns in front of them, evidently expecting resistance rather than the wide-open door. Right inside they stopped again, this time obviously stupefied, staring at the ocean of silver as if they had fallen into a trance.

"*Go farther in*," Taber muttered.

And then, as if in agreement, they moved forward, no longer warily, but greedily, hunched over and staring. The electric light from the string of bulbs played over the mounds of silver coin and ingots, which looked endless from the point of view of the camera: mounds and stacks and hummocks and pyramids of silver—a moonlit desert landscape, stretching on into the shadowed depths of the cavern. Postum stopped and turned his head to look at the open door, as if making sure of the way out. It was impossible to make out his expression in the dim light, whether it was of satisfaction or doubt. It seemed to Calvin as if there was something strange about him—as if he'd put on weight, or was wearing clothes that were slightly too small.

"One more step," Taber muttered. "Get on with it."

"He's wary," Calvin said. "He's wondering why the door's been left open."

"Greed trumps wariness here," Taber said, his hand on one of the switches, and sure enough, as if Postum couldn't help himself, he bent over to heft a big ingot. He turned it over and inspected the writing stamped into the bottom, then looked up, as if he had something to say and was trying to find the words. Defferson was moving around through the silver, lost in the gloom farther back. Yorkmint had fallen onto his knees and was running his hands through a mountain of coins. Behind Postum the tunnel door dropped down into place, pressing itself into its niche with what must have been an audible noise, because Postum looked back sharply, set down the silver, and strode toward it, saying something back over his shoulder.

"Heaven help me," Taber said. He looked at Calvin, his face pale. "Later on, remind me of the way they burned Shirley Fowler's store, and the way Postum killed Lamar Morris." His hand moved on the faders. The camera winked away, the scene changing to reveal the doors in the back wall, beyond which the river flowed. The doors began to open, sliding upward, and immediately river water was rolling in beneath them, flooding into the cavern and down across the steeply sloped floor. Again the camera switched away, focusing again on the door into the tunnel, which was still closed tight. Postum and Defferson worked to raise it, pushing their hands against it and leaning into it, trying to slide it upward. Yorkmint searched frantically around the floor, looking for a lever, maybe, but finding nothing but the shotgun he'd brought in with them. He picked it up and tried to jam the barrel under the door. Their mouths worked as they shouted at each other.

After a moment, when the water was knee-deep, they slogged away, clambering up the heaps of coin. Again the camera cut away. The river doors were fully opened, the arched doorways hidden behind the two torrents of water, which were rapidly filling the cavern, vast as it was. Taber looked at Calvin, whose face must have revealed the horror that he felt. "That's Bob Postum you're worrying about," he said.

"I'm not worrying," Calvin said. "It's just...*is* it Postum?"

"Sure it is. The man's greed personified. He got those trebuchets up and running and then came down the tunnel with the others. I'll bet ten dollars he's got a railcar waiting to come down. One thing, though, if you're squeamish—if he can tread water, he'll make it out of there alive. There's an outlet, and if he doesn't panic he'll be swept out in the current. He's got the advantage of bulk, so he'll float."

"But what if it's *not* him? What if it's someone who *looks* like him?" Calvin watched the monitor for another moment. The coins were submerged, the water still apparently flooding in through the doors. Then someone swept past at the bottom of the screen. It was a big man—not Yorkmint or Defferson, but not Postum, either. His hat was gone and his beard was half pulled away from his face where the spirit gum had given out. He slapped at the water, struggling to stay afloat, catching the false beard in his flailing hand and pulling it away, his face pudgy and moonlike now, his eyes terrified. He swirled out of view again, and there was nothing to see but dark water.

Calvin realized that Taber was talking on his cell phone now. "Out by the river gate," he was saying. "That's right, three of them." Then he stopped and looked sharply at Calvin. "Nettie didn't give you that veil, did she?"

"No," Calvin said. "She told me that you sent Doc Hoyle out to get it. She didn't give it to him, either."

"I sent Doc Hoyle out there to see what he could do for

Lymon. He's got no business with the veil. He shouldn't give any kind of damn about it."

Before Taber could say anything more, Calvin was out the door and loping past the wharf. They had sent a fake Bob Postum down the tunnel because the actual Bob Postum had someplace else to be.

THE FOURTH SECRET

Calvin ran down across Taber's little stretch of beach and had just passed the end of the dock when there was a shattering concussion. Something hit him in the head, and he slammed onto his shoulder in the sand. Water and debris rained down around him, and he curled up, shielding his head, his ears ringing with the reverberations of what must have been the fall of a monstrous stone. When he wiped his face, his forearm came away smeared with blood and water. He felt his forehead gingerly and found the wound at his hairline—a flap of skin torn away and hanging. He pressed it back into place, his head beginning to throb, and tried standing. He found that he wasn't going to pass out, and so stepped toward the dock, where a ragged terry cloth beach towel hung on a nail driven into one of the pier pilings. He yanked it down and dipped it into the river, wrung it out, and blotted the blood out of his eyes again, then pressed the towel hard against the wound, feeling half stupefied.

He saw what had hit him—a big, jagged splinter of wood blown off the dock in the impact. The dock had been shattered by the falling stone, and the end of it was pushed up out of the water like a broken ski ramp. The fireboat, its starboard side hammered in, was slipping away in the current, the mooring lines dragging dock pieces along with it as it drifted toward the island.

Taber's door slammed, but there was no time for idle talk. Without looking back, Calvin waved with the towel and jogged away around the curve of the bay, his head pounding with each step. Taber shouted something after him, but he waved his hand again, watching the scene out on the river where a pontoon boat with a camera mounted on it zipped alongside the slowly spinning fireboat, shooting the wreck from the decorated side, the painted plywood and oars still foolishly intact, spared by the stone. Someone on the camera boat tossed a big canister aboard and the fireboat went up in a whoosh of flame.

On the island Knights were running down the dock, and as the burning wreck drew near, they pushed it away with long poles, but it edged back in, dangerously near the gas pumps. Someone had started up the water cannon engine moored to the ferry dock, but it was so close to the wreckage that when the cannon let go it blasted burning pieces out across the water, nearly taking out the camera boat and its crew, knocking men and equipment into the river and spinning the fireboat safely out toward midstream, a burning wreckage of knocked-apart plywood. A ski boat with a couple of Knights on board put out from the island, angling around into the river to recover the burning fireboat, the whole scene drifting out of sight.

Calvin took the towel away from his forehead. Apparently the bleeding had slowed down. He used his teeth to tear through the hem of the towel, and then ripped off a long strip, which he tied around his forehead as tightly as he could. He threw the rest of the towel aside and set out again, skirting half a dozen riverside houses, his head still throbbing, and the wound sharply painful now that the initial numbness was wearing off.

The heightening pain seemed to clear Calvin's mind, and he thought about the rat Mifflin had told them about. Ten dollars said it was Hoyle. Postum had left his car in the lot at Beamon's because he didn't need it: Hoyle was giving him a lift into New Cyprus, probably in the trunk of his own car, which, if it was true, meant that Postum had been in New Cyprus for hours, maybe biding his time, maybe up to something more. The Bob Postum up on the hill with the trebuchets was another fraud.

Calvin waded through the last of the shallows and pushed through a stand of willow, up onto the beach in front of his aunt's den. The lawn chairs were folded and leaning against the side of the house, but the den door stood wide open. He stepped in warily, listening to the silence, and saw at once that the place had been ransacked—not carefully, either. Cupboards stood open; books and silver bookends and chair cushions lay on the floor; kitchen drawers were pulled out. The cupboards beneath the living room bookshelves had been yanked open, the false veil boxes ripped up and pitched aside. He moved up the hallway to the open door of the Lymons' silent bedroom, darting a glance inside, praying that the room was empty.

The clothes in the open closets were pushed aside, the blankets yanked off the bed. Dresser drawers had been pulled out and dumped. Calvin stepped into the room, not seeing the body on the floor until he had walked past the tilted mattress that was hiding it from view. It was Doc Hoyle, lying on his back, his eyes open and staring, his arm across his chest.

Calvin stood there listening to the drone of the swamp coolers, looking at Hoyle's upturned face, and then he turned away, thinking that he should close the man's eyes. He was staggered by a wave of dizziness, and he grabbed the bedpost to steady himself, seeing then that a scalpel with a bloody, inch-long blade lay on the floor, and that there was a bloody smear on the lampshade and a spray of drops on the wall behind it. For a stupid moment he thought that Hoyle had somehow murdered himself with his own scalpel, but then he saw the small, bloody hole in his shirt pocket, nearly hidden by the dead man's wrist.

Calvin backed away from the body, trying to make sense of things. Postum had ransacked the place looking for the veil, which he knew was in the house because Doc Hoyle had told him it was. Postum had met Hoyle here, Calvin reasoned, and when he discovered that Hoyle had failed to get the veil from Nettie, he had torn the place up looking for it. Had he found it? Or had he come up empty and shot Hoyle out of anger? Or had Hoyle futilely attacked Postum with the scalpel, making a last-ditch attempt to undo his bargain with the devil?

Calvin hurried back out through the kitchen, heading outside toward the cellar, pushing the door open and looking in carefully. The lights were on, but the cellar was empty and hadn't been ransacked. The wheelchair was gone. He walked across to the door to the passage, pushed it open, and listened to the hollow silence within the dimly lit tunnel, which stretched steeply away downward, under the bay and out toward the island. The roof in this section was supported by a scaffolding of railroad timbers, the air inside smelling of creosote and dust.

Had his aunt and uncle gone out through the tunnel, his uncle in the wheelchair? Or had Donna talked sense to Nettie and taken them somewhere safe—down to the Temple, maybe? Calvin set out downhill through the passage and into cool air. Better to find out what lay ahead than to search topside for them. He tried to think of where his uncle and aunt could have been headed if they came this way, but the throbbing in his forehead seemed to knock apart his thoughts. It came to him that he should call Taber to warn him about Postum, and he fumbled his cell phone out of his pocket, but of course there was no signal.

Turn around? He kept walking even as he was considering the possibility. The supporting timbers abruptly ended, the passage level now, cut out of solid stone. There was a porcelain insulator screwed to the last of the timbers, with the electrical wire running through it. Calvin's tiki hung incongruously over the outthrust insulator. He stood staring at it, trying to make sense of it and leaning against the tunnel wall for support, feeling dead tired.

Donna hung it there. There was no other explanation. She had gone down the tunnel looking for the Lymons, or accompanying the Lymons, and she had left this as a sign. Except that if she had wanted to leave a sign she could have left one back in the cellar, in writing, thumbtacked to the door. She didn't need to leave the tiki, which told him nothing except that she had come this way....

He lifted it off the insulator and clutched it in his hand, the obvious answer to the riddle dawning on him. Donna must have left the tiki as a message because she hadn't had a chance to do anything else. Why? She was with Postum? Maybe having walked into the Lymons' house when he was ransacking it? Calvin recalled the image of Doc Hoyle lying on the floor, the spray of blood on the wall and lampshade....

He tried to unclip the tiki to put it around his neck, but dropped it instead. Clumsily, he bent over to pick it up, feeling himself pass out in a dark rush, and then an instant later aware that he was sitting on the cold stone floor, which felt as if it were moving beneath him. Abruptly it stopped moving, and then shook again before becoming still. He waited another moment and then crept to his knees and picked up the tiki. He rose slowly, his head pounding again with his first tentative step. There had been an earthquake, coincidental with his passing out. A *portent*? Nothing that Lamar Morris had told him seemed the least bit unlikely now.

He heard the sound of footfalls, and a shade passed through the air in front of him, a flitting shard of bat-like darkness. Surprised, Calvin swung his hand clumsily, his hand and arm passing through the apparition just as it coalesced into the shadow of a man walking a few steps ahead of him. The figure wavered like a desert mirage, and as it disappeared he heard the faint sound of the footfalls passing away. Then, uncannily, he heard them again, but approaching from behind him this time.

He turned slowly around, wary of passing out again, and

in the semidarkness beyond the nearest hanging bulb, another figure, dim and transparent, appeared to be pacing toward him. It was Uncle Lymon, momentarily nearly solid, looking beyond Calvin as if he weren't there, and then evaporating and disappearing as he walked into the brighter lamplight, leaving Calvin alone again in the tunnel. He thought of Donna's ghostly miners, apparently displaced in time, and of the figure in the tunnel near the catacombs, and he seemed to hear a rising cacophony of footsteps around him, and the sound of picks ringing against stone.

A line of blood ran down his cheek like a crawling insect, bringing him to his senses, and he compelled himself to walk on and to order his mind. He worked through the alphabet backwards, resolutely mouthing the letters. Soon the strand of lights ran out, the way turned, and it was utterly dark. He trailed his right hand against the wall of the passage to keep his bearings, holding his left hand out in front. Flashes of light exploded before his eyes, keeping time with the throbbing in his head.

He felt the charged air that he had felt in the relics antechamber now. He sensed it again in his spine and along the back of his neck. And at the very edge of audibility he could hear the strange, creaky, antique music that he had heard before. The music rose and fell, the melody mingling with what sounded like the clacking together of wave-washed stones on a beach and the creaking sound of stone against stone, as if the earth were restless, turning over in its bed. The ground shook again, and he stood still, bracing himself against the wall, but almost at once the quake subsided, and he went on blindly.

Some distance ahead of him there was a feeble glow, like

moonlight, which broadened as he moved forward, a natural cavern opening up before him. He could see the tips of stalactites projecting downward, pearl-white and glowing in the light, and he heard the dripping of water, oddly loud against the strange music that seemed now to rise from the stone floor and walls. He couldn't make out the source of the diffused light, which was more like an illuminated cloud than lamplight.

At the entrance to the cavern stood the wheelchair, and for an instant he saw his uncle sitting in the chair, and his aunt standing behind it, and then it came to him that he was seeing his uncle through the transparent image of his aunt, but before he could understand what that meant, they had vanished, and on top of the vinyl wheelchair seat sat a cardboard box, clearly not any kind of figment. He picked it up, looking at the familiar Gas'n'Go address. It was empty.

He moved forward carefully, the cavern opening outward and upward, vaster than seemed possible, although its apparent size might have been an illusion of the glowing mist, which apparently filled the upper reaches, as if the cavern had its own atmosphere. There was the smell of water on stone, and from somewhere came the sound of the river flowing beyond the cavern wall.

He heard someone speak, and he peered into the recesses of the cavern, trying to orient himself before moving farther in. Illuminated like figures in a painting, the Lymons stood in the distance near a shoulder-high, rectangular white stone. Calvin was astonished to see that his uncle stood there unsupported, when only a couple of hours earlier he had been near death. Clearly Nettie had made use of the veil, as she had threatened—or promised. The white stone was the Cornerstone of the Temple of Solomon—the Fourth Secret. His aunt held the Veil of Veronica in her hands.

Water leaking through fissures in the floor above fell like a brightly beaded curtain between the Lymons and the stone. Other cut stones rose beyond the Cornerstone in an immense pile, pyramiding up and filling the end of the cavern, supporting the floor of the Temple. The glowing light clearly emanated from above, as if from an interior sun—light that seemed to Calvin to be alive with flitting dark figures like giant birds in a painting of a prehistoric world, or like angels in an antique illustration of Heaven. The figures coalesced out of the mist, glowing briefly like burnished gold in the light, and then became shadow again and disappeared altogether, back into the misty ceiling of the cavern as if into the vast, open sky of another world.

Calvin saw Postum now, standing some distance away near the far left wall of the cavern—the river wall. Water ran through the rock behind him, trickling down in little mineral-streaked rivulets. Postum's arm hung at his side, his hand holding a pistol. He wasn't moving, but was talking into a walkie-talkie, staring at the Lymons and at the falling curtain of water. Calvin edged toward him, keeping well out of sight, seeing Donna now, who sat on the floor of the cavern, apparently unhurt, her hands behind her, her ankles held together with a nylon zip-tie. A backpack lay on its side ten feet from her, spilling out hand tools, water bottles, assorted junk.

The ground shook again, and Calvin staggered, but caught himself, listening to the creaking of the restless earth, the ground trembling, and he told himself that if he wanted to see the sunlit world again, he'd have to do something besides stand and wait—something that wouldn't prompt Postum to start shooting up the place. His aunt and uncle stood stock-still, Nettie holding the veil up and out before her now as if it were an offering. The mist overhead dimmed and glowed, still alive with shadowy movement.

"That's right," Postum said, talking loudly. "Are you hearing me clear now? Good, because I'm getting a little nervous about these quakes. Like I was saying, it's old school. Black powder, a piece of PVC pipe from down at the hardware store, and some cannon fuse I ordered out of the Estes Rockets catalogue. It's a foolproof, thirty-dollar deal. All I want to do is breach that wall." He gestured with his left hand, which held the pistol.

Calvin spotted a heavy smear of black tar on the river wall, water trickling over and around it. Pressed into the middle of it was a foot-long piece of PVC pipe with the ends capped off. Several feet of fuse looped away from it. Calvin knew nothing about explosives, but he knew that Postum didn't have to use theater props down here where there was no audience. The bomb wouldn't be a fake.

"The river'll do the rest," he was saying. "How high it'll rise is a good question, but it'll sure drown anyone down *here*, which amounts to three people, me being the fourth. What I want is twenty-four hours. Then we'll be out of your hair for good and all, and no more collateral damage.

"Wait…you hear me out. I'm looking at the veil as we speak. Right now it's in the hands of an old woman who won't give me more than a moment's grief before she drowns. As for the silver, I'm banking on the water rising past the entrance to that passage that comes down out of the Temple there, which means that the *only* way into what you call the *mint* is down from the hills, and from your point of view that's enemy territory now. Whether that mint's underwater or bone-dry, we're going to take that silver right out of there in a trolley car. You all can come on up the Khyber Pass and gamble with us if you want, but I don't think you've got enough chips to see the bet. That's the end of my pitch."

He listened again, and then said, "You sure can try a man's patience, Miles. Give me just a second to up the ante here."

He walked across to the coil of fuse, took a cigarette lighter out of his pocket, lit the flame, and touched it to the fuse, which immediately sparked and burned. Calvin stopped himself from lurching out of the darkness right then and there, which would only end in him being shot—no doubt about it this time. He wiped his face with his forearm, then yanked off the saturated piece of beach towel and tossed it aside. The misty light around him seemed to have intensified, and sounds were strangely clear—the undertone of music, the sound of the river.

"It's done," Postum said. "Fuse is lit. Anybody shows his face at the mouth of the cavern is a dead man, according to my pistol. This cannon fuse burns at a steady rate, and you'd best believe I've timed it to the inch, so I know just how much time I've got to walk out of here, and it ain't long. All my chips are on the table now. You want to call my bluff, Miles, you go right ahead. Meanwhile, I'm going to secure that veil before the river looks in on us."

Move, Calvin told himself, and this time he didn't hesitate. He stepped out into the open and strode silently toward the burning fuse. Donna was looking straight at him, but her face didn't change. The Lymons were facing away, paying no one any mind. Nettie was talking out loud, what sounded like prayer, still holding the veil out before her. Postum paced toward the Lymons, intent on the veil, his back to Calvin. *Bomb first,* Calvin thought.

He stumbled, but caught himself, not knowing whether it was the knock on the head or the earth moving again, and not caring. *Jerk the wire loose?* He wondered whether it would explode like a holiday cracker. His ignorance of bomb making was profound. He sank his fingers into the roofing tar and clutched the piece of two-inch pipe, pulling it loose from the wall. Holding it out in front of him, he turned around and walked back toward the entrance to the cavern. The least he could do was carry it away, throw it to hell and gone up the passage. He ran his free hand up the long looping fuse until he found the end, feeling it burn his fingers. He pressed on it, trying to smother it, heading for the entrance to the cavern.

Donna shouted, and he ducked sideways fast, hearing the gunshot and spinning around, making himself small as he lunged away. Postum was coming straight toward him now, walking hurriedly and shaking his head, half smiling, aiming the pistol. Calvin lurched away, seeing the fuse sparking again. He hadn't put it out at all.

"You're going to blow yourself up, son," Postum said to him, his voice loud and nervous now. "Give me the bomb and take a seat with your girlfriend. Miles is going to come through here and solve this problem. You see if he doesn't. Do it right now, or I'm going to have to shoot you."

Calvin backed away, watching Postum's face. He yanked hard on the fuse, which popped out of the pipe bomb through a plug of roofing tar. They were jolted by another earthquake, hard this time, as if defusing the bomb had silently exploded it. Calvin hunkered down, riding it out, the bomb stuck to his hand. Fragments of rock fell from the roof of the cavern in a shower of dust, the falling debris causing Postum to throw his arms over his head. The walkie-talkie flew out of one of his hands, landing somewhere out of sight and taking Miles Taber out of the equation.

Calvin saw that Uncle Lymon had fallen, and that Nettie knelt next to him now, lifting the veil again with both hands, as if she had business to finish and no earthquake was going to stop her.

Postum recovered, raising the pistol again, and Calvin threw the bomb hard, but it stuck to his hand like a tar baby, the piece of pipe merely falling loose and bouncing on the ground. Postum bent over as if to pick it up, his head cocked upward so that he could watch Calvin, the pistol ready but aimed slightly wide. Calvin rushed at him without thinking, gripping the long fuse, looking at Donna and senselessly yelling, "Now!"

Postum spun sideways toward Donna, who still sat helplessly on the ground, and Calvin threw a loop of still-burning cannon fuse around Postum's head, thinking of Lamar Morris dead in the cardboard carton. Postum shoved his hand and arm into the loop before Calvin could yank it tight, and then turned to face him with no apparent effort, slugging him hard in the stomach. Grabbing both of Calvin's shoulders, Postum cracked his head against Calvin's forehead, and Calvin fell in a rush of darkness, holding on to the fuse, dragging Postum with him, gasping for wind, his eyes blurred with blood.

Postum pushed himself free and stood up, a bloody mark on his forehead, the pistol in his hand. He picked the pipe bomb up off the floor and wiped a gob of tar off the top of it, then fumbled to push the fuse back in, packing the tar around it carefully, glancing at Calvin but not apparently concerned with him.

There was a sound like ice breaking now, as if the floor of the cavern had split open like a frozen lake, and the undertone of music heightened, the sound of the river playing beneath it, the sighing of the water and the clacking of stones taking on a counterpoint melody. The cavern seemed to Calvin to be slowly spinning, and he braced himself, fighting vertigo, watching Postum shuffle sideways to stay on his feet, cramming his pistol through his belt and heading toward the river wall and the heavy smear of black tar, still working his plan.

Then he stopped abruptly. His attention wasn't on the bomb any longer. He was staring at the Lymons, who were on their feet again, standing before the Cornerstone.

Postum raised the pistol, but his hand moved wildly from side to side as if drawn by an erratically shifting magnetic source. Calvin stood up dizzily, trying to balance himself. The music was abruptly deeper, a symphony of earthly noise rising out of the bedrock on a draft of cool air that washed past Calvin, raising dust from the floor, the updraft catching the veil and lifting it from Nettie's hands. The veil fluttered upward, slowly ascending, casting golden rays where the light shone through it, until it was a small wafer of shadow against the misty aura of the ceiling. Calvin wiped blood from his eyes again, squinting upward, watching as the veil disappeared.

Uncle Lymon sat down hard on the ground, which shook again as if he had become so heavy that the earth could barely support his weight. The floor tilted sharply, and Calvin lunged forward, feeling the solid stone moving beneath him. Postum waded toward the cavern wall again like a man fighting against a waist-deep, heavy tide. He bent over the backpack and picked up what must have been a pair of wire cutters, clipping off most of the remaining fuse before throwing the cutters aside and jamming the pipe bomb back into the tar. He fumbled the lighter out of his pants pocket, clicked open a flame, and waved it at the fuse, but then staggered backward, trying to stay on his feet, glancing back at Calvin. Postum looked smaller now, old, worn-out. Fear played in his eyes, as if he had finally figured out that the stakes were higher than he had thought.

Calvin started toward the wire cutters, the cavern abruptly quiet. He snatched them up, moved to where Donna sat, and snipped through the nylon ties. He saw that his aunt and uncle were walking forward now, having passed through the veil of water, an aura of opalescent light around them that brightened and brightened until they simply disappeared altogether.

There was a crack like a gunshot, and Calvin saw Postum pitch forward, a hail of stones clattering down around his shoulders, and in the next instant Postum looked upward into the downrushing shadow of an immense, conical stalactite that pulverized him beneath a cloud of dusty rubble.

Calvin felt a hand on his arm, bringing him to his senses, yanking him backward, and a voice shouted "Run!"—a voice he obeyed without hesitation, the glittering dust whirling around him and the sound of avalanching rock filling the cavern. Donna's hand clutched his wrist, drawing him upward. He looked back into a cloud of illuminated dust, but the cavern disappeared from view as they ascended, and Calvin found himself in the darkness of the passage again, Donna still holding on to his wrist.

TOMORROW

Calvin sat in a lawn chair drinking a grape soda. There were a dozen bottles left from the case—two of which were dug into the river sand at his feet, keeping cool—but that would be the last of it, given what had happened to the Gas'n'Go and Shirley Fowler's moving out to New Cyprus from Essex. The thought made him consider the things that had come into his life and then had passed out of it again over the past few days, and, more happily, the other things that had come into his life and stayed.

By the time he had gotten home last night from the hospital in Bullhead City, Doc Hoyle's body was gone, and the bedroom and most of the house had been put right. This morning his forehead was tight with the stitches, and the aspirin hadn't done much to dumb down the pain, but he had awakened with a feeling of peace that was still with him. Out on the Temple Bar they were taking the fortifications down, eradicating all evidence of yesterday's invasion, the little Bobcats and Pullman carts running back and forth, the Knights putting things right. Calvin was reminded of holiday decorations coming down or of a theater set being struck after a show had closed.

He thought again about the strange ascent of the veil, and about the rest of the Knights' relics, or rather the relics that the Knights cared for. Taber apparently understood them to be symbols of Heaven on earth. His uncle had seen them as a way to change human pain into something bearable. To Bob Postum they had been objects that you bartered at the Coronet store with promises of a pillowcase full of paper money. But for Calvin the relics hadn't been the issue. New Cyprus was the issue—the ever-moving panorama of the river, the mountains glowing gold with the dawn light, the fall of evening casting long shadows over the trailers in the park....

They had found Postum's body beneath the rubble in the cavern. The Lymons had simply vanished along with the Veil of Veronica. "God took them home," Taber had told him. "Now and then He does that." Calvin had no reason to argue, and anyway, he wasn't in an argumentative mood.

The constant fisherman in the little aluminum outboard had a line out over on the Arizona side now, and beyond him a dust devil rose up from the field where Postum had been casting stones. It spun wildly for half a minute before abruptly falling still. *Dust to dust,* Calvin thought, tossing a stick out into the river and watching it bob away on the current. The water was emerald green even under the blue of the desert sky, and there were thunderheads over the mountains again. A breeze sprang up, carrying on it the promise of pending rain, of autumn and cooler days.

"There's your ghost," he said to no one, "blowing in from Arizona."

He thought about his uncle and aunt and about his father and mother and the inevitable passing away of the things of man. And then, hearing Donna's footsteps on the driveway, he said a few words on behalf of all of them to the close and holy silence of the desert morning, finished his grape soda, and headed around the side of the house to meet her.